"I promise I'll only call you Kat when we're alone. In bed."

Katherine's lips parted with surprise. "We won't ever share a bed," she murmured, but the protest was weak.

"No?" he whispered.

Slowly dipping his head, Dominic captured her lips. With a moan that came from deep within her, Katherine slid her hands up to clutch his arms and returned his kiss. The reaction sent a rush of longing through Dominic. The control he'd been so carefully practicing suddenly fled.

Startled, he used every ounce of strength in him to pull back.

"You *will* be my wife," he whispered, his lips just inches from hers.

She pulled back to stare up at him, her eyes misty with desire and unshed tears. "No."

"You will."

Other **AVON ROMANCES**

Coming Soon

And Don't Miss These
ROMANTIC TREASURES
from Avon Books

ATTENTION: ORGANIZATIONS AND CORPORATIONS
Most Avon Books paperbacks are available at special quantity
discounts for bulk purchases for sales promotions, premiums, or
fund-raising. For information, please call or write:

Special Markets Department, HarperCollins Publishers, Inc.,
10 East 53rd Street, New York, N.Y. 10022–5299.
Telephone: (212) 207–7528.   Fax: (212) 207-7222.

Jenna Petersen

Scandalous

AVON BOOKS
An Imprint of HarperCollins*Publishers*

AVON BOOKS
An Imprint of HarperCollins*Publishers*
10 East 53rd Street
New York, New York 10022-5299

Copyright © 2005 by Jesse Petersen
ISBN-13: 978-0-06-079859-8
ISBN-10: 0-06-079859-9
www.avonromance.com

First Avon Books paperback printing: October 2005

Avon Trademark Reg. U.S. Pat. Off. and in Other Countries, Marca Registrada, Hecho en U.S.A.
HarperCollins® is a registered trademark of HarperCollins Publishers Inc.

Printed in the U.S.A.

10 9 8 7 6 5 4 3 2 1

For Miriam, who reminded me I could.
For May, who told me I would.
And for Michael, because he is my hero.

Chapter 1

~~~⌘~~~

Dominic Mallory had never been one to debauch virgins, but he was beginning to think he should make an exception for this beauty. He took a quick glance around the wide stone terrace before he stepped farther back into the shadows. Good, they were alone. He ground out his cigar as he blew a last circle of smoke into the cold air. If he had it his way, nothing would disturb this moment. Rushing a seduction took all the anticipation out of it.

Seduction hadn't been his plan when he arrived at his family's estate. In fact, he'd come straight to the terrace in order to avoid the celebration inside. Now he knew he'd made the right choice. He could have a much more interesting party alone with this young woman.

She leaned on the terrace wall, completely oblivious to his presence. He had been more than aware of hers from the moment she slipped from the crowded ballroom into the frosty night. Now she stared up at the stars, giving him the impression that her heart and mind were leagues away. Her jet black hair matched the inky sky. Somehow during the evening, a few long, curly strands had come down from the elaborate pile on her head, leaving a tantalizing trail down the middle of her back. A trail he longed to follow with his lips.

He sighed softly. But, if she was a guest at his brother's wedding *soiree*, she was surely a virginal miss who would only be interested in a marriage proposal. If he revealed himself to offer her a night of pleasure, she'd probably swoon.

But then again, if she swooned, he could catch her.

Dominic grinned as he took a few quiet steps out of the shadows. He had the benefit of a thin dusting of snow on the stones, which muffled his approach. Even when he was right at her side, she didn't glance his way.

Perfect.

"Good evening," he whispered, just a touch too close to her ear to be proper.

She turned toward him with a blush and he finally had the pleasure of seeing the color of her eyes. Jade green. Magnificent. Even if this woman proved to be an unattainable challenge, he'd certainly chosen well.

"G-Good evening," she stammered as she straightened up to smooth the front of the gown that matched those jade eyes perfectly. She pulled a darker emerald shawl tighter around her shoulders as she smiled. "I'm sorry, sir, I didn't see you there."

He shrugged one shoulder and gave her his most dashing wink. Insincere, but always effective. "You were wishing on the stars. I wondered what you might have wished for."

He was being completely and inappropriately forward and he knew it. Judging from the wary surprise in her eyes that accompanied his impertinent question, she recognized it, too. Yet instead of hurrying away or calling for her chaperone, her face slowly relaxed and she said, "I didn't wish for anything. I have everything I've ever wanted."

Dominic frowned, all his lustful thoughts pushed aside, at least for the time being. How was that possible? No one ever obtained everything they wanted. There was always something lacking. At least, there always had been in his life.

"My, how lucky you are," he drawled, then shut his eyes in exasperation. His voice was brittle and forced. Not the way to talk to a lady he wished to seduce. With effort, he softened his tone. "But perhaps I'm not enough of a romantic to believe in wishes, after all."

She laughed and his eyes flew open at the light, melodic sound. Her pale face flushed, but this time it was with mirth, and her eyes shone like precious jewels in the moonlight. He wouldn't have believed it possible, but she was even lovelier when amused.

"Well, if you cannot be a romantic at a wedding celebration, perhaps you're a lost cause, sir," she teased.

He had often thought that himself.

With a shrug, he said, "Yes, well the wedding isn't for another three days. Maybe I'll find a little romance in me during that time."

He tilted his head to lock gazes with her. Now that he'd talked to her for a few moments, he was sure she was an unmarried, eligible lady. Still, he felt an inordinate amount of heat coming from her. Like there was something a bit wild hidden beneath all the pretty clothes and small talk. Something well worth exploring.

She broke their stare with a startled flash in her eyes, as if she remembered where they were and that they were alone. Her spine stiffened as she leaned away.

"I don't think this is a very appropriate conversation to be having with a stranger on a terrace." Her voice was breathy.

He stifled a laugh. There were the maidenly refusals. The wild thing was stuffed back under a layer of propriety. But oh, the challenge of coaxing her out again.

"So you're telling me we could continue to talk about things a little more interesting than the weather if we weren't strangers?" he asked with a cocked eyebrow.

Slowly, she allowed her gaze to flit to his face, but gave no answer.

He laughed. "Very well, my lady. Why don't you tell me who you are first?"

She backed away a long step and her eyes darkened. "D-Don't you know? I thought for sure you must. I'm—"

Before she could finish, the terrace door opened behind them and she spun around to face the intruder. Dominic stepped into the shadows instinctively. No use causing a scene with some fawning mama. Though the woman who interrupted them looked nothing like the one he'd been speaking with. No, the intruder was wide where this beauty was slender, and instead of ebony hair, this new woman's was mousy brown.

Not that Dominic had grounds to talk about anyone else's lack of familial similarity.

"There you are," the woman at the door said as she put her hands on her ample hips. "I have been searching for you for a full ten minutes."

Dominic's target looked as guilty as a thief. "I'm sorry, Eustacia. I needed a breath of fresh air. It was stifling inside."

The older woman now identified as Eustacia shook her head. "It's freezing out here. You'll catch your death. Colden is waiting for you. Come back inside so he can make the toast, Katherine."

Dominic's stomach tightened as he reeled backward, until he flattened against the house's stone wall. His sister had written to him about a woman with the name Katherine. But no. It wasn't possible. Except that it was.

The woman he'd been contemplating taking to his bed was Katherine Fleming, his older brother's fiancée.

Katherine turned and seemed surprised that he'd disappeared. Her voice was unsure when she murmured, "There was a man . . ."

Eustacia rolled her eyes, then held the door open a fraction wider. Her large, slippered foot tapped aggressively beneath the edge of a hideous red gown. "I'm sure it was nothing. Come along."

"Yes, I suppose you're right," Katherine said as she moved toward the house. At the door, she paused to take one last glance over her shoulder, then disappeared from view as the door swung shut behind her.

Dominic let out a low stream of curses that went from colorful to absolutely blasphemous. Once again, it seemed he was playing second to Cole. It was a competition he despised, no matter how accustomed to it he became. Though he had no interest in marrying, it rankled him that his brother possessed the first woman who held his attention in what seemed like months.

"I never should have come to the family estate," he muttered under his breath as he finally came out of the protection of the shadows. Now that Katherine Fleming was gone, the place had lost a great deal of its charm. In fact, it was nothing but a pile of memories from his youth. Most of them unpleasant.

Despite that, Dominic had no choice but to return to his childhood home. Cole had something Dominic wanted. And it wasn't Katherine Fleming. She had only been a momentary distraction. One he'd do best to forget.

Katherine forced a smile as she came across the crowded ballroom to her fiancé's side. Cole was chatting with his mother, Larissa Mallory and Katherine's guardian, Stephan Walworth. As she drew near, he stopped speaking and gave her a wide, dashing smile.

"There she is, my lovely future bride."

He offered his arm and she slipped her hand inside the crook. As always, she felt a swell of friendship for the man she was to marry. Nothing more.

Certainly nothing like the odd sensation she experienced outside on the terrace with the stranger who appeared and disappeared so quickly. Who was the man with the dark hair and stormy gray eyes who made her heart do the oddest kind of fluttering?

And what in the world was she doing remembering such details, like a stranger's eyes? She was to be married in three days to a man with blond hair and . . . and . . . brown eyes.

She took a sidelong glance at Cole to make sure she was correct. Yes, his eyes were brown. Relief filled her. Not that it made a bit of difference whose eyes were what color.

No, she had no business focusing on some forward stranger who hadn't even the courtesy to introduce himself properly. She had Cole, and Cole was exactly what she wanted. He was a good man and a friend to her. He wasn't anyone she could ever feel a great, overwhelming passion for, which was exactly why she had accepted his suit after years of waiting and refusing other men.

"Are you quite well, my dear?" Cole whispered.

She started at his voice and shook her thoughts away. "Of course. Why do you ask?"

"You seem a bit distant, that's all." He gave her arm a reassuring squeeze.

Her smile grew wider as she relaxed back into reality and forgot about her troubling musings. Cole always noticed her every mood. He was so considerate in that regard. Certainly no other man would be so attentive. And definitely not the man on the terrace.

Now, why was she thinking of *him* again?

She gave Cole a shaky smile. "I'm fine, just a bit distracted by all these people and the wedding plans. I'm sure it will pass."

"Of course."

He looked out over the small crowd of important people from the shire. They'd been invited to share in the joy of the impending marriage. It was a business move as much as a celebration. If the people were happy, Cole's life would be easier. Katherine understood perfectly well that making her new husband's life more pleasant would be a large part of her duties in the future.

"In just a few days, all this will be over," Larissa said with a cool nod for her future daughter-in-law. "Isn't it time for your toast, Colden?"

"Yes, Mother, I do believe you're right." Cole motioned to the orchestra and slowly the song they played trailed off. All eyes turned to Cole as he took a flute of champagne for himself and one for Katherine. As he handed her the glass, he announced, "I would like to thank you all for coming."

The crowd muttered appreciatively, though Katherine noticed they were shifting in the back, as if someone were elbowing his way through the masses toward the front. With a small shrug, she turned her attention back to Cole.

"As those of you in this room well know, the last few years have not been easy for me." He frowned and Katherine's heart ached for him. Cole's first wife had died just two years before. "But I'm happy to declare that Katherine has helped me during these trying times."

He opened his mouth to say more, but at that moment, the person who had been pushing his way through the crowd burst to the front and came to Cole's side. He was a nervous-looking wisp of a man, hardly taller than Katherine herself and nearly the same weight. She expected her fiancé to wave him away, but instead Cole paused to lean down and whisper for a moment.

Katherine knew something terrible had happened by the way her fiancé's normally calm face twisted, then paled two shades.

"Are you sure?" he said in low voice.

The intruder nodded at least ten times in rapid succession. "I spoke to her meself, my lord."

"Thank you," he murmured, then turned back to the crowd. His expression was tight and false. "Thank you again for coming and have a good evening."

The group seemed as confused as she was by the sudden shift in their host's mood and the abrupt end to his toast, but they quickly returned to the free drinks and lively music of the orchestra.

Cole's family, however, didn't accept his change of tone so easily.

"What is it?" Larissa asked as she took two steps toward her son. Cole's sister, Julia, made her way through the crowd with a look of concern on her face that mirrored Katherine's own.

Her fiancé clenched his teeth. "Come with me to my office."

Without even a glance for her, he started out of the ballroom toward the main area of the house.

The Mallorys followed closely behind, and though they hadn't been invited, the Walworths seemed determined to attend as well. Katherine took up the rear with a strange sense of dread filling her every fiber.

She had never seen Cole look so upset. Not even when he spoke of his late wife during their courtship of the last year. But now he seemed distracted beyond reason. She could only pray nothing tragic had happened. Her intended had already suffered more than enough loss.

She finally caught up with the main group as they entered her fiancé's office. She'd only taken half a step into the room when Cole turned to the small crowd around him and said, "I'm sorry to have been so rude, but this is an emergency."

Julia stepped forward. "What is it?"

The look on her face was enough to frighten Katherine. Since she met Julia Mallory nearly a year before, she had always been impressed with the other woman's poise and serene nature. Though she was classified as a spinster at the age of thirty-four, that never seemed to bother her. In fact, this was the first time Katherine had ever seen Julia look remotely worried.

Cole glanced in Katherine's direction with a troubled frown. "The man who interrupted my toast is a trusted investigator in my employ. He told me something very shocking. In fact, I can hardly believe it's true myself."

Larissa pursed her lips in annoyance. "Don't keep us in suspense, Cole. What is it? Is it something about your brother? Just tell us."

He shook his head as if he couldn't believe what he was about to say. "My late wife is—*She's alive.*"

Katherine's mouth fell open in disbelief at Cole's announcement, but she was too shocked to let out a gasp like the other inhabitants of the room. This couldn't be true. It just couldn't be. Sarah Mallory had been lost in a tragic accident at sea! Poor Cole never even had the peace that came from burying his wife, as her body had never been found.

Her heart pounded as her own thoughts betrayed her. Without a body resting in a peaceful grave, his statement could be true. Sarah could very well be the woman this investigator had seen. Certainly, there had been tales before of sailors believed lost who had turned up long after being declared dead.

Everything sank inside her. How had this happened? She'd chosen so carefully, made her plans so well. And now, with one sentence, her world was coming down.

She shook her head. Her reaction was very selfish. Here Cole had just announced his beloved wife was alive and all she could think about was how this destroyed her life. No, she had to focus. Later, she would consider the consequences.

Julia uncovered her mouth and finally broke the weighty silence. "Sarah? Alive?"

Larissa shook her head as she sank down into

the closest chair. "It's a lie. We were told by reliable sources that her ship went down and all aboard were lost. This woman, whomever she is, is an imposter."

Larissa's sure tone gave Katherine a brief moment of hope. Yes, perhaps it was a mistake. A misunderstanding. Her gaze flew to Cole, but her hopes were dashed immediately. He was shaking his head with just as much determination as his mother possessed.

"No. I don't believe she is. I trust my source completely."

"Who?" Julia asked with folded arms. "Who could you possibly trust so implicitly that you would believe your dead wife to now be alive without even seeing her? And why did you even have an investigator on this case after so long, even after you were meant to marry another?"

Cole blanched and Katherine's heart ached. The questions Julia asked were reasonable and deserved answers, but still her heart went out. Obviously Cole was in no condition to reply.

Julia cocked a brow when her brother didn't answer. "You seem less than shocked by this turn of events."

"Julia!" Larissa cried, but Cole interrupted.

"I—I—" he stammered, then took a breath and seemed to recover himself. "By God, Julia, you act as if I knew my wife was alive all along. The investigator is Father's old man in London. He was not investigating Sarah in any way, but apparently he heard rumblings." His eyes flitted to Katherine. "But I promise you, I knew nothing about this until tonight. Of course I would not have continued with an engagement if I thought there was any chance—"

"That is enough! This is ridiculous. Cole, you do not have to explain yourself further." Larissa glared at her daughter. "How can we be utterly sure this is true? Even if you trust this man as much as your father did?"

He sighed heavily. "We will know soon enough if the man is as trustworthy as he once was. The woman . . . Sarah will be arriving the day after tomorrow. If it is true, I'm certain she'll have a tale to tell as well."

Now that the shock was wearing off, Katherine let out a low moan. Any minute she'd wake up. This would all be a nightmare. She even gave herself a little pinch to hurry the process along, but nothing changed. This was reality. A bitter one.

In a few days, this woman would appear. If it were truly Sarah Mallory, she would take Katherine's carefully planned life. Of course, it had been the other woman's life first, but the thought still made Katherine sick to her stomach.

What would she do?

"See here, Lord Harborough," Stephan Walworth said. Her guardian's thin fingers were jammed into fists at his sides. Though he wasn't often an emotional man, now he looked furious. "We had an arrangement. If this mysterious woman is your late wife, what do you intend to do about Katherine?"

At once, all eyes in the room pivoted on her. Hot blood filled her cheeks. Having them look at her with such pity was almost worse than finding out the truth. The attention was suffocating.

"Yes," Eustacia agreed with a nod of her fat, red face. "We have a responsibility to Katherine, and so do you, my lord."

Katherine opened her mouth to protest, but Larissa was faster. "See here, Mr. and Mrs. Walworth, you certainly don't believe any of this is my son's fault. It isn't as if he knew his wife was alive when he made his offer for your ward's hand."

Cole was growing paler with each passing moment. "Quite so!"

"Whether he knew about his wife or not won't make a difference to the gossip mongers in London!" Eustacia snapped. "Katherine will be ruined by this scandal. Tell them, Stephan!"

The other man nodded like his head was on a hinge. "Exactly right. It isn't as if finding her a match wasn't hard enough."

Katherine winced as her guardians' statements pierced through her emotionally numb haze. Why did Stephan and Eustacia have to make it sound as if she were some toothless old maid? She hadn't made a match earlier because she hadn't met anyone she wished to marry. Unlike many of her contemporaries, she had *no* interest in reforming a rake or finding the great love of her life. And she didn't have the kind of family ties to make a match for political purposes. No, her reasons to marry had been far different.

And Stephan and Eustacia had argued every step of the way.

"This will destroy any chances she has left at marrying well." Eustacia let out a long sigh that made it clear Katherine's entire life was over.

She'd had just about enough. "Now—" she began.

This time, Cole cut her off and he looked livid. She'd never seen her fiancé's rage before. It seemed a force to be reckoned with. His normally placid, handsome face twisted with ugly emotion and darkened with heat.

"There is no need to raise your voice at me, Mr. Walworth! This is an untenable situation for us all. I certainly didn't wish for it to turn out this way."

"But it has! She's ruined! Ruined!" Stephan said, his voice going up on each and every word until the room rumbled with his declaration of her social demise.

"I'm not—" she said, before being interrupted yet again.

"Don't you think this will touch our family, too?" Larissa said in an icy tone that put everyone in the room in their place whether they had been out of order or not. "Good Lord, a wife returning from the dead, a fiancée thrown over. The Mallory name will be a laughingstock for years."

"We had an arrangement. We shook hands on it as gentlemen." Stephan folded his arms. "And now this damage must be repaired. How can we do that?"

"What if she married someone else right away?" Larissa offered after a brief pause. "I'm sure with our family connections we could find someone who will be happy to receive her fortune"—she glanced at Katherine with an apologetic expression, though it was obviously an afterthought—"and her charms as well. It will reduce the damage to us all."

"That's enough!" Katherine finally cried out in a voice no one could ignore or interrupt. The chatter in the room ceased as everyone looked at her, really looked at her, not through her. "I will not be married off to just anyone simply to make you all feel as if you've done right by me. I remained an unmarried woman for three seasons in order to choose the kind of man I wanted as my husband. You will *not* push me off on just any man."

To her surprise, there was a harsh bark of laughter behind her. She hadn't realized anyone else was in the room. Spinning on her heel, she nearly fell over when she realized the man who laughed at her plight was the same one who had approached her on the terrace.

"My, my, my," he drawled in that gravelly voice that brought her body to full attention. "This Kat has claws."

Heat filled her face again, but it wasn't from em-

barrassment this time. No, some other emotion
made her blush, though she had no name for it, or
for the shaking that accompanied it. This man was
mocking her, but still all she could do was stare
into his gray eyes and be sucked in by his presence.

The room had gone into a shocked silence again.
Why? Except this stranger was now intruding on
what was obviously a family moment. Worse yet,
he seemed to be enjoying it. There was a devilish
twinkle in those eyes that raised her ire.

"Who are you?" she asked with as much icy disdain as she could muster.

He smiled. "Don't you know? I thought for sure
you must." He mimicked her words from the terrace and her blush grew hotter.

Cole stepped forward to place a possessive hand
on her arm. "Katherine, this is Dominic." As he
spoke, the two men's eyes locked in a hostile gaze.
"My derelict *brother*."

Katherine let out the gasp she'd been unable to
express when she heard her fiancé's wife was alive.
This was Cole's brother?

Over the past year, she'd heard references to the
man, but never met him. Cole had led her to believe
Dominic Mallory was a black sheep who was cut
from the family tree with little regret. Larissa left
the room whenever he was mentioned. Only Julia
spoke of her youngest sibling with any affection.

Now this man who had no place in his own family was staring at her, drawing her in. And she

could not turn away. He was nothing like she'd pictured from her fiancé's description. In fact, he was completely different from the rest of the fair-haired Mallorys. No, he was dark, square-jawed, and looked hard. And uncommonly handsome.

Dominic responded to her shock with a cocky half-smile. Straightening her back, she turned away. But despite not being able to see him any longer, she still felt him behind her. Like the heat from a blazing fire, his presence seeped through her.

Ignoring the shocked stares of the Mallory family, which had now shifted from her to Dominic, she tried to return the focus to the problem at hand, but Eustacia was faster.

"Katherine, watch your tongue! Lady Harborough was only trying to consider your future and you should, too."

"My lady, I'm sorry if my answer was sharp," Katherine began with an apologetic glance for Larissa. Her ladyship hardly seemed to be attending as she stared at her youngest son. "But I still insist that I don't need—"

Cole placed a hand on her forearm to silence her. "Katherine, this is a very upsetting situation for all of us. Nothing is set in stone as yet. Let's leave the arguments for later, shall we?"

His touch was the same as ever, but now she found it lacking. Especially when compared to the heated form of his brother, whose presence she still felt throughout her. And he wasn't even touching her.

"Cole—" she began.

He shook his head. "Why don't you go back to your chamber and rest. This news must be troubling to you."

She drew her arm away to stare at him with wide eyes. *"Troubling?"*

What was she, a child who needed placating when her toy was taken away? The word *troubling* was an insult to her roiling emotions.

He nodded with a sympathetic smile. "In a while, I'll call on you and we'll try to find a solution to this mess that is acceptable to all parties involved."

Cole turned away before she could respond and faced his brother. The gentleness that had always been in his eyes disappeared, replaced by a hard edge Katherine had never seen before. She couldn't help but step another few inches away from him, not that he even noticed her anymore.

"I need to speak privately with my brother," Cole said. "I believe he has some reason for being here."

She shook her head. She didn't want to be shoved aside so Cole could explore some lifelong rivalry with his younger brother. She wanted to sit down with him and discuss what they should do. To be treated like an equal in this terrible turn of events, rather than some child.

"But Cole—"

"Later." His voice was cold and clipped.

Finally, Katherine dared to do what she'd been

trying to avoid. She looked at Dominic Mallory over her shoulder. Like Cole, he had a dark, angry look on his face. But Dominic used that look with more skill than her fiancé . . . *former* fiancé.

She shivered as she drew away from them both. There was more going on between the two than she understood. And she didn't want to know for now. Not when her own world and future were in such danger.

"I believe Colden is correct," Larissa said with a worried glance between her sons. Still, she did not greet Dominic. What had the man done to deserve such censure? "Come along, I'll accompany you and the Walworths back to your chambers."

With a gentle hand, Larissa hustled Katherine's caretakers from the room. At the doorway, she turned back. "Come."

Julia gave her a sympathetic glance as she, too, departed. "I'll start moving the guests toward their carriages. There's no use continuing an engagement party now, I suppose."

Katherine frowned as she attempted to lock eyes with Colden, to get some kind of sign from him that all of this would be resolved. But he refused to meet her questioning stare. He hardly acknowledged her at all except to place a soft hand on her back and give her a little shove toward his waiting mother.

Stunned at his chilly dismissal, Katherine turned back to ask him to reconsider, but Dominic was there, closing the door in her face. As the barrier moved closer, she made the mistake of looking up into his eyes. The gray steel drew her in, warmed her in a way she'd never felt before.

Then, to her utter surprise, the grin returned and he gave her a saucy wink.

And then he was gone, and she was only staring at the solid wood between them. And trying to control the way her knees threatened to buckle.

Chapter 2

"**D**rink?" Cole asked with a thin smile for Dominic.

As desperate as Dominic was to dull his emotions with liquor, he shook his head. He'd learned from years of bitter experience that he couldn't give his older brother even the slightest edge. A clear head was the only way to face Colden. To demand what he'd come home to take. Later he could indulge to his heart's content.

Especially if the meeting didn't go well.

"No." He remained standing just inside the doorway while he watched his brother mix a drink for himself, then stroll over to the desk and settle in.

Cole raised his brown eyes and Dominic had a

sudden flash of their father. Harrison Mallory had called Dominic into this very room for lectures so many times over the years, he'd lost count. And for punishment. His gaze automatically flitted to the fireplace, but the thick switch Harrison once kept there was gone.

Cole smiled maliciously. "I put it away. No use having it there until I have sons of my own."

"As if *you* ever felt a blow from him in all your years," Dominic returned with more heat than he intended. Immediately, he cursed himself for showing any emotion, even anger, and quickly tamped it down.

Though Cole's eyes sparkled with delight that he'd gotten a rise out of his younger brother, to Dominic's surprise he made no further comment. Cole rarely let a shot go untaken.

His brother motioned to the chair across from his desk. "Sit."

Dominic's first urge was to refuse, but he reined in his rebellion. Let Cole feel drunk with power for now. It was only a temporary state.

"So what do you want?" Cole asked as he took a slow sip of his drink. "Or have I already guessed?"

"Perhaps I'm here to celebrate your nuptials."

Dominic arched an eyebrow as he waited for his brother's response. Any response. It was as if Cole had forgotten Sarah was alive and he was going to have to find a way to compensate for Katherine Fleming's soon-to-be-public humiliation.

"You?" Cole sneered. "Offer me congratulations? That's a rich joke."

Dominic remained silent as his brother's ugliness faded and his twisted face relaxed.

"No," Cole continued. "I think you're here to talk to me about Lansing Square." He leaned forward. "To *beg* me about Lansing Square."

Dominic bit the inside of his mouth until the taste of blood tainted his tongue. "Judging from the mess I just witnessed a few moments ago, you've got more pressing problems." He shrugged. "I *am* here to talk about Lansing Square, but it can wait."

It was a lie and his mind revolted with a silent scream of protest. It couldn't wait. It had bloody well waited for three years. Long years when the estate had invaded his dreams and been his sole obsession. The idea of putting off his final demand for access actually pained him. But rationally, he was aware that his only real hope was to stay his assault until Colden was most open to his wishes. The only chance Dominic had to win the prize was to play his game wisely.

He settled into the chair as if years and hatred didn't separate him from his brother. "I can't believe Sarah is alive," he said in the most conversational tone he could muster.

"Hmmm." Cole's brown eyes went distant as he rotated his glass in a slow circle. The amber liquid within created a whirlpool. "Yes, my wife's reappearance is unexpected. But now that she's returned from the dead, I find myself in a bit of a situation, don't I?"

Shock and confusion moved through Dominic. How could his brother remain so damned calm? Cole and Sarah had certainly made no love match all those years ago, but their union had always been full of high emotion. For his brother to sit so coolly when he believed his wife was back from the dead made no sense.

Dominic leaned back, determined to stay as detached as Colden somehow managed to be. "A situation. I would say so. You now have both a fiancée and a wife. If, indeed, this woman is Sarah."

"I've no doubt she is who she claims to be." Cole met his gaze evenly. "I trust my source implicitly. And I suppose we'll all see firsthand when she arrives."

"How can you remain so composed?" Dominic asked in wonder. This certainly wouldn't be his reaction if the situation were reversed.

His thoughts turned to Julia's earlier comment. She'd said Cole didn't seem shocked by the news. Was his brother simply stunned into numbness . . . or was it possible he had known of Sarah's existence before tonight, despite his protestations to the contrary?

The calculating cruelty of that idea made it hard for even Dominic to believe.

Cole laughed. "Unlike you, my dear brother, I'm

able to control my emotions. What good would panic do at this moment? No, what I need right now is a plan."

"What kind of plan?"

Dominic shoved his doubts aside as he realized this was the first time he'd had any semblance of polite conversation with his brother in what had to have been eight years. Under normal circumstances, Cole would have started a fight by now. Suspicion sluiced through him. His brother wanted something.

"I need a plan for Katherine's sake, of course. She'll be ruined by this."

Dominic nodded. For the first time since she left the room, he allowed himself to think about his brother's beautiful fiancée. Katherine hadn't reacted to the news of Sarah Mallory's impending return the way many of her contemporaries would have. There had been no swooning, no tears or hysteria. In fact, she had enough wits about her to argue with his mother, of all people.

And now she would be free.

Not that Dominic cared, of course. The seduction he planned for her when he first caught sight of her on the terrace hadn't included taking advantage of a broken heart.

"Why are you telling me this?" he finally asked carefully. He didn't want to reveal too much. "You've never made me privy to your schemes or plots. Why now?"

Cole ignored his question. "Yes, Katherine's future is at stake, but so is mine. The money her inheritance would have brought into the family was sorely needed." His face clouded. "As was a particular piece of property in her possession."

Now all Dominic's attention was focused on his brother. He hadn't realized the family was in financial trouble. *He* certainly wasn't. The thought made him smile.

"Can't manage your estate, eh?" he asked with a wicked arch of his eyebrow.

Fire flashed in his brother's eyes and Dominic readied himself for the appearance of Colden's famous temper. The one he had inherited from his father. Instead, Cole clenched a fist on the desk and ground out, "I admit I made some bad investments. But our father"—the cruel gleam reappeared—"or should I say, *my* father, did the bulk of the damage himself."

Dominic winced inwardly. Cole had always taken a great deal of pleasure in reminding Dominic of his status. By-blow. A bastard. A Mallory in name alone. After fifteen years, Dominic supposed he should have been used to it.

He rose to his feet. This conversation wasn't getting him anywhere. "Well, that's too bad for you, Colden. I hope you find a way to amend the damage to your purse and your life. But I think I made a mistake coming here today. I'll go."

With a nod for his brother, he turned to leave, but before he could, Cole's voice stopped him.

"Dominic, I want you to marry her."

Dominic nearly tripped on his sudden stop. Shock rippled through him as he turned back to face Colden. His brother hadn't risen from the desk, nor did his face reveal anything, but tensions increased as he awaited Dominic's answer.

Which Dominic was too shocked to render.

"Who? Katherine?"

He let out a bark of laughter at such a foolish idea, though in the very depths of his soul the thought gave him a brief, but powerful, pause. After all, being married to Katherine would assure her presence in his bed, at least until he tired of her.

But no. It wasn't worth it. All the marriages he'd been witness to were ugly affairs that only lead to unhappiness for all parties involved. Marrying a woman who thought herself in love with his *brother* could only spell further disaster.

"Why in God's name would you think I'd do that for *you* of all people?" he asked.

Cole's smile was thin. "I'd be a fool to have missed the way you looked at her earlier this evening." He rose to his feet with a cold laugh of his own. "But then, you've always been partial to my women, haven't you?"

The urge to hit his brother had shadowed Dominic his entire life. He'd even given in to it a few times, but now he was old enough to know a brawl wasn't going to improve anything. It wasn't worth the temporary pleasure.

He shook his head with a disgusted snort. "I don't have to listen to this. Enjoy your bankruptcy."

Again he turned to leave, and again his brother's voice stopped him. "You can have Lansing Square."

For a moment, Dominic stopped breathing. He couldn't inhale because his heart had leapt into his throat. With all his strength, he gripped the doorjamb and put on the face he used while playing cards. Unreadable. Hard.

Slowly, controlling every breath, every motion, he turned. "Excuse me?"

Cole's expression remained impassive. "You heard me. I'm offering you a deal. Do you wish to negotiate?"

Dominic considered it, or tried to pretend he was, but his mind kept repeating the same refrain over and over. Lansing Square. His. The past revealed to him without having to ask permission anymore. The place responsible for his very existence in his possession. Only his.

But was it worth marriage, even to an alluring stranger?

He took the chair across from his brother for a second time and leaned back with what he hoped resembled boredom.

"This woman might not even be Sarah," he insisted, determined to steer the conversation slowly.

Cole clenched his fists in frustration. "The man who found her is the same one who discovered the proof of our mother's disgusting affair. You know, the one that produced *you*?" His brother glared at him. "I have no reason to doubt his thoroughness or truthfulness."

Dominic cocked his head. His brother's dig about his parentage rolled off his back this time because deep in Cole's eyes he saw a wild desperation. A need for his help.

It was a beautiful thing.

"Perhaps you believe this man because you already knew the truth. Perhaps you knew Sarah was alive before anyone brought the news to you tonight."

His brother's eyes widened and his cheeks paled. For a long moment, he seemed to struggle with an explanation or denial. Finally, he folded his arms.

"I don't have to explain myself to you. Do you wish to negotiate for Lansing Square or not? I won't ask you again."

Dominic stared. Cole had all but admitted he had some knowledge of Sarah's existence before the scene tonight. That meant he had been playing a part in a cruel fraud against Katherine and her guardians for weeks . . . perhaps longer. Sudden, powerful anger flowed through his veins, and for once it wasn't the righteous indignation about his own treatment that spurned it.

It was the flash of pain he'd seen in Katherine's eyes.

He shook those wild thoughts away. Cole's lies weren't his concern. Katherine's hurt certainly wasn't. He didn't even know the woman.

"What are your terms?" he asked with little joy.

Colden's eyes narrowed with triumph. "You will marry Katherine as soon as possible. Within the week if we can manage to convince her. That will mitigate the damage this scandal will do to the Mallory name."

"And to her," Dominic said in a flat voice.

Not that he believed for a moment his selfish brother really cared about Katherine's comfort one way or the other, especially if he knew about Sarah. Katherine may have been drawn in by Cole's act, but years of bitter experience made Dominic all the wiser. Cole looked out for Cole. God help anyone in his way.

"Yes, yes." Cole waved his hand as if to dismiss Katherine completely.

"And the terms?" Dominic asked. "Because I know this arrangement isn't as simple as you wish to make it sound. If it were only a matter of arranging for a new marriage, I would be the last person you turned to for help."

Colden arched an eyebrow as if he were a tiny bit impressed by the way his brother saw through his act. "There are a few stipulations," he admitted. "I want her money to come to the family. I want her dowry and whatever inheritance you, as her husband, will have control over. But most of all, I want that bit of property I mentioned earlier."

Dominic's eyes narrowed at the unexpected request. "You want me to take Katherine as my wife and then *steal* from her?"

It wasn't that he was some heroic figure, but there were unspoken lines a man didn't cross. Stealing from one's own wife was one of them.

"Why?" he asked.

Cole shifted uncomfortably. "The truth is I wagered away her property in a card game a few weeks ago. Since I was to be her husband, I had the deed turned over to the gentleman already. You can imagine the trouble it would bring me if that fact were to come to be public knowledge."

Dominic's eyes widened in shock. His brother's lies were layered so thickly on top of one another he was unsure where each began and ended. "You ass. How could you take what was hers? How could you expect me to?"

Cole's eyes grew wilder and some of his practiced, manipulative control fell. "It isn't as if she'll need the money or the estate. I'm well aware of just how much you've brought yourself up in the world. Perhaps you traded on my father's name because no one knew the truth, but whatever you did, you are living more than comfortably."

Dominic slammed a palm down on the desk. "I *never* traded on the Mallory name. I never wanted to."

His brother shrugged. "The point is that she'll never miss what she's lost. But I need it."

Suddenly everything became very clear to Dominic. Sickeningly clear. "That's why you were marrying her, isn't it? Her inheritance."

The room was silent for a long moment while Cole considered that. "Yes, partly. And of course, you must have noticed how beautiful she is. It's a pity, really. I would have enjoyed having her."

Though he hadn't yet agreed to take his brother's place as Katherine's husband, Colden's vulgar admission caused a rush of protective rage to course through Dominic.

"Does she know the real reason behind your suit?" he asked with ice on each word.

Cole let out an ugly laugh. "No! Of course not. Do you really think I'm that stupid? Thanks to the help of her countrified guardians, I was able to turn myself into the spitting image of what she looked to find. You see, they were to be given a special stipend if they were able to marry her before her twenty-first birthday. After she threw off so many suitors, they were a bit desperate themselves."

Dominic snorted in disgust.

"Once she saw me as the prince she had been searching for, she took what I offered eagerly enough." Cole leaned closer. "If you know what's good for you, you'll not breathe a word of my true motives, either. Katherine trusts me, and if this plan is to work she'll need to go on trusting me."

A bitter taste filled Dominic's mouth. He knew what it was like to be on the receiving end of both Cole's lies and his venom. He felt sorry for Katherine.

As much as he longed to walk out of the office with nothing but a well-placed punch for his brother, he managed to rein in his fury and choke out, "And what will I get out of this? Because I had no wish to marry. Not now, not ever. I'll be giving up a great deal if I take your fiancée for my own."

Cole arched an eyebrow as if his brother were an idiot. "As I said, you'll get Lansing Square."

"A rather lopsided deal, won't you admit?"

Actually, it was far from lopsided. Cole didn't know what really hid in Lansing Square.

His brother laughed harshly. "Don't be an idiot, Dominic. Not only is the property worth a great deal, but you have been after me to allow you access to it for years. I know owning that land, being master of that house, would make you feel legitimate. Society may not know you're a by-blow, but you know. And it eats at you."

"Thanks to you," Dominic muttered.

"Thanks to our mother," Cole shot back with heat. "But regardless of who is to blame, don't think your indifference to my offer fools me. You want Lansing Square. Now the question is how much? Because if you don't do this, if you don't take my very generous offer, you'll never so much as see a glimpse of the estate, let alone set a toe over its borders."

Dominic blinked, because for a moment he looked at his brother and saw his father's face. Harrison Mallory always used threats, too.

He glared. "You won't allow me access at all unless I marry Katherine in your stead?"

Cole nodded, a smug smile just below the surface. "And I will sell Lansing Square. It's not wrapped up in entail, I am within my rights to do so. There are plenty of interested parties who'd like to buy it."

Dominic pursed his lips. "I already told you I'd buy it from you. For twice what it is worth."

"No, I won't sell it to you. In fact, I'll sell it to the gentleman who wishes to tear it down. He'll slash and burn the estate and whatever it is inside that you want so desperately." With a grin, his brother leaned back in his chair and folded his arms. "So what will it be? All? Or nothing."

Dominic stared at his brother with bitter hatred churning inside him. How he wished he could laugh in Cole's face and leave him to scandal and bankruptcy. But two things kept him from doing so. One was the need to take what Cole offered.

And whether he ever admitted it out loud or not, the other was the look on Katherine's face when he shut the office door earlier in the evening. The pain in her eyes had been a pain he'd felt himself so many times. Loss.

But marriage? It wasn't something he ever considered. Not with his bastard secret and firsthand knowledge of how ugly and twisted a match could become. His own mother had been trapped in a loveless union with a man she despised. And on one drunken night, she had admitted she wished to be free. That she once had dreams of being with the man who sired Dominic. But those dreams were taken by the prison of a wedding ring. That was the only thing she ever said to him about his real father, but it was enough.

He had vowed never to find himself in such a trap. In London he was free to come and go as he pleased. His mistresses knew better than to lay any claim on his heart. If they tried, he settled with them immediately and cut them free.

In his own element, he could have as many debauched nights in the hells as suited him. He answered to no one. He was responsible for no one. If his heart changed, no one was hurt. Not the woman in his bed. Not him.

The idea of giving that carefree existence up was sobering. But the idea of finding the truth he sought about his past was just as tantalizing.

What was a wife anyway? Katherine hadn't chosen him, there was no love to be lost between them. As long as he was open with his desire to remain free of emotional entanglements and allowed her some small level of the same freedom, she wouldn't be hurt. Until he bored of her, she would be his for the taking in his bed. He certainly felt a strong draw to take her there already. Stronger than he'd felt toward a woman in a long time.

The advantages to his brother's twisted bargain seemed to far outweigh the disadvantages.

"I suppose the terms of the deal are satisfactory," he muttered with a shrug. "But will Katherine go along?"

Cole nodded. "I'll speak to her tonight. By the time I'm finished, she'll believe she's doing this for the best of everyone involved. It's easy enough to play on what she wants and needs."

Nausea churned Dominic's stomach. Colden, the master manipulator. He had no doubt his brother *would* guilt Katherine into accepting the new arrangement. But that wasn't how Dominic wanted to begin a life with this woman. If their marriage was to be built on deceptions, at least he wanted them to be his own.

"No." He shook his head firmly. "Katherine is mine now, I don't want you manipulating her any longer. I'll handle this in my own way. And I won't talk to her until tomorrow. She's had enough shock for one day."

With a shrug, his brother rose to his feet. "Very well. But I warn you, Dominic, she may look like a fragile dove, but Katherine is more of a fighter than you realize. You'll have to keep a short leash on her."

"Actually, Colden, from the first moment I laid

eyes on her, I knew she wasn't fragile." Dominic opened the door and gave his brother one last glare. "And if she's a fighter, then perhaps she's more my match than she ever would have been yours."

With that, he slammed the door behind him and stalked away. But the farther he got from his brother, the more his own words rang in his ears. A fighter he could understand.

But the idea of a perfect match terrified him.

Chapter 3

~~~~⌒◯◯⌒~~~~

Katherine pulled the fur-lined shawl closer to her shoulders before she leaned against the low terrace wall to look at the winter scene below. The rolling hills and trees were covered with a blanket of snow and the air was still and peaceful.

She would have enjoyed the image if it wasn't so completely opposite to her own tormented emotions. She was pulled from all sides as she tried to adjust to last night's news. How could Cole's wife be alive? And what did it mean for her?

Despite her protestations to the contrary, Katherine knew there was some truth to the overly dramatic statements her guardians made. When word of this shocking turn of events became public knowledge, she would be hurt socially. Perhaps even ruined.

"It's so cold," Julia Mallory proclaimed, pulling the terrace door shut behind her. As she buttoned her long woolen coat she said, "No matter how frigid the weather, you're always out here. Why?"

Katherine kept her eyes ahead and continued to stare across the expanse of white stretching out before her as far as she could see.

"It helps me think." She sighed as she turned to face Julia with a weak smile. "It clears my head."

Julia's eyes softened as she reached out to touch Katherine's forearm. "You have much to think about. I'm so sorry. I was looking forward to having you as my sister."

"As was I."

Katherine saw the tears that glimmered in Julia's eyes. Exactly like the ones that pricked her own. She'd been an only child. Julia had been her one glimpse of what having an older sister would have been like. Now she was going to lose that, too. It wasn't fair.

With a shake of her head, Julia turned away. "This woman claiming to be Sarah will arrive tomorrow, I suppose."

Katherine shrugged. "Colden seems to believe without a doubt that it *is* her. Part of me hopes it's just wishful thinking." She sighed. "But if it is true, I have to be happy for him, even if Sarah's return does alter my future irrevocably. He loved her so much."

To her surprise, Julia turned to her with a start, her brown eyes wide. "We-Well, they did have an . . . interesting relationship, I suppose. But I wouldn't say . . ." She shook her head. "Never mind. It isn't my brother I'm worried about, it's you."

Katherine drew away. Though she and Julia had grown close during the past few months, she was surprised Cole's sister would be more concerned about her than her own brother. He was family, after all.

"What will you do, Katherine?" she asked quietly.

Swallowing hard, Katherine contemplated the question. She'd been pondering it all night. "I'm not sure. The general consensus seems to be that I'm ruined. Ruined!" She raised her hands in a mockery of Stephan's theatrical proclamation, but couldn't seem to maintain the falsely jovial mask. Her arms fell with a sigh.

"You know why everyone is saying that." Julia looked at her with pity. "They're only trying to protect you. When word of this gets out, it's going to be a scandal. Without controlling the gossip . . ." She trailed off as if the rest of her thoughts were self-explanatory.

And if Katherine was honest with herself, they were. "The Walworths agree with your mother. They've made it perfectly clear they expect me to marry someone else right away. Eustacia is already making lists labeled ELIGIBLE GENTLEMEN WITH CLOUT."

Katherine covered her eyes with her hands as a dull throbbing began in her temple. The idea of marrying someone who fit that description was downright depressing. She'd spent three years searching for someone who fit her needs completely. She wanted a husband who had no need for her fortune. And she wanted him to be a friend, not someone she could ever fall in love with. No use tempting that part of her that could so easily be swept away by passion. That could be blinded by desire and an empty hope for love. She'd seen the damage those kinds of strong emotions could cause.

Colden Mallory had fit the bill entirely. From the first moment she met him, he said and did all the right things. She hadn't hesitated to accept his offer of marriage.

That future was gone now. Replaced by uncertainty. Exactly the condition she tried so desperately to avoid.

With a start, she realized Julia was speaking.

"Marrying quickly isn't a bad idea."

Her mouth dropped open. "Oh, Julia!"

Julia raised a hand to cut off any remaining protest. "You don't want to end up like me. Alone. If you don't do something to mitigate the harm now, that's exactly what you may be."

"I've always thought being unattached might be pleasant," Katherine said, once again looking out over the snow. "To have no one to answer to, no one to disappoint—"

"No one to hold you when you need to be touched." Julia's voice was flat and emotionless, but Katherine looked up in time to see pain flicker in her friend's eyes.

"Julia." She stepped forward to say more, but before she could, the terrace doors opened and awareness ripped through her. It stole any thoughts and all emotions, leaving only the tingling of anticipation.

Dominic Mallory.

Dominic had a keen sense he was interrupting something important as he stepped from the warm house onto the packed snow that lined the stone terrace floor, but he came out regardless. What he was about to do was important, too. Probably one of the most important moments of his life.

Nausea swept through him at the thought. Was a house worth all this?

No. But the past was. The truth was.

He plastered a false smile on his face as he strode toward the two women. In response to his appearance, Katherine dropped his sister's hand and took two steps away. But there was something about the look in her eyes, just the smallest fraction of heat in the cool green that pushed his nervousness aside and replaced it with desire.

He broke his gaze away from Katherine with difficulty to smile at his sister. Julia's face lit up and the shadows that had been there fled as she stepped forward to hug him. Dominic squeezed her back. When he divorced himself from his family, the loss of his sister's company was the one thing he regretted. Her letters had always been a source of comfort to him.

"I'm so glad you're here, Dominic," she whispered as she let him go. "I know it's . . . difficult for you."

Yes, Julia did know. She'd seen everything that had transpired in this house. A few times she'd even tried to shield him from some of it, to her own detriment. How he wished she had found her own happiness. For some reason, Julia never married, yet, despite her advancing years, she was still as beautiful as ever.

He turned to face Katherine and found her staring at him with a look of wonder on her face. Almost as if she couldn't believe what she was seeing. Then she dropped her stare from him with a warm blush.

"Julia, I need to speak with Katherine alone."

His sister met his eyes with a gasp of shock. Unspoken communication rushed between them and he realized she knew why he wanted to talk to his brother's fiancée.

"Y-Yes," she muttered before she threw a fleeting look in Katherine's direction. "Come speak to me later, if you have need."

Katherine edged closer with a genuine smile for Julia. "If I can't have you as my sister, I'm pleased to keep you as my friend."

With an awkward nod, Julia gathered up her skirt and fled. When the door shut behind her,

Dominic turned back to Katherine to find she'd paced away to the middle of the wide expanse of the terrace. Apparently he was going to have to chase her if he wanted to make her his.

A thought that wasn't entirely unpleasant.

Dominic stalked toward her. This was a business deal, nothing more. It was simply going to take some finesse.

"I'm sorry I interrupted you," he said as he approached her side. He maintained a distance, and was surprised he could smell her lavender scented skin. Even more surprising was the strength of his body's reaction to just the sight of her. He tensed and hardened as much as he would to a familiar woman's touch.

She shrugged as she dared a sidelong look in his direction. "Julia wasn't telling me anything my guardians didn't repeat over and again to me all night long."

With a smile, Dominic sidled closer. She tensed at the subtle movement but didn't turn away. In fact, her gaze lifted more fully to his face.

"This must be difficult for you," he said softly.

A sudden desire to touch her had him lifting his hand from his side, but he forced it back. Now wasn't the time. Touching her would gain him nothing except the pleasure of feeling her skin. He hadn't yet, but knew instinctively it would be smooth as silk.

Instead of responding to his statement, Katherine

slowly turned to face him fully. "I—I wish you had told me who you were last night."

Her voice was soft and had just the tiniest husky timbre. Enough to heat his blood.

"You too," he murmured.

For a long moment, only silence hung between them. Her green eyes were full of emotion, but he couldn't sense which feelings boiled in them. He thought there was some pain in those depths and even a bit of anger, but there was also a touch of something else, too. That hint of heat, passion, he sensed whenever he came so near. It seeped through him until his vision began to blur from strange, sudden desire.

He stepped back as the cold winter wind reminded him of reality.

Clearing his throat, he said, "It seems you're in a predicament." Did his voice tremble? No, it seemed calm enough. He hoped she couldn't sense his sudden lack of control. He wasn't ready to share that weakness. Yet. "One I may be able to resolve."

The strange mix of emotions on her face was replaced by one very strong one. Anger.

"I wonder why it is that everyone, including a total *stranger*, feels compelled to tell me how much trouble I am in?" She gifted him with a pointed scowl. "It isn't my fault if Sarah Mallory is alive. It isn't anyone's fault. In fact, I'm pleased the poor woman is coming back. Her death was very difficult for Cole."

Dominic shook his head. If only she knew what he now suspected. That her "beloved" fiancé had lied to her. He could only imagine her reaction if she discovered Cole's hopes for their engagement, to fatten his own meager purse despite knowing his wife might still live. Katherine wouldn't be so certain all her wishes had nearly come true then. And Dominic doubted pity for Cole would be what darkened her eyes.

Even now, he wasn't sure pity was her overriding emotion. She could pretend all she liked, but she couldn't truly be happy Sarah was returning, ruining all her plans. To take away the man she cared for enough to say she would marry him.

That last thought put an unpleasant taste in his mouth. Pushing that reaction away, Dominic returned to his duties.

"You're right that none of this is your fault," he said softly. "But it *has* happened and the concerns of others are valid. This is about more than just you, Katherine. It will undoubtedly put a stain on my own family's name if it isn't resolved with as little difficulty as possible."

She tilted her head to catch his eye. "I was under the distinct impression you didn't care much for your family."

Dominic froze. "Who told you that?" His eyes narrowed. "Cole?"

This time she laughed, though it was as incredulous as the look on her face. "No. I'd be a fool if I didn't see it myself." She shook her head. "My goodness, Cole and I have been courting for a year, and engaged a quarter of that time. You were mentioned so few times, I could count them on one hand. I was hardly aware of your existence before I stumbled upon you lurking on this very terrace."

Dominic couldn't help the smile that twitched to his lips. This one was sharp. Perhaps too sharp to fool, despite Cole's pronouncements to the contrary. But then Dominic's brother had never been one to recognize the strengths in others, only identify weaknesses to exploit.

Dominic couldn't deny how much he liked Katherine's wit and her utter lack of fear or pretense. The fact that she was one of the most beautiful women he'd ever encountered didn't hurt either. Especially in the snow. Her dark hair and bright eyes stood out even clearer on the flushed pink of her cheeks. It was like she was a snow queen who had wandered from her own realm and found herself here. With him.

"Skulking," he said quietly.

She drew back in surprise. "I beg your pardon?"

He leaned in closer and breathed in that hint of lavender again. He was too close, but he didn't give a damn. "I was skulking on the terrace last night and *you* are changing the subject."

And then he saw something in her eyes that he

never would have expected. A subtle shift that took her from fear and anger to desire. Hot desire, as hot as his own, glittered in her eyes and heated her face. If he touched her, she would melt.

But he couldn't do it. Not yet. Despite just how much he wanted to. Or perhaps *because* of how much he wanted it. The first time he touched her, it was going to be to prove a point, to stake a claim. Not because he was out of control.

"You know what I am going to propose."

Somehow he maintained his distance, holding her captive only with his stare, not his touch. A stare she didn't seem to be able to turn away from, even when her eyes widened and she shook her head.

"No." Her voice wavered.

"Yes, you do."

Desperation flashed in her eyes. "But we don't know if this woman is who she claims to be."

Her whispered statement was a plea that tugged at Dominic's long-hardened heart. His brother had used this woman in the worst way possible. He'd used her desire for a match she chose, he'd used her guardians' greed. Dominic had to amend for that somehow. He didn't know why, but he did.

But all he could do was remove her false hope.

"Cole believes he has irrefutable proof. Sarah's coming here is a formality in his mind, not a test. We must prepare for the very high likelihood that Sarah is alive."

He dared to reach out, finally took the prize he'd been longing to claim. He brushed the back of his hand against her cheek, then cupped her chin to tilt her face up. For a moment, she let him hold her so close that her hot breath brushed his face, then with a start she stumbled away.

"N-no. You shouldn't do that. I'm engaged to your brother."

Her lips formed the words of protest, but her eyes told a different story. She liked his touch, liked his closeness. Deep inside, in places she'd been taught to ignore, she wanted him. A surge of triumph and rekindled desire caught Dominic off guard.

He smiled as he edged closer again, thoroughly enjoying the hunt in a way he hadn't for a long time.

"A married man can't be engaged, Kat."

That made her turn and she steadied herself on the terrace wall when she realized how close he was. But she didn't step away.

"You shouldn't call me that." Her voice trembled like her hands.

"Why? I like it. It fits you." He edged even closer and touched her face a second time. This time she leaned into his palm with a small, almost imperceptible whimper. "But I promise I'll only call you Kat when we're alone. When we're in bed."

Her lips parted with surprise. "We won't ever share a bed," she murmured, but the protest was weak, indeed.

"No?" he whispered.

With a slow dip of his head, Dominic captured her lips. Though she didn't pull back, she seemed frozen with shock and didn't respond immediately either. But that was just part of the challenge. Gently, Dominic nibbled her lower lip, tasting the sweet honey of her skin until she opened her mouth to him with a gasp. He took the access she granted and tasted her. He continued to be gentle, exploring rather than plundering. There would be time to ravage and pillage later.

Finally, with a moan that came from deep within her, Katherine slid her hands up to clutch his arms and tentatively returned his kiss. The reaction sent such a rush of longing through him that it nearly unmanned him. The control he'd been so carefully practicing suddenly fled.

Startled, he used every ounce of strength in him to pull back.

"You *will* be my wife," he whispered, his lips just inches from hers.

She pulled back to stare up at him with jade eyes misty with desire and unshed tears. "No."

"You will."

"I can't," she said on a half-sob.

He shook his head. "Why not?"

"Because you're . . . you're not—" She broke off with a shiver.

Realization shot through him and doused his desire as efficiently as an icy bucket of water. "Who?" He released her to rake a hand through his hair. "Cole?"

She drew away at his harsh tone. But before she could respond to his accusation, the terrace door opened and the very man he would never be strode outside to interrupt them.

Katherine stared at Colden with enormous guilt weighing her down. She'd been kissing her fiancé's brother! And worse than that, she liked it. No, liked wasn't a strong enough word. She was consumed by it, devoured by the tingling sensations his touch left coursing through her body. Even now, she ached to continue what had begun in that all too brief moment.

Cole smiled, but it was a knowing smile, not the one full of kindness he normally bestowed upon her. Katherine stepped away. Dominic was right. Colden was no longer her fiancé. That was as clear as the ice that clung to the stones at their feet.

And worse, it looked as though he was well aware of Dominic's offer to be his replacement. Perhaps Cole was even behind it.

Though she doubted he was behind his brother's sinful kiss.

Her eyes naturally moved to Dominic's mouth. How could such an innocent-looking pair of lips leave her feeling so . . . wicked? Worse yet, how could they reside on a face that was far from innocent? With thick dark hair that was just a fraction too long to be decent, piercing gray eyes, and the hard lines of his face, Dominic Mallory was sin embodied.

"So you have been talking?" Cole asked with a smile as he reached her side.

"Yes. Talking." Dominic shot her a look that she desperately tried to avoid.

"You two cannot be serious about this!" she managed to say with what was an amazing level of clarity, considering her turbulent mind.

Cole's smile turned to a disapproving frown. "Katherine, I really think this arrangement could work out for the best for everyone involved."

Her doubts were wiped away, replaced by a strange sense of disappointment. Somehow she hoped Cole, her friend, a man she'd grown to trust, would understand her opposition to a quick, new marriage. Certainly not arrange for it himself. And behind her back.

"So you *did* send your brother here. You want me to marry him instead?"

"No." Cole took a few steps toward her to catch her hand. Unlike all the other times, she felt no safety in his touch. "I wish none of this were happening, but since it *is*, I want you to be protected. And to do my duty for my family."

"And just how will this protect me?" she snapped, shaking away his hand. Her anger and frustration bubbled up again. "Our engagement was announced in *The Times* and we've had so many parties hosted for us in London and here that I've lost count. Regardless of what you do, everyone will still know your wife returned from the dead. They will know I was thrown off and foisted on to your brother!"

Dominic gave her the half-smile that turned her knees to mush. "No one is foisting anyone. And my name is Dominic."

Hadn't she called him by name yet? She'd learned it the night before, and thought of it, him, a dozen times or more, despite how inappropriate her thoughts were.

He continued, "And trust me, my lady, the fact that I'm Colden's brother is only one of many facets of my personality."

Despite everything else, Katherine's face twitched as she fought a smile at his retort. This man wasn't only handsome, but he was challenging. Of course, he had no decorum. This wasn't the time to try to soften her with witty banter, but still . . .

Cole glared at his brother as if he, too, shared her thoughts about Dominic's inappropriateness. "We'll make explanations. We can act as if you were to marry Dominic all along. We'll say everything else was simply a misunderstanding."

Katherine stared at Cole for a moment in utter disbelief. How thick did he think she was? Very if he expected her to fall for that line of reasoning. Or anyone else for that matter.

"Ha!" she barked out.

With a disgusted sigh, Dominic shoved his brother aside. "Really, Cole, you're terrible at this." In two steps, he caught her shoulders and drew her closer. A fresh stab of heat burned through her. "Katherine, everyone will obviously know the truth, but if you marry me you'll maintain the protection of the Mallory name. My protection. We'll turn any tide with the support of my family, and of key people who"—he smiled—"owe me."

He released her, but instead of feeling relieved she was out of his arms, she felt strangely bereft.

Running a hand through his already tousled dark hair, he said, "If we handle this the proper way, there will be a cut, but it doesn't have to scar."

She turned to Cole one last time, hoping he would change his mind. Praying he would save her by saying this wasn't the only way. But he had a look of relief on his face that let her know he wouldn't rescue her ever again. In fact, this was the best solution for him. All Cole had to do was hand her over and he could be free of the entire mess and only have to deal with the return of his wife. How very convenient.

He met her eyes as if he realized she was waiting for him to say something. "It will be difficult to see you with my brother."

Katherine stepped back. *That* was all he could say? That lie? She and Cole never shared the kind of relationship that would make it difficult for him to see her with another man. They had exchanged a few brief kisses, but she knew they were flat and chaste even before Dominic swept her into his arms and showed her how a woman was meant to be kissed.

And that was the problem. Passion like that was the last thing she wanted.

"This will be for the best." Dominic's rough voice had her looking at him. His gray eyes were gentle with compassion and that expression touched her strangely. "For everyone."

All the fight slipped from her as she stared at this stranger. This man who wanted to take her as his wife. "You aren't really asking me, are you?" she asked softly before glancing back and forth between the two men. "Either of you."

To her dismay, both shook their heads.

With a purse of her lips, Katherine threw up her hands. "Then why pretend to ask me?" She shot both men a look. "Take care of it. You two work it out and I'll do whatever you think is best."

With that, she pushed past them and headed toward the sanctuary of the house. Before she went in, she made the mistake of peeking back over her shoulder. Dominic stared at her with a look so intense it nearly pinned her where she stood. Instead, she forced herself to close the door to his stare. Once inside she leaned against it with a shuddering sigh.

Now that the decision had been made, one thing was clear. She was going to have to focus all her attention on protecting her heart. Dominic Mallory was exactly the kind of man who could blind her to everything else but him, break her heart . . . cause her unending grief. But she wouldn't allow it.

She couldn't.

Chapter 4

"I don't understand why my presence is even necessary," Dominic snapped as he shifted his weight from foot to foot. "Sarah's arrival should be a private moment between Cole and his wife."

His mother was the only family member in the small group standing in the parlor who heeded his statement. She glared at him with a quiet "hush" before returning to the endless wringing of her hands.

Dominic rolled his eyes before casting them to Katherine. To his surprise, she was staring back at him with an expression that made it clear she agreed. And that it irritated her they shared the same sentiment about anything.

He gave her his most wicked grin. Yes, taming

his Kat was going to be an interesting exercise. One
he looked forward to with increasing intensity.

Though he'd never been long without a bed partner, in the last year he had been bored with his
choices. Yes, they were all beautiful, amorous,
skilled mates, but his interest waned after a few encounters, if even that. The challenge of his wife
might prove to be very enjoyable. He would have
the opportunity to introduce her to ultimate pleasures.

And if he lost interest after he claimed her? Well,
then their marriage would be no worse than three-
quarters of those in the *ton*. He only had to make
the boundaries of their marriage clear to avoid
heartache. Later today he planned to do just
that . . . and then kiss Katherine until she trembled.

The parlor door opened, interrupting Dominic's
musings, and Cole's butler stepped in. He gave the
assembled family a quick bow before announcing,
"L-Lady Harborough."

From the look on the pale man's face, it was clear
he believed the woman to truly be Sarah. And if
Dominic had any doubt remaining, it was pushed
aside when she swept into the room with all the
aplomb he remembered.

The family let out a collective gasp. Sarah hadn't
changed since her "death." She had the same thick,
luxurious blonde hair, the same vibrant violet-blue
eyes. And her mouth still had a cruel tilt, like she
was laughing at everyone around her.

Dominic knew from bitter experience that most of the time she was.

"Oh my, I've earned the family greeting," she murmured as she looked from one face to another. Her gaze halted on his brother and her smile grew wider. "Colden. Haven't you anything to say to me? After all, I've been 'dead' for so long."

His brother stepped forward and the expression on his face was heated and desperate. Dominic couldn't help but shake his head. Despite everything, it seemed their relationship would instantly return to its previous pattern. Passionate and hard, whether in the bedroom or in their nasty arguments. The ones they shared even when others were present.

He had always watched his brother's relationship with the interest of a passerby observing the clean-up of a carriage wreck. As much as he wanted to turn away, it was just too fascinating. Or at least, it had been until that moment when Sarah somehow showed up in his bed at his London town house.

Had he been tempted by her? Hell, yes. What normal man of a certain age wouldn't be lured by her lush curves and experienced touch? He'd even indulged for a brief moment in her kiss. But she'd tasted bitter. Dominic had pushed her away. Even so, the whole thing went to hell when Cole discovered them. Any hope he had of a real relationship with his sibling flew away that night, dashed on the rocks as much as Sarah's ship had supposedly been just a few weeks later.

The timing matched so closely, Dominic had to wonder . . . was that why she hid away for nearly two years? Why she allowed the world to believe her dead? Had Cole threatened her somehow because of the indiscretion and a false death seemed better than his alternative punishment? Just how big a role had Dominic played in his brother and sister-in-law's deception?

"Sarah," Cole murmured. His hand stirred at his side to touch her, but she was quicker and leaned up to place a hot kiss on his mouth.

Beside him, Katherine turned her head. Dominic frowned. When she sucked her breath in through her teeth and stared at the ground in misery, it was impossible to forget that he was her second choice. He wasn't her choice at all. Despite knowing that, and even claiming it was better that way, the obvious exhibit of Katherine's pain raised his hackles. He suddenly wanted to make her forget any emotions she felt for his brother.

Sarah broke off the kiss with a feline smile. "Delicious, as always."

Cole took his wife's arm and moved to Larissa. Their mother was pale as she searched Sarah's face.

"Sarah," she whispered. "Where in God's name have you been?"

"Hello, Mother Larissa." Sarah smiled as if she had only been gone for an evening before she turned her gaze on Julia. "And Julia. My, are you still unmarried and living under *our* roof?"

Dominic's sister stiffened. Her breath came harsh. "Sarah, please tell me you forgot who you were. Tell me you did not put your family and ours through hell while you knew we believed you to be dead."

"Direct, as always." Sarah glanced at Cole from the corner of her eye.

Dominic sucked in a breath as he followed her gaze. Cole looked positively sick. Was he waiting for his wife to reveal her own secrets? Or his? He was certainly curiously silent.

"Sarah!" Larissa's voice cut through the tension. Its normal sharpness returned now that the initial shock had passed. Even Sarah's smug expression flashed with momentary surprise. "Where have you been?"

Sarah looked at Cole one last time before she began to speak. Her voice was flat and monotone. "As you know, our marriage was . . . failing. At the time of the incident, I planned a trip to Spain to visit friends. When I arrived at the port in London, there were two ships bound for the Continent. I was meant to depart on one, but when I saw the accommodations on the second, I decided to change."

Julia shook her head. "And when you heard your original ship was lost and all aboard feared dead, why in God's name didn't you send word home?"

Dominic noted Sarah's hesitation as she searched for words to explain the unspeakable, but his attention was drawn to Cole. As their mother and sister interrogated his wife, his brother stood by watching. There was no emotion on his face, save anxious waiting. As if he hoped these explanations would simply pass.

Sarah shrugged. "I planned to let Cole suffer for a short time and then return home."

At his side, Katherine winced. Dominic looked down to see her shaking her head in shock at the other woman's callousness. If only she shared his suspicion that Cole had some knowledge of his wife's deceit, perhaps she wouldn't reserve so much pity for her former intended.

"But life in Spain was so entertaining. I could do what I liked, when I liked, with whomever I liked. So I never got around to writing or coming home." Sarah's smile fell as her eyes narrowed. "Until I heard word from an investigator I hired to watch over Cole that my husband was planning to marry another woman."

Now she turned on Dominic and Katherine with sudden fire in her stare. Dominic felt an odd urge to throw himself between the two women. To protect Kat from the bile Sarah was sure to throw her way.

"I assume, little mouse, that *you* are the woman Cole promised to wed?"

Katherine's hand tightened on Dominic's arm, but she did not burst into tears or turn away from the challenge apparent in Sarah's every gesture and expression. Dominic thought about the words Cole had used to describe her. Katherine was a fighter. Apparently, he was about to see proof of that fact.

"Yes, my lady," she said with as cold and hard a voice as Sarah had ever managed. "I am."

Dominic wanted to applaud when Sarah's eyes narrowed. She wasn't used to being faced head on. That Katherine was staring at her unflinchingly was obviously a disappointment.

"Perhaps if you had been more considerate of your husband and family's feelings, you would not have had to hear such bitter news," Katherine continued. "Cole mourned you extensively. No one should be forced to endure the hell he faced."

"Did you, Cole?" Sarah turned on her husband with amusement. *"Did you?"*

Cole cleared his throat uncomfortably.

Katherine shook her head. "Our engagement has obviously been dissolved," she said as she looked up at Dominic. Her hand tightened on his arm again and warmth spread from the spot where she touched him.

Sarah's mouth opened and she laughed with incredulity. "Don't tell me! You? And Dominic?"

Dominic smiled as he placed a possessive hand over the one Katherine had on his arm. "Yes, Sarah." He gave Katherine an adoring stare, if only to irk Sarah and Cole. Though he had to admit it was far more pleasant to face their poison with someone taking his side. "So some good has come from your deception. I'm very glad you're home unharmed."

Sarah's eyes narrowed to slits. "Are you now?" she whispered. "Well, I'm surprised you would settle for your brother's leavings. Again."

Katherine let out a most unladylike snort and released his arm. She opened her mouth to retort. Before she could say too much and begin an all-out war in the sitting room, Dominic put himself between the women and clasped her arm again.

Though she put on a good front with Sarah, when he touched her, he felt her tremble. It was the first sign of weakness she'd shown in this trying day, and it roused an urge to comfort her that was as strong as any he'd experienced before.

Pulling her a fraction closer to reassure her, he said, "Katherine is marrying me now. From this moment on, we will behave as if the engagement between Colden and Katherine never happened. All of us. Publicly and privately."

His gaze moved from one family member to the next, holding longer first on Cole and then Sarah. To his relief, his brother nodded grudgingly. Dominic prayed Cole would convince his wife to behave accordingly.

"And now my fiancée and I are going to take a bit of fresh air. I assume Colden and Sarah will want a moment alone. Good afternoon." With a nod for his mother and sister, Dominic gripped Katherine's arm tighter and led her from the room.

But as they passed through the doorway and headed toward the terrace, he had to wonder where this strange protectiveness came from. And where it would lead him if he chose to allow it to continue.

As much as Katherine tried to control the wild beating of her heart, she couldn't seem to manage it while Dominic's large, warm hand was on the small of her back, leading her onto the terrace where she first met him. First kissed him.

While the parapet had once been a snowy retreat for her, now he owned it. Everywhere she looked, she was reminded of him. Of his taste. Of the gravelly timbre of his voice.

But then, it was better than being in the stifling parlor with that harridan Sarah Mallory. Katherine somehow hoped the woman would have a good explanation for her long absence. To hear her so callously dismiss the grief she caused made Katherine's stomach turn. Never in her wildest imaginings had she believed Cole's first wife would be so cold. So cruel. So ugly that she demanded a retort.

With a shiver at the memory, she stalked away from Dominic to give herself a safe amount of distance.

What was it Sarah said . . . something about Dominic taking his brother's "leavings"? What did she mean? That Katherine's soon-to-be husband had been involved with Cole's romantic partners, perhaps even Sarah herself? She shot a quick glance at Dominic, who was staring at her evenly, but without advancing on her position.

Did it really matter? It only cemented the things she already believed. That Dominic was a threat to her if she let him get too close.

Which didn't explain the sting in her heart when she thought of it.

"Th-Thank you for taking me out of there," she murmured as she stared absently at the terrace stones.

"It was awkward for everyone involved," he said softly.

"Yes." She flashed back to Sarah's cold viciousness. "I didn't expect her to . . . be like that."

He was quiet for a long moment, as if contemplating what she said, then he answered, "Sarah has always been exactly as she was in the parlor today. Her time away obviously hasn't changed that. She thrives on competition and ugliness. Whether she encourages it in others or participates in it herself."

Her gaze flashed up at the distaste in his voice and she found herself looking at her future husband's face. The hard lines were softened slightly by the compassion he obviously felt for her in her plight. His eyes captured hers and it took nearly all her strength to move her gaze to a spot slightly lower—his square jaw that somehow already had just the hint of a beard.

"You don't like her."

Hearing this statement come from her own lips surprised her. It was an inquiry of a highly personal nature. To hear his answer would only lead her into a deeper understanding of this man. Though he was to be her husband, it was the last thing she wanted. Distance was key. It was far too dangerous to be involved in his life any more than she had to be. Yet she still waited with bated breath for his response.

He laughed. "As you so astutely pointed out, I'm not particularly fond of anyone in my family. Except my sister."

"Then why are you marrying me?" She cocked her head. "If you don't care for them, why protect their name?"

He dodged her glance and shuffled. For a moment he seemed lost for words. But then the smooth smile returned to his face, yet his eyes remained cold. "It's my name, too."

She opened her mouth to press further, but he edged closer to her. All thoughts fled, replaced only by awareness of his scent, his heat, the nearness of his body.

"Regardless of why, we will be married tomorrow. I procured the special license and made the final arrangements today."

Her heart leapt. "So soon?" she asked with a desperate lilt.

His smile faded. "We were only waiting for a confirmation that Sarah was indeed alive. Obviously, she is. The sooner we marry, the sooner everyone can forget and the scandal around us can fade. Cole and Sarah's scandal is another story. I'm not sure the family will ever recover from that."

Tears pricked her eyes. Somehow she dreamed she would escape this nightmare of a situation, that something would happen to change the inevitable. But now that Dominic said they would marry tomorrow, realization hit her. In twenty-four hours she would be Katherine Mallory. But it wouldn't be the same Katherine Mallory she planned on becoming. There would be no staid life full of dependable security and companionship.

Only uncertainty, and startling passion she neither wanted nor needed.

With a shiver, she stepped away from Dominic to sink her hands into the snow along the top of the low wall. Though her thin gloves weren't made for it, she didn't care. She wanted to feel the sting of the cold, to remind herself of reality. That though the snow looked soft and beautiful, it could cut. And so could Dominic Mallory.

"Katherine!" he said, pulling her hands away from the icy water. In a few swift movements, he peeled the sopping kid away from her skin and cradled her damp, cold hands between his own. His skin was hot and slightly rough.

She attempted to tug back to no avail. "Please don't trouble yourself with me," she whispered, willing herself not to look into his face. Not to be pulled in by the heat of his eyes. "You should go and enjoy your last night of freedom."

Dominic held tight to her hands with one of his own, while with the other he tilted up her chin until she was forced to meet his stormy gaze.

"Don't worry, Kat. I intend to."

With that, his mouth came down on hers to claim her in a way she had never been claimed before. Their last kiss was warm and gentle, an exploration. This kiss devoured, consumed. And in her surprise, she responded. She slipped her hands from his to wrap them around his neck and into his hair. The dark locks slid like warm silk through her chilly fingers and the friction of the action caused her to kiss him deeper.

He tasted very faintly of cigar smoke tinged with just the sharpest hint of whiskey. She never would have thought that taste would please her, but somehow it fit him. Smoky and tangy melded together in a way that made her knees go weak.

Not that she needed their support. The moment their lips touched, Dominic crushed her against him and became her support and her prison all at once. A prison she didn't feel any desire to escape.

In comparison to the air and the cold of the snow, he was as hot as fire. She was molded against a hard, lean body that melted her defenses and made her groan.

"Dominic," she whispered against his lips.

He smiled between hot kisses. "So you do know my name. Say it again." Instead she lifted her lips for another kiss, but he held back. "Say it."

"Dominic," she repeated, so low he barely heard it. But it was loud enough for now. Later, he would make her cry out his name. It would be a plea and a prayer as he took her careening over an edge he doubted she even knew existed. Yet.

Just the thought of that made hot blood pump harder through him and he brought her even closer. Slowly, he moved his mouth away from hers and began a leisurely trail down her throat. To his delight, she arched against him with a quiet moan as her fingers dug into the layers of his coat.

Emboldened by her passionate response, he pressed her back against the terrace wall as one hand brushed up her body until he cupped her breast.

Her eyes flew open in surprise, but within the green depths he saw no fear, rather a haze of desire and surrender. With a half-smile, he kissed her again, this time with more control as he gently massaged the nipple thrusting out even through her heavy gown.

Her mouth came open with a gasp of pleasure and he drank deeply of her taste. He wanted her. Now. Tonight. Tomorrow wasn't going to come fast enough.

"Come to my room," he asked as he brushed his lips up to her ear.

Her body tensed beneath his hands and he knew instantly he'd gone too far. Damn.

"No." She whispered it at first, but then her voice grew louder, as if she'd woken from a dream. "No!"

With all her might, she placed her hands against his chest and pushed until she had enough space to slip away. He shut his eyes for a long moment before he turned to face the woman who would be his wife in just a few hours.

"You know that display wasn't all me a moment ago. Deny it if you want to, Kat, but you responded to me the same way I responded to you."

She shook her head, but it was clear he'd struck too close to a raw nerve. "You don't know me. And I—I don't want to know you."

Her lip trembled as she spun away toward the door.

He let her take three steps before he called out, "Katherine."

Stopping, she clenched her hands into fists and slowly eased back around. She arched an eyebrow in haughty question.

"You can run tonight, but tomorrow you won't want to. I guarantee that." He said the words softly, but from her stunned expression, it was clear she took the powerful meaning beneath them.

She swallowed hard, then nodded coolly, as if they had been talking about meaningless things. "Good afternoon."

As the terrace door shut behind her, Dominic let out a sigh of frustration. He'd been so close to the heaven of her embrace. So close, and then to have it snatched away.

By her virginal sensibilities, perhaps. But there was more to her withdrawal than only propriety and fear. He thought of her downcast eyes when his brother kissed Sarah. Perhaps Cole was part of the reason she denied him. She'd begun to give in, but her loyalty and memories of Cole stopped her.

Had his brother ever kissed her that way? Touched her that way? He'd be a fool if he hadn't. Yet, from the way his brother talked, Dominic was fairly certain he hadn't had Katherine in his bed. No, Colden would be proper, at least on the surface.

Unlike him. Dominic would have swept her away and made love to her all night if she allowed it. Marriage vows—or lack thereof—be damned.

But she hadn't. And for some unfathomable reason, that stung.

With a curse, he turned to look out over the dusky shire. Tomorrow, he would erase all memory of Cole from her mind. Tomorrow, he would claim Katherine as his own.

Katherine cursed her shaking hands and body as she ran into her chamber and slammed the door behind her. She felt as if the hounds of hell themselves were at her heels, but of course it was only one devilish man. Still, she had no doubt Dominic might get it in his head to pursue her. And judging from the way she lost all sense when he kissed her in that sinful, heated way, her greatest fear was that she would give in to the pleasure he offered.

And be well on her way to the fate she watched her father cause her mother, where desire and love blinded her to everything else. She couldn't let Dominic wield such power over her.

"Not now, not ever," she said under her breath.

"Are you talking to yourself?" Eustacia asked as she came out of Katherine's bedroom to enter her dressing chamber.

Katherine jumped in surprise. "I didn't realize you were here. Shouldn't you be getting ready for supper?"

Just the thought of food had her own stomach churning, but it was usually a quick distraction for Eustacia. Judging from the determination in her guardian's eyes, it wouldn't be this time.

"Since you are to be married tomorrow, I believe you and I ought to have a little chat." Eustacia settled her large frame into a wing-backed chair with a tight-mouthed frown for Katherine. "Sit down."

She opened her mouth to protest, then gave up and did as she was told. Eustacia and Stephan Walworth had been her guardians since her parents' deaths when she was thirteen. In those seven and a half years, she'd come to realize while her mother's distant cousins were never cruel, they didn't love her, either. And they didn't like to be disobeyed. That point had been made abundantly clear during so many arguments over her lack of interest in her suitors. It had only gotten worse as her twenty-first birthday loomed ever closer. Only her engagement kept them at bay recently.

"What is there to talk about, Eustacia?" she asked as she rubbed her tired eyes. "I would have been married to Cole in a few days if his wife hadn't resurfaced. You never mentioned wanting to have some kind of special talk with me then."

"Well, I had no doubt Lord Harborough would school you in the marital bed with gentleness and care. But his brother . . ." Eustacia trailed off as she fanned her face with one large hand. "Well, *he* is an entirely different beast. A man like that will have expectations. Needs."

Katherine drew back in utter horror as the purpose of her guardian's visit became all too clear. "You've come here to talk to me about the marriage bed?"

Her guardian's face reddened, but she managed a curt nod. "If your mother were still alive, you would be having this conversation with her."

Katherine shuddered to think of how that exchange would have gone. This one was trying enough in itself. "I—"

Eustacia interrupted with an uncomfortable smile and a raised hand. "Now, now. It's natural for you to have some nervousness, but this is a conversation you must have before you depart for Mr. Mallory's estate tomorrow."

"Oh, good Lord," Katherine breathed. Her temples pounded. As if her shocking reaction to Dominic's touch weren't enough, now she had to go through this torture.

"A man will expect you to perform your wifely duties." Eustacia squirmed uncomfortably, as if she didn't know what to say. "He will want to put his . . . his . . . stick inside you."

"His stick?" Katherine repeated, raising a hand to cover the most ridiculous urge to laugh.

"Yes." Now her guardian was nearly purple. "The one between his legs." Her voice dropped. "His man stick."

Katherine bit her lip. Hard. "Man stick," she repeated with difficulty.

"And though it isn't the most pleasant experience, you must lie still and endure it. Because that is the way the Lord enables us to reproduce. Afterward, he will likely be very tired and fall asleep. If you're lucky, he'll return to his own chamber to do so."

"Well, that was very . . . enlightening." Katherine stood and faced the window as giggles wracked her. She only hoped she could keep them inside until Eustacia was gone. The last thing she needed was a lecture to top off this already trying day.

"Yes." Her guardian sighed. "Well, you'll soon see. I just think it's better if you're prepared."

Katherine turned and somehow managed to keep

her mouth from twitching. "Well, I thank you, Eustacia. Now you'd best get ready, and so must I. I shall see you in an hour or so."

"Yes, my dear."

Once her portly guardian slipped from the room, Katherine threw herself on her bed and stifled her peals of laughter in her pillow. Man stick? If only Eustacia knew the kinds of books her parents left sitting about in their bedroom.

At twelve she found one. It was mostly pictures, but she remembered quite clearly that the women did not look as though they were "enduring" anything.

Beyond that, Katherine had already seen the results of a great passion. Despite his philandering ways and cruel treatment, Katherine's mother had been blind to everything but her father's charms. She had allowed herself to be humiliated just because her husband knew how to manipulate her desire for his love. That was the power a woman gave a man when she surrendered her heart. And when she took too much pleasure in his touch.

That blind faith in an undeserving man had killed them both. Katherine never wanted to slip so far into another person that she would be unable to see the truth.

Something that would be far too easy to do with a man like Dominic Mallory.

Her laughter was long gone now. Dominic was obviously skilled with women. And the animosity he had with his family made her wonder even more about his character.

Yet somehow, when he looked into her eyes, when he pressed his lips to hers, she forgot her doubts. That was why she couldn't trust him. She could never forget herself with him.

Not if she ever wanted happiness. Not if she ever wanted peace.

Chapter 5

Katherine's gown was the one she chose months before. The minister she had met a dozen times. The wedding breakfast was exactly as she specified. Even the ring on her finger had been chosen by Cole.

The only thing that made her wedding different from the one she meticulously planned was the man sitting to her right. Her new husband.

Dominic Mallory.

With a disgruntled sigh, she stole a glance in his direction. Unlike her, he seemed unmoved by their current situation. In fact, he was chatting with his sister as if he hadn't a care in the world.

She folded her arms with a deep scowl. The

blasted man. Didn't he know everything was falling apart? She was married to the wrong Mallory. While Colden sat at the other end of the table, watching the new couple through narrowed eyes, she was with his brother. The man who was full of dark heat. Instead of toasting her future with the brother who made her feel secure and safe, she had to start anew with the one who already made her feel the beginnings of the things she wanted to avoid.

She might be married to the wrong Mallory, but that didn't mean she had to surrender to the odd, scorching feelings he evoked. From now on, she would keep him at arm's length. Eventually he'd lose interest and simply go away. She had seen it before.

The electricity of his touch on her bare wrist snapped her back to reality.

"It's nearly eleven," he said as he attempted to meet her eyes.

She ducked away to examine the gilding on the gold plate. There was no time like the present to start putting distance between them. She felt his frown rather than saw it, but it brought her no joy or flush of triumph.

"We should depart," his voice was softer with this second attempt at conversation.

A few seats away, Sarah rose to her feet with a smirk. "Oh, must you?"

Katherine winced at her new sister-in-law's harsh tone. The woman was an utter nightmare. Why in the world had Cole ever married such a witch? Her beauty was the only pleasant thing about her.

"Sit down, Sarah," Cole said in a low voice that made even the minister glance up from his ham.

Dominic settled Katherine's hand in the crook of his arm and ignored the entire exchange as if it had never happened. "The sooner we get on the road, the sooner we'll reach Lansing Square. Once we're there, the talk and the gossip will begin to subside."

"And Lord knows, that will be the best for us all," Larissa agreed with a false smile as she rose to her feet and looked from one son to the other. "We must avoid more scandal at all costs."

"You've always believed that, haven't you, Mother?" Dominic muttered coldly as he began to lead Katherine from the dining room toward the foyer. Behind them, the family followed.

"Shut up, Dominic," Cole snapped.

Dominic spun back to face his brother. With wide eyes, Katherine watched the two men square off. Both looked like any word would lead to a strike. More troublesome was that Sarah stood nearby, grinning as if this fight were an entertainment and not something to be prevented. It put her to mind of Dominic's comment the previous day. That Sarah liked to instigate trouble, or at least bear witness to it.

Katherine stared between Sarah, Dominic and Cole. There was obviously no love lost between the trio, but why did the tension exist? Sarah's comment the day before about Dominic taking Cole's leavings rang in her head again. She could hardly trust Sarah's implications, but Cole was another story. She respected and liked her former fiancé. His disdain for Dominic made her wonder about her new husband.

Julia stepped forward and inserted herself between the two men. "Come now," she said softly, staring evenly at Dominic. "Say goodbye to me."

Dominic's face softened as he hugged his sister. Then he turned back to Katherine with eyes that pinioned her. "Say your farewells. It's well past time we departed."

Katherine nodded slowly, barely able to move under her husband's close stare. As she said mechanical goodbyes to the Mallorys and her guardians, she stole another look at Dominic. He stood impassively by the carriage door, waiting to help her inside. Whatever kind of man he was, it was too late to turn back now. She was Katherine Mallory. And she was being led away from the life she'd so carefully planned by a man she both desired and feared.

Dominic looked up from the papers in his lap to slant his new bride a glance. Though he knew she sensed his stare by the way she tensed, she made quite a show out of turning the next page in her manuscript like he wasn't even there. Stifling a grin, he leaned over the expanse of space between them and placed a finger at the top of her book. With just a nudge, he lowered it until she was forced to look at him.

"Good day, Mrs. Mallory," he teased with his most dashing grin—one, it appeared, she wasn't completely immune to. Her cheeks dusted pink and her eyes widened. Then she smiled and Dominic's world changed.

Whether he wanted her or not, this was his wife. And at present, he wanted her very much. That would change in the future, of course, but he intended to enjoy every moment of the desire while it lasted.

"And a good afternoon to you, Mr. Mallory." Her expression wavered as her blush deepened. "Was there some reason you interrupted my reading?"

With a short burst of laughter, he leaned back to fold his arms. "What is your story about, Kat?"

She blinked. Once. Twice. "E-Excuse me?"

"You've been 'reading' since we began this journey nearly five hours ago. What is your book about?" He slipped the tome in question from her hands and flipped through the pages. "We could start with the main character's name. What is it?"

Her mouth dropped open. She struggled for an answer. "It's . . . it's . . ."

"Matilda." His smile widened. "And our illustrious hero?"

"Of course, his name is . . ." She twisted her mouth, then shrugged in surrender.

"Gerald." He cocked his head as he looked again. "Good God, those are awful names." With little fanfare, he tossed the book on the seat beside him and leaned closer. "Now, why don't you tell me *why* you've been pretending to read? Am I such very awful company?"

"Well . . ." she trailed off with a sparkle of teasing in her eyes that took him off guard.

"Oh, that's good for a man's ego," he laughed.

"I doubt your ego suffers much," she said with a grin of her own. Then she turned serious. "I'm just . . . I feel awkward," she admitted with a shrug of one slender shoulder.

"You, awkward?" he asked to lighten the mood. "Impossible."

She shook her head, refusing to continue the banter they shared a moment before. Dominic was filled with sudden, unexpected disappointment at that fact. Though he had not invited it, he liked the spark between them, the connection he had not shared with any woman in his memory.

She sighed. "You know what I mean. We hardly know each other, and yet we find ourselves bound for the rest of our lives. What can you say to bridge that fact?"

Gripping the seat edge, he leaned forward until they were just a breath apart. "How about what's your favorite color?"

She laughed despite her widening eyes. "I've always been partial to lavender."

Taking a breath of her scent, he nodded. "Of course you are. And my favorite color is green. Jade green."

He let his gaze linger on that very color, reflected in her shimmering eyes. His compliment didn't fail to hit its mark, for she turned those jade eyes away with a small smile.

Silence surrounded them again, but it was no longer the awkward one that plagued them earlier. This time there was comfort to it. Then she glanced back over at him with a guilty look.

"Do you mind if I ask *you* a question now?"

With a shrug, he answered, "It only seems fair. Ask away."

"Where have you been all these years?" She caught a wayward strand of her black hair and began to curl it around her fingertip in a nervous circle. "Why did you leave your family?"

He drew back in surprise. He had asked her favorite color and she responded with a question that was deeply personal, and dangerously close to the truth behind why he wed her. Those facts were something he wasn't ready to reveal yet. Perhaps he would someday. It wouldn't be fair to keep her in the dark indefinitely.

Clearing his throat, he turned to look out at the snowy road passing by his window. "With my family, it's complicated." There was an understatement if ever he made one. "It always has been."

"Family is," she said quietly, more to herself than

to him. "But that doesn't explain where you've been."

So avoidance wasn't a tactic she would accept. He made a mental note as he glanced back her way. Perhaps he could reveal part of his story without telling it all.

"When I was sixteen I had a break with my family. My father and I had a row, partly caused by something my brother told me a few years before." The memory caused him to swallow back bitterness that filled his mouth.

"What did he tell you?"

He shook his head. "It isn't important now. Perhaps I'll tell you another time."

"Very well," she said softly, and there was no pouting in her demeanor or promise of punishment to come in the future. Unlike most women, she seemed to understand his need to keep a part of himself private.

He continued with a growing respect for his bride. "After I left, I returned to school and befriended several men who became benefactors to me. They tutored me in business, cards, and I'll admit, a bit about being a proper rake."

She laughed quietly. "Well, if I ever meet them, I shall compliment them. The last lessons, at least, seem to have taken."

"You haven't seen the rake in me yet, dear lady," he teased. When her eyes widened with interest, heat spiked through his blood. He had to struggle to regain focus and continue. "And I'm sure you shall meet them. The man who was closest to me, Baron Adrian Malleville already planned to meet with me in a fortnight. I extended him an invitation to Lansing Square as soon as you agreed to marry me."

"I'll do my best to make him welcome," she promised. She hesitated and he thought the conversation was concluded, but she continued, "It was good you had friends, but it must have been difficult to be so young and cut off from your family."

He waved her concern off with one hand, though he knew in his heart how much truth she spoke. It had been a lonely existence until he taught himself not to feel the rejection. He had dragged himself up and now he no longer questioned his value or worth.

Only his heritage.

"It isn't important."

A small shiver wracked her. "Yes, it is. I know from my own experience how frightening it is to be alone in the world."

"How?" he asked, eager for insights into her life now that he'd inexplicably shared such a large part of his own. Giving her so much information hadn't been in his plans.

Her face twitched with emotion he couldn't place. "My parents were killed when I was just thirteen."

Pity moved him. "Oh, Katherine, I'm sorry. I didn't know."

Somehow he had assumed her guardians were a later addition to her life. Now he could clearly picture her as a frightened young girl. The image struck a long-hidden chord in him.

Reaching out, he weaved his fingers through hers for a gentle squeeze. To his surprise, she didn't pull away.

"Why would you know?" she asked with just a small choke to her voice. "After all, favorite colors aside, you and I don't know each other at all."

For a moment, he only looked at her. She returned the gaze evenly, as if in challenge, but the defiance hid a plethora of pain and betrayal. These past few days had been a trial for her. Now that they were over, he wanted to reassure her that the rest wouldn't be so difficult. Even if he never gave her much of himself, he still wanted her to feel safe. Secure.

Slowly, he moved across the coach to sit beside her. He brushed a lock of hair off her shoulder with light, tender fingers. "In time, that will change. We will come to know each other."

She drew in a harsh breath through her mouth as he raised his hand, but this time drew it across her cheek. Her eyes fluttered shut as if she were resigned to a fate she couldn't control. Neither could he. He was going to kiss her. There was no choice, only that fact.

Slowly, deftly he gathered her into his arms and eased his lips down on hers. She whimpered a response as her fingers slid through his hair and shots of fire raced through his body. The kiss deepened, the feelings intensifying each time he stroked his tongue over hers.

With each little moan she breathed against his lips, a point of no return moved ever closer, a place where his thin band of control just might break. He didn't want her first experience with lovemaking to be in a drafty carriage. But that didn't mean he couldn't touch just a little, enough to give her a preview of the pleasure to come, but not snap that wire of restraint.

Now her hands slid down from his neck to his chest. He thought her plan was to push him away as she had so many times before, but instead she slipped them inside his coat to where his body heat was trapped. He could have sworn she purred with pleasure and that small noise nearly undid him.

Slowly, he kneaded her thigh through her gown. Her breath caught when he made contact and she tensed a fraction. Still, she didn't pull away and her kiss continued with just as much desire as before. Gently, he massaged until her legs fell open a fraction. He glided his hand up until he brushed the apex of her thighs where he was greeted with intense heat, even through the confining layers of her gown.

She pulled back immediately with a gasp of surprise. Panting, she stared at him. Her eyes were moist with desire, but there was wariness there, too. But why wouldn't there be? She had never been here before, the new experiences were bound to startle her.

"I won't hurt you," he whispered as he placed another featherlight kiss on her lips while he stroked her with his hand.

Though she didn't pull away, she shook her head. "You can't promise me that, Dominic."

His hand stilled and he didn't go back in for a second kiss. He stared at her. Why would she say that? Because her reply seemed to be about more than just a simple kiss or touch. Did she truly believe he would physically harm her?

Before he could ask that very good question, the carriage began to slow. It shuddered as the driver climbed down. Reluctantly, Dominic returned to his own seat across from her. Katherine straightened her wrinkled skirt, but refused to meet his eyes. Instead, she kept her gaze focused on the damp carriage floor.

"This is the inn, Mr. Mallory," the man said as he opened the door.

Dominic kept his eyes on his wife for a moment before he nodded. "Thank you. I'll help Mrs. Mallory down. You tend to the bags."

"Yes, sir. Very good." The man turned away, but left the door open for Dominic to exit.

"Are you ready?" he asked, but even as she murmured her answer in the affirmative, he wondered if he, himself, were ready. Because when they entered that inn, it would be as near strangers, but by morning they would know each other intimately.

"There is only one bed," Katherine muttered as the innkeeper's wife bustled into their room ahead of them and motioned around her.

"This is our best, Mr. Mallory," the woman gushed, obviously pleased to have a wealthy man like Dominic as a guest. She seemed more than eager to impress him. Enough that she hardly even acknowledged Katherine's presence beyond a polite greeting upon their arrival. Was Katherine the only woman not completely taken in by Dominic Mallory's charms?

She blushed at her private question. No, she wasn't *completely* taken in by her husband. Only partly.

But much more than she should be.

The innkeeper's wife continued. "When the carriage arrived, I brought up a tray of food and wine. Is there anything else you'll need tonight?"

Dominic shot his gaze in Katherine's direction and heat flooded her cheeks. It was clear the look was meant to say, *I need you.*

"No, this looks wonderful. Thank you."

"I'll have bath water for you in the morning." The slender woman gave the two of them a knowing smile that made Katherine all the more aware of what was expected that night, then backed from the room and shut the door behind her.

"One bed," Katherine repeated, more to herself than to Dominic.

He swept up one of the glasses of port by the fireside table and took a long sip. "What did you expect, Kat? This *is* our honeymoon."

She shook her head as she began to yank off her gloves. Tossing them on the table, she looked around. The room was large, but it was still dominated by that bed. A big bed. A bed meant for two people to roll around in. And she had a sneaking suspicion it had seen little sleep over the years.

She fiddled with the hem of her sleeve, but couldn't pretend not to see the way Dominic stared at her from the short distance between them. A predatory look.

Yes, she was in a great deal of trouble if she didn't manage the situation, and quickly.

"You must be hungry. Why don't you eat?" she said, motioning to the small spread laid out for them. If she stuffed him with food and plenty of wine, perhaps he would pass out.

"I'm not hungry," he said softly as he took a small step in her direction. "Not for food, not yet. But if you are . . ."

She shook her head. Yes, eating might put him off for a while, but her stomach was already aflutter with anxious butterflies. Adding food to the mix would only make her feel more unsettled.

Eustacia's advice about a wedding night returned to her. Just lie there and bear it. She didn't think that would be possible with Dominic. His hands forced a response in the carriage right before they arrived at the inn, one she'd somehow known to give even without any experience. It was a far cry from what she once imagined this night would be like with Cole.

Cole would have been businesslike. Not emotional. Gentle. And though she didn't believe Dominic would hurt her, there was an animal quality about him that struck a nerve she'd long ago buried. Dominic would expect—no, demand—her response, just as he'd done in the carriage. There would be nothing polite or tidy about it.

Her wayward thoughts drifted again to the books in her parents' home. Only instead of thinking about the naughty drawings she'd seen on their pages, she pictured Dominic acting out those images with her. His hands on her bare backside. His mouth on her breast. And God help her, she pictured touching him, too. Gliding her hands over his bare skin and tasting him.

Trembling at the powerful desire those images created, she spun away from his dark, heated stare. Desperate, she searched her mind for a diversion.

"Shouldn't you be outside, er, g-guarding the carriage?"

Oh, she was a blithering idiot. Years of schooling

and the best she could come up with was to ask the man to guard their carriage?

His smile was fast and wide. "This is the best inn along our route, possibly one of the best in the country. The rooms are expensive enough that the place can afford a night guard." Another step brought him ever closer. She could almost smell the musky heat of his skin. Her nostrils flared in anticipation of the masculine, good scent. "Besides, that's what I hire grooms for. I have duties tonight, but keeping watch over our carriage is not one of them."

He stopped talking, but kept moving, and Katherine found herself backing up until she was nearly in the fireplace. His smile fell.

"Are you afraid of me?"

She shook her head, but a shiver belied her denial. "You must understand, I didn't even know you just a few days ago. I wasn't supposed to face"—she looked around her at the softly lit room—"this for a few days more. When I did, it was meant to be with . . . with—"

"Cole." He cut her off in a voice as cold and hard as ice.

She shut her eyes at the anger that lay just under the surface of his every move and word. It was clear by the way he reacted every time she said Cole's name that Dominic thought she preferred his brother to him. Although she hated to do so, using that belief might be her only chance at salvation.

Slowly, she nodded. "Yes, with Cole. I need time to adjust to my new circumstances. Perhaps you could get another room—"

"Ha! On my wedding night?" His laugh was brittle. "We're trying to avoid a scandal, Katherine, not create a new one. No. We will share a bed, as we were meant to do, but I will make you this promise. I swear I won't do anything you don't consent to." Again he advanced, and because she had nowhere else to go, she held her ground. "Is that agreeable?"

No. No, it wasn't. Sleeping in a bed beside this man was going to be difficult. She had somehow hoped he would take her offer and go away, but of course that had been folly. A man like Dominic Mallory wouldn't be ordered about by anyone, least of all her.

"Er, very well." She turned to the changing screen by the fire. Her valise was close by and someone had already taken her nightclothes out and laid them in easy reach. "I'll just put on my nightgown, then we can go to b-bed," she stammered. "To sleep. We can go to sleep."

Dominic arched an eyebrow, and with a quiet curse, Katherine grabbed her night shift and scurried behind the screen, safe, if only for the moment, from her husband's stare.

But not from the ever-growing knowledge that no matter how she tried to avoid the inevitable, tonight she would become his in every way.

And she secretly thrilled at that thought.

Chapter 6

Even behind the so-called protection of the changing screen, Dominic could see every line of Katherine's body in the firelight. He supposed he should feel guilty, but that was the furthest thing from his mind as he watched her shadow stoop to pick up her nightgown.

By God, she was perfect. From the soft curve of her breasts as the shift slipped over them, to the long lines of her arms and legs, it seemed her body had been plucked from his most detailed, sinful fantasy.

With a growl of frustration, he turned away. This wasn't helping his raging desire any. He wanted to finish what they began in the carriage. Suddenly, he wanted to make Katherine his, to erase any claim Colden had on her—but she couldn't, or wouldn't, let his brother go. Her comments a few moments before proved her hesitation had to do with lingering feelings for Cole.

That stung.

The only way Dominic knew to combat her remaining desire for Cole was to make her want *him* more, which he had promised not to do, or at least not to force.

With a blush, she came around to the front of the screen. Her nightgown was high-necked and plain. It allowed him no access to her body, except for the visions he created in his mind.

"A *modiste*," he muttered under his breath as she moved with uncertainty toward the bed. Yes, he was going to have a dressmaker come to Lansing Square as soon as he could convince one to travel. His wife needed new nightclothes. Ones that didn't make her look like an old woman. He wanted access, at least visually, to her skin. He wanted to see the way her breasts curved. To watch her hips sway when she walked.

"What was that?" Her voice trembled.

"Nothing."

"I'll ring for someone to take my hair down." The tremor in her voice grew stronger and struck both a primal and protective chord in him.

"No." He held up his hand to keep her from crossing to the bell at the door. The idea of someone invading their privacy was actually physically painful to him. "I'll do it."

"Take my hair down?" Her eyes widened. "You?"

Nodding, he motioned to the dressing table. She sat and he found himself staring down at the crown of black satin that was her elaborate hairstyle. Had he ever taken a woman's hair down? He didn't think so, but the scent of lavender that seemed to hang around her addled his mind and filled his senses until he couldn't have moved if she paid him good money.

Slowly, he eased his fingers into her hair and she let out a long sigh as he massaged her scalp.

"Did I hurt you?" he asked, surprised he could breathe, let alone speak.

"N-No." In the mirror, her eyes darkened and dilated.

If that was her reaction to his touch, he planned to take her hair down each and every night. With trembling fingers, he set about finding the pins. Finally, her hair cascaded down her back in a long, flowing cloak. It wafted out sweetness as a few strands brushed his legs and fell to her hips. He might have believed he'd died and was in heaven if he weren't so aware of his body's sinful reactions to touching her.

"Brush," he requested softly.

She complied with shaking hands.

Stroke by stroke, he glided the brush bristles

through her hair—gently, so as not to hurt her, he smoothed the waves. How had he not known how erotic a woman's hair could be? He prided himself on his experience, but for the first time in a long time, he questioned his prowess.

It affected her, too. In the mirror he could see her shut her eyes, and apparently try to bite back soft moans each time his hands weaved through her hair. Triumph coursed through his every nerve and vein.

"Thank you," she murmured as she suddenly skittered out of the chair. She touched her hair briefly, then shook off whatever effect he had on her, and glanced toward the bed. "I—I'm tired."

It was a lie, and he knew it. It wasn't sleepiness he saw glittering in her gaze. No. It was time for a seduction. If she pushed him away, so be it, but he had no choice but to try. Not when his body called so insistently.

"Very well. I'm tired, too." Slowly, he eased the buttons open on his shirt. She watched him, swaying slowly in his direction before she yanked herself back.

"Uh, you're going to take off your clothes?" she asked.

He gave her a grin. "Well, I normally don't sleep in my full regalia."

"What do you sleep in?"

He couldn't resist. "Nothing."

A little strangled groan escaped her lips before

she controlled it. His smile broadened. "But for you, I'll keep my trousers on tonight."

Relief lightened her face. "Very good."

She dove into the bed and under the covers as if she could hide from him there. She was so very wrong. When he pulled back the blankets on the opposite side of the bed, she stiffened again.

"You're going to sleep under the coverlet?"

He laughed. "Kat, it's the middle of winter. Surely you don't want me to freeze."

Her pause was just long enough that he knew she was considering the merits of letting him do just that. "No, of course not." She turned her back to him. "Good night, Dominic."

He didn't answer but edged himself into the middle of the bed. Slowly, he wrapped his arms around her waist and pulled her back against his stomach.

"You said you wouldn't force me to—" she yelped.

"I'm not forcing anything," he drawled close to her ear. "But is there any harm in holding you? Not anything else. Just holding you."

A tremor quaked through her. "No, I suppose not."

She settled back, but there was tension in every muscle in her body. Every part of her that touched him. And he ached to ease those tensions in the most pleasurable way imaginable.

"What about a good-night kiss?" he asked softly, amazed he was keeping any semblance of control in either his voice or touch. All he wanted to do was flip his wife over onto her back and taste her, touch her, plunge deep within her until they had become one body. Until he had purged all memory of any other man.

There was a long pause. "Dominic . . ."

"Just one."

Slowly, she rolled over to stare up into his eyes. "O-One."

He delved his hands into her hair and splayed his fingers out as he lifted her head to meet his lips. She let out a gasp at his ardor, but her surprise didn't keep her from returning his kiss with the same passion she exhibited in the carriage earlier.

Cupping one breast, he rubbed his thumb over the peak of her nipple as he continued to devour her mouth. The nub hardened beneath his touch as she arched with a moan that broke the contact of their lips.

True to his word, he released her. She stared up at him with eyes that flickered in the dying firelight. "You . . ."

He shrugged as he propped himself up on his elbow to stare down at her. "You said only one."

Surprise flashed over her face. Then she swallowed hard. "Was—was that a whole kiss?" She blushed and her stare dropped from his. "I don't think that was a complete kiss."

His smile widened as he slipped an arm beneath her head. She let out a little sigh as he gathered her against him. "The more I kiss you, the harder it's going to be for me to stop."

Her eyes fluttered shut and with a small sigh she whispered, "That is a risk I'm willing to take."

What was wrong with her? Was she crazy? Had she really just said making love to her husband was a risk she was willing to take? She couldn't. She shouldn't. And yet . . .

His mouth came down on hers to claim a second time and all her thoughts faded away on an explosion of desire and pleasure. There was no way she could resist his touch or the promise of all there was to come.

More to the point, she didn't want to. From the moment they stepped from the carriage into the inn, she had anticipated this very moment with as much eagerness as anxiety. And now that she was here, with Dominic's breath mingling with hers and his hands holding her steady while he kissed her, she forgot her fear.

Tomorrow she could remember.

She wrapped her arms around the strong curve of his shoulders and kissed him back. He was like granite beneath her hands, hard and smooth and so very male. And for that moment, so very hers.

His hand slipped to her breast and another burst of sensation rolled through her. Her thin shift didn't protect her like the woolen gown had in the carriage. His touch pierced through it like the cloth wasn't there at all. New feelings, ones she hadn't even imagined, followed in his hand's wake. Flames shot through her and any residual resistance melted away.

"Dominic," she whispered as her lips settled against the throbbing pulse point at the base of his throat. As she darted the tip of her tongue out to taste his skin, he let out a low groan that reverberated against her lips.

Shoving the covers off both of them, Dominic glided her shift up her legs. Every inch revealed more creamy skin, and guided him ever closer to the heaven he had longed to experience from the first moment he laid eyes on her on the terrace. He thought she looked like a Snow Queen then, but it wasn't true. If anything, she was a goddess of fire. The hidden heat below her surface could easily rage out of control if he touched her just right.

At present, each and every touch was the right one. When he cupped her kneecap, she shivered. When he stroked from the outside line of her thigh to the inside curve, she gasped with pleasure. Her fingers kneaded his shoulders as her eyes fluttered shut, her lips trembled.

Katherine arched under him as he settled his hand between her thighs. It took every part of him to remember this would be the first time she made love, that he couldn't take her with the animal intensity he craved. At least, not yet. Not until she would feel no pain when he entered her. After that, well, it was too much to imagine just how many ways he wanted to be with her.

And until he could, there was only one way to ease his own frustration: Make her writhe.

Slowly, he eased one finger inside her hot sheath to find her already wet and ready. But from the dazed look in her eyes, she was still as uneasy as she was aroused.

"Does that feel good?" he whispered as he leaned down to press a kiss on the flat of her stomach, just along the edge of the nightgown he'd pushed up.

"Y-Yes," she stammered, even as she grasped a section of the sheet and balled it in her fist.

"Tonight, I want everything to feel this good for you." He looked down to meet her gaze and was lost in a sea of green. "I want you to be ready for me. There are things I want to do to make you ready."

Those eyes widened until it seemed that everything that mattered was tinged with misty emerald. "What do you want to do?"

He withdrew his hand to glide the shift over her head, baring her to him and giving him the first glimpse of her nakedness that wasn't in the form of a fantasy. Her cheeks flushed red as she maneuvered to cover herself, but he gently pinned her arms to her sides.

"You're perfect. Never hide from me"—he cupped her chin to place a light kiss on her lips—"ever."

Katherine was surprised that her eyes tingled

with tears when he said those words. All she *could* do to protect herself was hide from him. Yet he made it sound like it would be so easy to open herself and allow him in. Despite everything, in this blissful moment, he made it seem simple . . . and perfect.

Then his mouth was gone from hers, instead blazing a hot trail down her throat, over her collar bone and finally, shockingly, over her breast. He caught one hard nipple in his lips and sucked ever so gently. Awareness ripped through her and she let out a cry of pleasure. It was like she hadn't really been alive until his touch, because she never imagined such intense feelings were possible.

But they were. Pleasure so focused it was almost pain. It was new and powerful. She craved more of it.

She clasped her hands around the back of his head and urged him to continue as she wound her fingers through his hair. And he didn't disappoint, only shifted to her opposite breast to suckle there.

Her body sang with need and she found herself not only enjoying his touch but returning it with fervor. Her hands smoothed over the taut muscles of his back, his arms, exploring every contour as if she could memorize them. Her palms glided around to his chest, then down to his stomach. Was there nothing about the man that wasn't perfectly formed?

"You should take off your clothes," she whispered, then placed a soft kiss on his shoulder. He even tasted good.

"Oh, yes?" he asked with a half-smile, though each time her mouth dragged across his skin, his gray eyes fluttered shut, proof that he didn't possess as much control as he wanted her to believe. It gave her an enormous sense of power.

"Why?"

She blushed. "Because if you're naked, too, perhaps I won't feel so shy."

Truth be told, she no longer felt shy, only curious. She wanted to know every part of her new husband's body. She wanted to look at him as intimately as he looked at her.

Before he acquiesced, he dipped his head and caught her lips. But this kiss wasn't gentle, it was completely passionate. He delved his tongue between her lips, tasting her, branding her. Just as she melted, he pulled back and rose to his feet. In a few swift motions, he shrugged out of his remaining clothes. In the dwindling fire and candlelight, nothing was left to Katherine's imagination. And now she knew just what all the fuss was about.

The man was like a god. From the broad shoulders to the tapered waist, the strong arms and legs, to the hard thrust of an erection that jutted proudly between his legs, he was what a higher power had imagined when He created Man.

As her husband climbed back into their marriage

bed, she felt shyer than she had a moment before. Because now the full reality of this moment hit her. This man, Dominic Mallory, of the flashing gray eyes and perfect body, was hers. And she was his. Forever.

Dominic brought his mouth down on hers, coaxing a hot kiss from her with insistence and teasing gentleness. As she rose up beneath him to wrap her hands around his shoulders, he maneuvered to lie on top of her. The entire length of him pressed against her, not one inch of her lush curves was secret to him. But still, it wasn't enough. He wanted to be completely joined with her, one body.

"Dominic," came her soft voice between kisses.

"Hmm?" He was far beyond the ability to form coherent words now. All that existed for him was sensation. Anticipation.

"I'm ready." Her eyes sparkled with desire. "You said you wanted me to be ready, and I am."

His body actually twitched at the innocence of her words. She had no idea what would happen when he entered her. No idea that a shock of pain would welcome her into the realm of physical joining, no matter what he did to make her more comfortable. But he could hardly wait any longer, and he knew he could make up that one moment of pain with a thousand more of pleasure.

"Very well," he whispered while he massaged her thighs a bit wider. Slowly, he took a position there, just nudging the tip of himself against the cleft of her womanhood.

Katherine's breath hitched as he brought his weight down on her. Then he was moving and she forgot to breathe at all while he filled her inch by marvelous inch. Her body was made to stretch around him, to accept him as if he were meant to be a part of her. She shut her eyes and allowed herself to believe that perhaps he had been.

He paused. "I'm so sorry, Kat. This is going to hurt for a moment."

Before she could nod or stiffen in preparation, he grasped her hips and entered her fully. A shock of pain made her shut her eyes with a sharp intake of breath, but it passed nearly as quickly.

"I'm sorry," he repeated as he kissed her damp neck and brushed dark hair from her eyes.

"No," she answered as she tilted her head and pressed her lips to his. "It doesn't hurt now."

His tongue swept lazily along her teeth, her lips, until any pain was forgotten, replaced by a wondrous sensation of belonging to him.

"I *am* going to make up for it," he whispered, low and close to her ear. "More than make up for it."

Then he moved, rotating his hips in slow, smooth circles. Katherine shut her eyes with a low groan at this new experience. How could something so simple feel so devilishly good? Yet it did. And it was feeling better by the second. He circled and thrust, fast and slow until she found her hips rising to meet him.

She clenched her hands into fists against the solid planes of muscle across his back. Her breathing came heavier, but so did his, rasping like music to her ears as she realized he was fighting for control as much as she was. As he thrust faster, the pleasure rose again. Her muscles trembled, her hips lifted uncontrollably and moans she couldn't hold back were ripped from her lips.

They built ever closer and closer to a moment. She knew it was coming, but didn't know what it was. Only that she wanted it more than she could remember wanting anything in her life. She craved release, but also that he wouldn't stop.

And then she couldn't think at all as the bubble of pleasure that had been building inside her burst free. She wailed low and loud as she collapsed back on the pillows.

Dominic gripped Katherine's shoulders as she thrashed out a release so powerful he felt it coursing through his own body. Somehow he managed to keep his rhythm, bringing her along as far as he could before he lost all control and joined her, pouring into her with a hoarse cry that echoed in the room around them.

For a long moment, neither moved. Katherine continued to hold him close with no indication she wished for him to leave her body. And he wasn't sure he could. He was lazy with sated warmth, and the idea of staying inside her for a few moments longer brought him a new level of pleasure he'd never felt before.

Normally, he couldn't wait to disentangle himself from his lover's arms after he spent. He'd never been much for the false words of love whispered in the dark, or the empty caresses that spoke of more emotion than he felt.

But with Katherine, these moments were somehow . . . different.

"Am I hurting you?" he whispered as he placed a soft kiss behind her ear.

She was silent for a long moment, then she sighed. "Not yet."

With reluctance, Dominic rolled away from her, but only to pull her to his side. As she rested a soft cheek against his chest, he breathed in her scent. Now she was his. No other man could say he had a greater claim on her than Dominic did. Not even his brother.

"I'm sorry if it stung," he whispered in the darkness as she pulled the covers up around them. "It only hurts the first time."

"It wasn't anything," she said after a long pause. "And the end more than made up for the beginning."

He shifted until she was fully pressed against him. "I promise you, it will only get better each time. I'll learn your body and you'll learn mine."

"Eventually you'll tire of me," she said in a brittle voice that cut the darkness. "All men tire of their women eventually."

The words hung in the air between them. Bitter and cold. Quickly he sought to erase them, even though he knew them to be true, at least in his experience.

"I don't foresee that happening any time soon. Judging from what just happened, I predict we'll be completely enamored of each other for some time to come. Completely . . ."

"Obsessed," she whispered, though it seemed more to herself than to him. Her tone troubled him, for it was distant and pained.

With a gentle tug, he rolled her over to face him. Her green eyes were wide and full of tangled emotions. Fear and worry and even the glimmer of remaining lust. He bent to place a gentle kiss on her lips.

"Only if we're lucky." Then gentle turned more possessive and the stiffness in her body relaxed as he drew her closer.

Yes, he could very easily become obsessed with his wife. And he intended to have her just as addicted to him.

Before Katherine opened her eyes, she knew she was alone. Dominic's presence didn't overwhelm her as it did when he was nearby. Carefully, she opened one eye to scan the room. The rumpled bed contained only her and a carefully folded note on the pillow beside her head.

Pulling the sheet around her breasts, she rose to a sitting position and was greeted by aching muscles. Well, what else could be expected? She had spent a night making love to her husband, she'd earned being sore. Of course, he was right that each and every time grew better and better. He'd proven that so many times during the night, she'd lost track.

She was slipping further and further under his seductive spell.

With a groan, she read his note.

You looked too beautiful to wake. I will be down checking on the horses and ordering our breakfast.

> *Dominic*

Why did her body tingle when she read his words? Why did she blush with pleasure that he'd written she was beautiful? And *why* was she examining every swirl and curve of his handwriting as if it mattered to her?

With a quiet curse, she balled the missive up and tossed it toward the fire. So much for self-control and careful detachment. Those things deserted her the moment Dominic pulled her against his chest and offered her heaven in his arms. A heaven she'd taken despite knowing how dangerous it could be.

True to her fears and the memories of her parents' marriage, she had all but forgotten her doubts the night before. Her suspicions about Dominic's other women were lost the moment he pulled her shift over her head. Her fears of growing too close to him were gone when he filled and claimed her.

Even when it was over and her doubts returned, she hadn't pushed him away. When he'd said he couldn't see them tiring of each other for "some time to come," it had proven to her that he wasn't the kind of man to make lifelong commitments. But had she put her night rail back over her head and gone to sleep? No, it had only taken a few brief moments for him to smooth her fears away with skilled hands and tongue.

She flopped back on the bed. Did he know the power he held over her? A man like him, a man who had doubtlessly been with many women, would surely know the power passion and desire could hold. He had talked of surrender the night before. Of obsession. Those were things she never wanted to feel.

They were things she'd seen her own father demand from her mother. He had been a rake, too. And like Dominic, had been forced into a marriage not of his own choosing. When her mother's love suited him, he used it to get what pleased him. He didn't care about the damage he caused fragile Elsie Fleming when he took his mistresses out in public or disappeared to carouse for days on end. He didn't care that his only daughter had been the one to comfort her mother when he disappointed her over and over.

The lies and fighting and pain had grown and festered until it culminated in that horrible night nearly eight years ago. Katherine still remembered her mother's scream. The blood. Her own wail as it echoed in the dark night. And the long walk through the dark that seemed never ending.

"Kat?"

As the door flew open and Dominic took three steps inside, she sat bolt upright. She wasn't in the past. She could force herself not to relive all that heartache with this man, a man whose interest in her would surely fade in time, whether or not he admitted it now.

"My God, I should keep you in bed all the time. You look magnificent," he said as he quietly shut the door behind him and stalked toward her with purpose in his stare.

With a glance down, Katherine realized she hadn't pulled the sheet up. Dominic raked his gaze over her half-exposed body in a long, hot motion. Despite herself, she shivered with anticipation before she dragged the sheet up as a protective barrier around her.

"You should have woken me," she stammered as

she stood up and backed away from his approaching form.

He paused with a frown. "You were exhausted." His expression turned to a wicked smile. "You earned a long rest after last night."

Though it took every ounce of strength in her body, she managed to keep her tone icy. "Yes, well, the sooner we get to Lansing Square, the better. If you'll excuse me, I shall ring for my maid and begin getting ready."

"We could stay here another night," he said softly as he reached out to glide his fingertips down the length of her bare arm. Sparks of awareness crackled in the wake of his touch, and the urge to shut her eyes and sway toward him was almost overpowering. Almost.

"No," she said, a bit louder than she intended her voice to be. "No. I think we should just move on. Please, let me get ready."

His brow furrowed. "I'll help you."

Her mind flitted to the image of him taking her hair down the night before. His touch had been so sensuous and gentle it had softened her to him. She couldn't let that happen again. Especially since she guessed once he got the sheet off of her, he would pull her into the bed and they would be back where they started.

A temptation she had no choice but to resist.

"No, thank you." She pulled her arm away and paced to the low fire. Staring into the flames, she did her best to keep her thoughts on what she had to do, not her husband's touch or taste. "I would rather just ready myself."

When he was silent, she allowed herself a peek over her shoulder. His eyes had turned from light gray to stormy seas, and his frown set his jaw in a way that left no doubt he was both annoyed and frustrated by her resistance.

Guilt stabbed through her. Guilt she tried to deny.

"I'll send your maid up right away. If we leave within the hour, we can reach Lansing Square by nightfall."

He turned on his heel and walked out the door, closing it behind him with little gentleness. After he was gone, she took two steps in his direction. All she wanted to do was follow and call him back. To ask him to help her ease the ache that had as much to do with her heart as her body.

Of course, doing that would only make her more vulnerable to him. Doing that was entirely out of the question.

Chapter 7

Trying to pretend an uncomfortable silence was an amiable one was a feat worthy of Hercules. Katherine was far from the mythical god. In fact, it took all her strength not to burst into inane conversation just to avoid the heated, quiet stare Dominic had fixed on her for the past quarter of an hour.

Instead, she bit her lip and turned the page of the old copy of the *Morning Chronicle* she held in her lap. The fact that she'd already read this particular edition four days prior made feigning interest all the more difficult. Still, she had little choice since her husband had already caught her in a lie about her novel, so there was no use pretending to read that.

With a sigh, she glanced up. To her relief, Dominic was looking out the carriage window. It was her first moment of freedom since they left the inn hours before.

He had attempted conversation for a while, and she had to admit, avoiding that was a difficult prospect. Dominic Mallory was much more than a darkly handsome man. He had knowledge of history and literature, as well as a cunning wit that made it difficult to pretend she didn't care for his company. Under any other circumstances, she would have called him a delightful traveling companion.

Instead she called him husband, and that changed everything. His comments were often punctuated by a light, yet seductive touch or a suggestive word that made her heart pound with the promise of pleasure she remembered all too well. He knew it, too. His smile grew each time her body lurched with reaction to his closeness. Each time she remembered his arms around her the night before.

No manner of distraction changed the fact that she'd wanted him then. If she allowed herself to admit it, gazing at him across the carriage as he examined the passing winter scenes, she wanted him now.

"Finished with your paper?"

His soft voice cut the space between them. She jolted at his words. Clearly, he was aware of her scrutiny even though he seemed distracted.

"Yes," she said before she stopped to think. Damn, now she had no excuse not to talk to him. "Would *you* like a glance at it?"

Gray eyes moved over to capture hers. "No, I read that particular issue a few days ago. Right before I gave it to *you* at breakfast that same morning."

The color that warmed her cheeks bled away. Did nothing get past this man? He seemed to remember every detail, every moment that could be used against her in the future. It was something to keep in mind as she navigated the volatile waters of their new marriage.

"Did you?" she asked when she found her voice.

"Yes."

"I must have forgotten."

To her surprise, he didn't press, but turned away to return his focus to the outside world. After a few moments he seemed to have forgotten her entirely. It seemed the closer they got to their destination, the more distracted he became. When he spoke, it was obvious it was with effort, and the sensual undercurrents that had been a constant between them faded, if only a fraction.

With a frown, she folded her paper and set it on the seat beside her. The entire day, her husband had pursued conversation with her like a setter on a scent. Now he barely acknowledged her existence. Why?

And why did she care? This was exactly the respite she needed. Still, now that she was being ignored, it was far less pleasant than she guessed it would be.

"Dominic?" she ventured softly, leaning forward. For a moment, he didn't answer. Then he shook his head like he'd been in a dream and said, "Yes?"

"How much longer?" she asked, not necessarily because she cared, but just to say anything.

"Not much farther, I'd wager," he said, but he hardly looked her way.

She frowned. What happened to the teasing, sensuous man who had married her?

"Why don't you tell me about this place . . . Lansing Square is it?"

Instead of dragging him from his current state, her question seemed to darken his mood. His mouth turned down sharply. "Yes, Lansing Square."

For a long moment she waited for him to elaborate, but he said nothing. "Well? What else can you tell me aside from the name?"

He finally looked her in the eyes and some of his focus seemed to return. He even managed a small smile, just a ghost of his usual cocky smirk, still it struck a chord deep within her. One that left her wanting to comfort him, despite her vows to avoid that kind of closeness.

"There isn't much to say." He accentuated the statement with a shrug. "I would guess Lansing Square is much like any other estate in the country. I know it's large and has brought in a modest income over the past few seasons."

She wrinkled her brow. "You act as if you've never seen the place before."

"It's new to my holdings," he said.

He shifted as if the subject made him uncomfortable, though she had no idea why he wouldn't want to talk to her about the home she would live in, at least some of the time. Unless . . . unless there was something about the home he didn't want her to know. Perhaps he kept a mistress there in the past, or intended to in the future.

Bitterness tainted her mouth before she shook off her jealous reaction with a scowl. These were exactly the emotions she wanted to avoid.

He cleared his throat. "Katherine, I think you and I should talk about our marriage."

She started as her heart lodged itself in her throat. There was something ominous about his tone, especially given her thoughts.

"Now?" she croaked.

He nodded. "We should have discussed it before we wed. Certainly before last night, but circumstances intervened and I never found the right time. It is my fault and I apologize."

She tilted her head as confusion and anxiety flooded her. What could he want to say to her that should have been said before they made love?

He continued, "Our marriage was not one either of us chose."

She winced, though he said nothing that wasn't true. She had no call to be stung by his directness.

"No," she admitted softly.

"But that doesn't mean it cannot be successful. It is a matter of reasonable expectations. Most marriages turn . . . ugly when one party feels trapped or disappointed."

Katherine nodded as she fought to keep her expression bland. Dominic was only voicing her own fears and expectations of the future, but somehow hearing him outline their marriage in such cool terms was like a dagger.

"If we are to avoid those complications, I think we ought to be clear about our desires now, so there will be no surprises."

She cleared her throat. "Very well."

"In London, I have a certain kind of life." He shifted again.

She folded her arms across her chest as an ineffective shield. This was not a surprise to her, but she somehow wanted to protect herself from it.

"You mean you have a mistress."

He drew in a shocked breath that she would be so frank. "Not at present, but I won't deny I have had them in the past."

She frowned. "And you wish me to know you will find one again. I understand."

She looked out the window to the gathering dark. The forlorn winter scene certainly reflected her emotions. It was one thing to guess your husband's activities. It was quite another to have him tell you outright. Never mind that this distance he was putting between them was exactly what she claimed to desire.

Dominic shook his head. "No. As I told you last night, at present, I have no plans to take another woman to my bed."

She glanced at him with unwanted hope lightening her heart. Hope she quickly quashed as she remembered how her own father had promised not to take a mistress only to appease her mother. Those promises had been broken. Again and again. She had no reason to believe Dominic's wouldn't be broken as well. A rake was a rake.

"You give me enormous pleasure, Katherine," he said, his voice turning soft and seductive. When he touched her hand, she found she couldn't pull away. "I am very happy to save all my desires and attentions for you."

"At present," she said with an arched brow. "But in the future, that might change."

He tilted his head as if he didn't understand. "I— I suppose so."

"And then you would take a mistress." When he didn't answer, she shrugged. "May I take a lover, as well?"

His face changed instantly and he withdrew his hand. A hot flash of jealous anger darkened his eyes and hardened his jaw.

"You would want that?"

Actually, she couldn't picture sharing her body with any man but the one across from her. But she couldn't let him know that. To do so would be giving him all the power to wield over her. She turned away so he couldn't read her emotions.

"It seems unfair for you to find pleasure with another woman while I sit at home alone," she murmured.

The vein in his neck popped as if he was reining in powerful emotion. He clenched his hands into fists in his lap as he nodded slowly.

"A point well taken . . . I suppose. But not one we must explore now. I have no intention of leaving you unfulfilled for the foreseeable future."

The anger and disappointment that rushed through Katherine surprised her with their intensity. On one hand, she was furious that her husband would bring up such a subject on the day after their wedding. That he would all but admit he was the cad she feared him to be.

But the other part of her had to respect his brutal honesty. At least this way she knew what to expect. And she could more easily keep her vow to lock her heart away from him.

Still, his admission about wanting her and only her, even if only for a short time, made her heart skip. It gave her a shameful thrill that seemed to override her other, more measured reactions.

"As you say, this is no love match," she said with more difficulty than she wished. "We're both aware of that. There is no reason why you should not continue your life as before. And I will find things to fill my time that do not require me to pine for my husband's heart."

He nodded, though he looked less than pleased at her swift agreement to his terms. He opened his mouth to speak just as the carriage began to slow. Dominic looked out the window and whatever he wanted to say was lost as his attention was reclaimed by the outside world.

The carriage stopped, but before the driver or footmen could climb down to offer assistance, Dominic wrenched open the door and stepped down into the snow. He blocked her own exit, so she simply watched him.

With a sigh, he looked up, obviously examining the house and main grounds, but from his expression she couldn't tell if he was pleased with what he saw or not. She waited for a few moments, then slid closer to the carriage entryway and cleared her throat.

He jumped as if he had forgotten her presence, then turned to her with a sheepish smile. "I'm sorry, Katherine." He motioned for the step to be set outside the door, then offered her a hand to help her down.

The storm had passed and a brisk breeze blew the clouds back until a full, bright moon reflected pale light from the snowy drifts. For a moment, her eyes adjusted to the darkness, then she looked up.

The house was large, as large as any country estate she'd seen, but it was rundown from what were obviously years of neglect. A few of the upper windows had been boarded shut, the stone was chipped and discolored, and the paint was peeling in some places. Though the house had obviously once been a showplace, it wasn't anymore.

Still, it had enormous potential. The windows were large, and many would get beautiful direct sunlight for a considerable portion of the day. The gilding and design details on the house were lovely, and would easily shine again with little work.

"Well," he asked, and there was an endearing nervousness to his tone, "what do you think?"

She smiled. "It's different than I thought it would be."

"As I said in the carriage, it's a new addition to my holdings."

He shrugged as if he couldn't care less, but she knew this estate had to be important. After all, why would he bring her here instead of going to London or to one of his other properties unless this place meant something to him?

"I can see why you acquired it." She tilted her head to look up again. "It has lovely lines. It's been neglected, but it has potential."

He ignored her statement. "It's freezing out here. Let's go inside."

He held out an arm, and she hesitated before taking it. Touching him was a dangerous prospect. Why, just taking his hand to exit the carriage brought heat to her blood. When he pulled her up against his side to lead her wherever he wanted her to go, it sent a shockwave of awareness through her.

After their conversation a moment ago, it was clear she had to keep herself separate from him whenever possible. He did not intend to share anything deeper than his body with her, so she could not give him a part of her heart.

Not that she wanted to.

As they reached the top of the stairs, the door opened to reveal a butler. He had a gentle face, white hair, and the eyes of a man who wasn't sure if this change of ownership would bode well or poorly for him.

"Good evening, sir," he said as they came into the warm foyer. "You must be Mr. and Mrs. Mallory."

Katherine's eyes widened at this surprising introduction. From his phrasing, the butler made it clear he'd never even met Dominic before. She stared up at her husband. "This really *is* a new addition to your holdings."

He smiled, but answered the butler. "Yes, I'm Dominic Mallory. And you must be Matthews."

"Yes, sir." He motioned for the footmen to take the bags and their coats and the men did it with swift efficiency. "We have been working hard to ready the estate for your arrival, sir, but it's been difficult—"

Dominic waved off the man's apologies. "Don't give it another thought. Mrs. Mallory and I don't plan to stay here at Lansing Square for long. I'm sure whatever accommodations you've made will be more than adequate."

Matthews' eyes grew more wary at the curt response. Katherine was surprised her husband would talk to the man that way. Obviously the staff was nervous about their new master and mistress. Only a few reassuring words could have eased their troubled minds and let them know the new couple had no intention of eliminating their positions. In fact, if she had her way, there would be more funds going into this estate for upkeep and renovation.

"Matthews," she said softly, smiling at him as kindly as she could to make up for Dominic's brusqueness. "The house is lovely. I know we shall both be happy here."

The man's face softened, but only a fraction. "Thank you, madam. Let me escort you to your rooms, then I shall let the cook know of you arrival. Unless you'd like me to assemble the servants for immediate inspection."

Katherine began to nod, anxious to make some kind of connection with the staff, to ease their fears. And also to begin her duties as lady of this house by making an overture to the servants.

"No, Matthews, it's late," Dominic interrupted. "Just have someone bring up a tray for us. We'll greet the servants tomorrow."

The no-nonsense tone of her husband's voice kept Katherine from arguing, at least in front of this stranger. But she was again surprised at Dominic's dismissal. He behaved as if this house and its staff were nothing but a bother to him. After his anxious response to seeing the home, she was surprised.

Matthews bowed and motioned to the staircase. He led them through a winding hall to a large double door. When he opened it, he revealed beautiful master quarters, with a huge pillared bed, a roaring fire, and the most elegant furniture Katherine had seen in the house so far. It was evident the staff had gone to a great deal of trouble with the room, and she was touched.

"I'm afraid the other chambers aren't ready, but we did the best we could with the master suite," Matthews said with an apologetic bow.

Katherine started at this news, that separate quarters hadn't yet been prepared. But she did her best to keep dismay from her face. The staff had obviously done their best to make their homecoming a welcoming one. Her upset would only be taken as censure.

How was Matthews to know she didn't want to share a chamber with her husband? If she had her own room, she could at least feign a headache to escape Dominic's sensual charms. Now there would be no such respite. It would take pure willpower to keep from giving in to what she knew he would offer.

"Thank you, this is magnificent," Dominic said with the first smile he had spared for the kindly man. He looked anything but upset by this turn of events.

"I will have someone bring a tray for you. Good evening." Matthews bowed to them, then began to close the doors. A twinge of panic twisted her heart. The moment that door was closed, temptation would begin.

"Good evening," Katherine replied weakly.

The door closed behind him and she found herself alone with her husband.

"You could have been friendlier," she said softly as she paced around the room.

It really was lovely, though her eyes couldn't help but continually stray to the four-poster bed across from the fire. It had been made for sin.

"What did I do?" he asked with false innocence. His eyes never left her, catching her every move with the intensity of a hawk on a hunt.

She did her best to focus on her scolding despite the growing awareness in her and the rising heat in the room around them. Even after all his statements about their marriage, she couldn't control her physical reaction to him. She was drawn to him like a moth to a flame. It didn't seem to matter that he could burn her; she craved his heat and light.

"You were short with him. And you gave him no reassurances when it was obvious he and the rest of the staff need them."

She plucked at the worn curtain before daring to meet Dominic's gaze. The gray pulled her in, warmed her. Made her want and made her forget.

Wordlessly, he took a long step closer. She drew

in a sharp breath of anticipation. It was so hard to resist him when he looked at her that way. Those bright eyes and half-grin melted her insides. She found herself actually swaying.

"Y-you must be tired," she stammered as she gripped the curtain even tighter. The brocade dug its pattern into her palm, but she worried it was the only thing keeping her upright at the moment. The only thing grounding her.

"I'm hungry," he whispered in that gravelly voice that touched her very core.

She grasped at the lifeline his words offered. "Yes, well I could ring and see where the food is. Or we could go down and explore our new dining room." She flinched at the desperation in her voice.

He cut her off with a wicked grin. "I wasn't talking about food. I'm hungry for you."

Her knees buckled, but she managed to stay upright with a stunning show of self-control. A voice in her head screamed at her to resist, but her body didn't seem capable of listening. Everything tingled like he had already touched her, and her lips throbbed for his kiss.

"I—I will perform my *wifely duty* if I must," she said shakily, hoping her use of the term would put him off.

His eyes lit up, but he chuckled rather than turn away. She cursed herself. Obviously he could see how much she wanted him, despite her protestations. She turned to face the window so he could no longer read the need in her eyes.

"Was last night so terrible, then?" he asked.

Suddenly, he was at her back, his breath caressing her neck before his lips descended to claim the skin left uncovered by her gown. She stiffened as hot sensation rushed through her, enveloping her in a web of desire.

"I-it was fine." She fought to breathe as he unfastened one button at the back of her gown and flicked his tongue across the flesh he revealed. "If you like that sort of thing."

He responded with a low laugh that reverberated across her skin. Her eyes fluttered shut as she barely held back her answering moan.

"And you don't?" he asked.

"No. It's too . . ." Intoxicating. Wonderful. Tempting. "Messy."

Another button slid through his fingers and his mouth followed the trail with a whisper of breath against her spine. She tried not to arch with pleasure and failed. He smiled against her skin.

Damn.

"Hmmm. So you don't want me to do this?" He slipped the last button of her gown open and bared her back to the heat of the fire and his equally burning touch.

"N-no," she whispered, though her voice cracked.

"Or this?" His hand slipped beneath the layers of

gown and chemise to brush against her skin. Slowly, he eased the dress over her shoulder and reached around to cup one exposed breast.

"No." Her voice was even softer and less sure.

She couldn't remember anything anymore. Not why she'd been lecturing him, not why she had to keep him at arm's length. Nothing but the fact that he melted her, and it was folly to try to resist.

"And definitely not this." He flicked his thumb against her nipple and wet heat rushed through her, settling between her legs where she began to throb with a want to bring him inside her.

"Oh God," she sighed and finally leaned back against his chest. "Please don't."

She was begging him. Begging him to stop, urging him to continue. His knowledge of what she secretly wanted and needed overpowered any ability to resist.

Slowly he turned her until she faced him. With primal possession in his eyes, he gathered her into his embrace and kissed her until her knees were water and her blood was boiling.

"And not that either."

He drew back and stared at her, waiting for . . . something. She wasn't sure what.

"No."

He pursed his lips and pulled back. "Very well. I won't take something you don't offer freely."

When he stepped away, Katherine stared at him.

He was going to go? Just leave her like this with her dress halfway around her waist and her body trembling with unfulfilled need? Simply because she asked him not to take her again? It was unexpected. It was unfathomable.

And it wasn't what she wanted. Deep in her heart, she'd expected him to force his suit until she surrendered like she secretly wished to. But now *she* had to make the choice. Do what she wanted. Or what she needed.

The first one triumphed.

With trembling legs, she stepped closer. Meeting his eyes, she reached out to take his hand, then returned it to her breast. His eyes widened, but he didn't pull away.

Her voice trembled. "I won't refuse you. It's clear you know that."

In silence, he put a hand around her waist and drew her closer. He caught her mouth for a long kiss as he swept her into his arms and carried her to the bed. His bed.

Their bed.

Laying her down on the coverlet, he brushed a few loose locks of hair away from her face, then eased the rest of her gown to her waist. She arched under his touch as he massaged her breasts, dragged his fingertips down her stomach. No matter what she said, or how she reasoned with herself, she wanted him. And she would be forced to find another way to stay in control when it came to her heart, because she had no intention of giving up these stolen moments. Not ever again.

His mouth came down on hers, claiming her and taking her thoughts. It followed the trail of his hands. His tongue darted over her breasts, teasing the nipples into tight beads, then dipping into her bellybutton as he stripped her of the rest of her garments.

Dominic leaned back to look at his wife. Her ebony hair had come down from its confines and spread out like a fan over the pillows. Her face was flushed with desire and she arched up when his fingertips brushed the soft mound between her legs.

For the first time in years, he felt lucky. Lucky to share this moment with her. Lucky to claim her as his wife. It was both a terrifying and an exhilarating sensation.

Returning his mouth to her stomach, he inched lower. She tensed as he nipped at her inner thigh.

"Dominic," she gasped from above him. "What are you—?"

He didn't allow her to finish before he pressed the most intimate of kisses against her. With a hoarse cry of surprise and pleasure, she gripped at his shoulders. Her nails dug into his skin as he stroked his tongue along her sex, tasting her like the sweetest wine. With each sinful kiss, he felt her move closer to the brink. He loved being the one to take her there.

By God, she was the most responsive lover he ever had. Though she was inexperienced, she was a quick learner. Her body was made for him to take and to give. And he relished every moment.

Katherine's vision blurred as Dominic slipped a finger inside her and continued to kiss her in that scandalous, fantastic manner. Her body was alive, aware in a way she hadn't been before. The pleasure was focused and intense as he quickened the pace of his tongue and fingers. And then, just as she was sure she couldn't bear the intensity any longer, she fell over an edge and experienced a release more powerful than any the night before. Her body thrashed wildly as she cried out over the long, insistent waves of her climax.

Before she had even a moment to breathe, Dominic rose up to kiss her mouth. She tasted her own desire on his lips as he eased into her in one, fluid movement. She hadn't realized he'd undressed, and would not have even been aware if the house was burning down around them.

Her body bucked at his first hard thrust. Then another and another as the pleasure built again with shocking speed and intensity. She scraped her nails across his back and kissed him with all the heat he created in her. She arched and writhed and finally cried out his name as she found release a second time, made all the better by the way he stiffened and climaxed deep within her.

It took her a long time to realize he'd moved and gathered her up against his chest. She was warm and sated, and feeling dangerously close to caring for this man she hardly knew, who could so easily make her forget the vows she'd made on the long, dark night her parents died. Make her forget she couldn't surrender the wavering control she held over her heart.

Letting out a deep sigh, she began to trail a small pattern through his wiry chest hair with her fingernails. Perhaps what she needed was a new plan. One that allowed her this pleasure at night without growing any closer to Dominic.

Already, his deep breathing indicated he was almost asleep. She propped herself up on one elbow to take a clear look at him. He was far too handsome for his own good. With a scruffy hint of a beard and the hard angles of his jaw, he looked more like a warrior than a pampered second son of a rich society member.

Though judging from the story he told her about separating from his family at such a young age, perhaps he hadn't been so very pampered.

Not like Cole. Cole didn't have an edge to his face. He didn't have any edges at all. He was all gentle, rounded curves. Safe and manageable.

As she looked down into her husband's dark face, Katherine realized just how boring safe and manageable would have been. Dominic fascinated her, and that was more terrifying than she could imagine.

Which was why she had to come up with a new plan.

She could share these passionate moments with Dominic in their bed. But in order to protect her heart and keep from becoming far too enamored of the man, she would make sure she didn't spend her days with him. She wouldn't find out more about his past. She wouldn't ask him to share his plans for the future. That lack of interest was what Dominic said he wanted, so it would be easy enough to manage.

The estate required enough work to keep them both occupied. She would simply throw herself into making their new home a showplace Dominic could be proud of.

With a small smile, she rested her head back against his shoulder as his arms tightened around her. But as she drifted into an exhausted sleep, a voice in her head whispered that this plan would never work.

Chapter 8

For three long days this had gone on. Three nights of going to sleep beside a warm and willing woman, only to wake to find her gone, not to be seen until a meal or another night. Even then, Dominic received no explanation for her absence. His wife had become quite adept at night, distracting him before he asked too many questions.

He slammed the door as he entered the hallway. He *should* have been interviewing the servants who might have been in residence around the time he was conceived. He *should* have been searching the attic for evidence.

But he wasn't, because he was on the hunt for Katherine.

He'd woken alone and disappointed . . . again. He'd been having a particularly pleasant dream he hoped to act out with his lovely wife. Reaching over to find her side of the sheets cold left him grumpy as a bear in winter.

So now he was storming through the house, searching for a woman who was hiding. Hiding from *him*! What had he done to her except make her cry out his name with pleasure for long hours each night? He paused with a wicked smile at the thought, before his irritation returned.

Damn it! It was time he and his wife had a little discussion about her refusal to spend time with him.

He stopped with a shake of his head. What was he thinking? A wife who submitted willingly, even enthusiastically in his bed and required nothing else from his heart, was perfect—more than he ever could have hoped for. So why did it bother him so much?

Perhaps because the moments they did spend together, particularly at meals, were as stimulating as the moments in their bed. Katherine had a sharp wit. Her laughter, though rare, warmed him. And she was intelligent as well. She often made observations about items in the morning paper that made Dominic think.

He *enjoyed* talking to her. Had that ever happened with another bed partner? He didn't think it had, and that made his wife's disappearances all the more irritating.

With a growl, he spun on his heel to go back to his duties in the attic. He wouldn't look for her anymore. If she didn't want to spend her time with him, that was fine.

"Oh, Matthews, this really is lovely."

He stopped at the sound of her voice in the room just a few doors down.

"You're telling me you found this folded in a trunk in the old servant quarters?" she continued.

Dominic found himself moving toward her voice like a sailor to a siren's song. He could only hope she would be less dangerous. Though he feared she was much, much more so.

With a sly glance, he peeked around the corner into a dusty parlor. He hadn't even known this room existed. Of course, he paid little attention to the house at all, beyond his fruitless searching. Why bother? He didn't want to live here. Only lies existed in these walls.

Katherine rubbed a fold of bright blue fabric between her fingertips with a nod for the butler. Matthews had a boyish grin on his wrinkled face like he'd done something to please his pretty schoolmistress. Dominic scowled. All the servants, especially the male ones, adored Katherine. Sometimes he thought they tolerated his presence only because it accompanied hers.

"Thank you so much. I believe you're right, it will be just perfect on the chair here in the corner.

Especially with that dusty blue I plan to order for the settee," she said.

"Excuse me." Dominic took two long steps into the room. Immediately, Matthews straightened up with a blush. Katherine spun to face him, then gave him a diminutive nod and returned to examining the ream of fabric in her hand.

"Good morning," she said.

Turning her attention back to the butler, she continued her discussion as if Dominic weren't standing there. "Will you ask Claudia and Irene to continue cleaning the ballroom? I know they've been working hard and the room is nearly ready for my ideas. I appreciate—"

"Matthews, step out," Dominic snapped, unsure of why his frustration was rising. All he knew was that he wanted his wife's attention. And while she was prattling on to the servant about ballrooms and fabric and who knew what else, he wasn't going to get it.

"I beg your pardon?" Katherine's eyes grew wide as she fixed her gaze back in Dominic's direction.

"I asked the butler to leave so that I may have a private word with you," he said in a no-nonsense tone Matthews obviously recognized immediately. With a bow, he hurried from the room and closed the door behind him.

Katherine set her precious roll of fabric onto a chair, folded her arms, and glared at Dominic.

"That was very rude. Matthews and I were having an important discussion."

Dominic motioned to the fabric with a dubious look.

"Yes, fabric is important! I'll have you know I intend this room to be the main sitting area in the house." She turned to motion to the streaked window. "It has the best light and will be warm and comfortable in the afternoons."

Dominic arched an eyebrow. His irritation was fading. How could he be annoyed when his wife had a smudge of dirt across the creamy perfection of her cheek? He stepped forward to wipe it away with his thumb.

"Why did you leave our bed this morning?" he asked.

She jumped at the contact of his fingers on her skin, but didn't pull away. "What do you mean? I woke up and went to my chambers to dress."

His annoyance returned at her reminder of the work she had been doing on the lady's chambers adjacent to the master suite. He didn't like the idea of her wanting another bedroom.

"Ah, yes, your chambers. How soon will your work be done there?"

Shrugging one shoulder, she paced away from him. "Soon. A few days I would think. And then you'll no longer be troubled by my constant presence."

"Where, in my bed?" he asked with a wicked

grin at her blush. "Ah, Kat, you may trouble me in bed any time you like. Even now."

Her skin colored even darker, but she struggled to maintain a posture of outrage. "Were you looking for me for any particular reason, sir, or just to practice your considerable talents as a rake?"

He hesitated. What could he tell her? That he'd spent a good part of an hour searching the house because he missed her? Even if that suddenly felt so true, it wasn't something he intended to admit. It broke all the boundaries they established the evening they arrived at Lansing Square.

Besides, those feelings weren't real. His desire drove him to her side, not something deeper. The fact that he was beginning to like her was completely separate from the fact that he longed to touch her.

"You've been avoiding me," he said instead.

She blanched at his directness. Pacing away, she motioned wildly around the room. "I—I . . . Perhaps you would like to see my plans for the estate?"

He sighed. The house again. Every time she didn't want to have a meaningful exchange with him, she brought up Lansing Square and her plans. He had heard enough about paint and carpeting to last him until his dying day.

"No." His tone was much harsher than he planned it to be. Enough that she stopped short with a glimmer of hurt in her eyes.

"No?" she repeated.

"You heard me. I don't care what you want to do with the house. In fact, I don't *want* you to do anything with the estate. I don't want the servants disposing of one thing," he continued, tamping down his guilt over her upset and confused expression.

"I don't understand," she said softly. "The furniture is innumerable seasons out of date and the walls need new paper and paint. I would love to purchase a new rug for the west library. How am I to make this estate one you'll be proud to hold if you won't allow me to make even the simplest of changes?"

He frowned. "I'm telling you I don't care about the estate. I've no plans to keep it. I intend to complete my business here and then we will return to London. My town house there is in no need of repair or renovation. You'll find it more than comfortable. In town, you can spend your days shopping—"

Her mouth fell open. "You don't intend to keep up Lansing Square?"

"I thought I said that," he snapped, sharp again in the face of his discomfort. He never expected her to become attached to the worn-down place so quickly. Actually, he never imagined she would be interested in it at all.

She shook her head in protest. "But this is a lovely estate, Dominic. With a bit of care and money—"

"Neither of which I want to venture."

She drew in a shuddering breath. "Then *why* are we here? You claim indifference, but you could have easily taken me straight to London or another of your properties. What kind of business could you have when you search the attic all day and keep yourself—" She stumbled over her words. "Occupied with me all night?"

Dominic clenched a fist. There was no way to explain his motives. Not without telling her the truth, which he wasn't prepared to do.

"My business is none of your affair," he said softly.

She barked out a burst of laughter. "I'm your wife."

"Which does not entitle you to be privy to everything I do."

She frowned. "Very well. Perhaps you *will* tell me what will happen to the servants if you don't utilize this estate? Are they to continue on such a small pittance that they can't even have half the rooms open? That they would be embarrassed to present the estate to visitors?"

He ran a hand through his hair. How had the conversation gotten so far out of control? He had plans when he found her. Topics to broach. This wasn't one of them.

"I have no idea. I'll be sure they have references when they depart, of course—"

"You're letting them go?" Her face twisted in horror.

"When we are finished here, yes, I intended to close the estate completely and send the servants away."

"No! Why? Why not sell it to someone who will understand its full value? Or use it yourself?" She gripped his arm to accentuate her plea, and he winced with guilt at the contact.

There was no way to explain how hateful he found this place. Here he'd been conceived from some kind of affair. Here his father had turned away from him. Shutting up the estate like it was unimportant always seemed like poetic justice to Dominic. It turned Lansing Square from an ugly part of his history into a piece of land he could do with as he wished. A memory he could discard as easily as he had been discarded. He certainly had no wish to live amongst the reminders of the past.

"This is none of your affair!" he growled.

She held out her hands in mute entreaty. "Sell it to me."

Dominic froze. Her words were a sharp reminder of how he had given Katherine's money to Cole. She had nothing to buy the estate with. Guilt filled his every fiber. Along with a strange urge to tell her everything. About his father, why the estate was so important, and how he had come to inherit it. Even how he made a devil's bargain with Cole to take her in trade.

Instead, he turned away. There was no purpose in sharing those things with his wife. To do so only confused their marriage and opened him to emotions he had controlled for a long time.

"This subject is closed, Katherine. We won't discuss it further."

"But—"

He spun on his heel. "There is nothing more to say."

She stared at him with hurt and anger flashing in equal measure in her eyes. Her lip quivered as she nodded briskly. "You may dismiss me like you would a child, but you cannot stop me from continuing on as I have been. I won't ask you for funds, but I *will* continue to give this estate the attention it deserves."

With that, she stalked from the room and slammed the door behind her. Dominic stared at the place she stood a moment before, his heart giving the oddest ache.

"Damn," he muttered to himself as he took a long glance around the room she wanted to make their main parlor.

She was right, the window was lovely, affording visitors a full glimpse of the large lawn and cluster of trees in the distance. In another life, in another house, he would have let her do as she wished. He might have even helped her, if only to watch the unexpected pleasure she took in making a home. Their home.

But not here.

* * *

Dominic slammed the trunk shut and sat down on its lid. With a curse, he wiped his brow with a handkerchief, then rubbed his eyes. He wasn't to the halfway mark of his search yet, and he had found nothing. No clues to who his real father was, or where the man was now.

Of course, it was silly to expect an instant answer, but his patience was wearing thin. He had pursued these answers for so many years, he could hardly remember a time when they didn't plague him.

After Cole told him of his bastard state that ugly night, he had turned to his mother first. As a child, he felt the distance between them, the coldness she displayed more toward him than Julia or Cole. Yet, he still prayed she would give him the answers he sought.

Instead, she responded to his query with shock, anger and denials so shaky they only confirmed his brother's story rather than put it to rest. Repeated questioning only gave him the same results.

Except for one night.

He'd found his mother crumpled by the fire on the floor of her private library, sobbing uncontrollably. She was normally so cold and collected, the perfect image of a lady, but that night she had been drinking. He could still recall the sharp scent of sherry on Larissa's breath when he ran to her, thinking she had been injured.

For once, she hadn't shaken his help off. In fact, she clung to him, weeping as he helped her to her feet, begging him not to tell Harrison Mallory what he had seen.

There had been a brief moment when he thought of doing just the opposite. Let his mother feel the wrath she had never protected him from. But he couldn't do it. Instead, he had quietly led her up the back stair to her room.

Only then had she whispered the one thing she ever admitted about his real father.

"I loved him, Dominic. If I hadn't been forced to surrender him by Harrison, everything would be different."

She had truly looked at him then and touched his face with the only warmth he remembered feeling from her. And then promptly slipped into drunken unconsciousness before Dominic could take advantage of her unusually candid mood.

But the next morning, she claimed no memory of the encounter. The rift between them grew ever wider until he stopped asking questions she refused to answer.

With a sigh, he shook off the memories. Reliving the disappointments of the past served no purpose. Not when there was still so much to be done here. So much to search.

He peered around him. Trunks and boxes were scattered with no rhyme or reason across the attic floor. The ones he'd opened, he moved over beside the pianoforte by the round window in the corner. Odd to see such an instrument all the way up here, but Matthews said the piece was damaged. Oddly, it had not been destroyed.

That was the problem. Nothing in this house seemed to have been thrown away. He had hundreds of years of history to examine in order to find one tiny clue. And he hadn't even started on the other rooms in the estate and hiding places on the grounds.

"Blast!" He rose to his feet and gave the crate a kick. Sometimes the search seemed hopeless.

Exhaustion suddenly overwhelmed him. He wasn't getting enough rest at night, though he had no complaints about Katherine in that respect. Then there was their disagreement earlier that afternoon. Her hurt face danced before his eyes every time he paused in his work.

He pushed away the guilt. It was only fatigue and hunger that made him dwell on emotions he normally kept at bay. After a bite to eat he was sure he would be able to forget Katherine's questions and face yet another crate.

With a slightly lighter step, he hurried down the many flights of stairs toward the parlor below. Already, he could taste Mrs. Matthews' tea and scones. The woman wasn't just his butler's wife, but a magnificent cook and housekeeper.

Just as he was about to turn to the last flight of stairs into the foyer, he heard Katherine's voice. Katherine's laugh, to be more specific. It was a sound he hadn't heard more than two or three times since he met her, and none of them had anything to do with him. Yet he found the sound soothing after his tumultuous days of hide and seek with the past.

"Oh, Matthews, you needn't worry about that!" she said and he could hear the smile on her face. If he closed his eyes, he could picture it. "No matter what Mr. Mallory said, I assure you, I'll make sure everything works out. Whether or not he wants it, I'm going to change his mind about this place. I'm going to make him proud."

"I hope so, madam. I shall make those arrangements right away."

Despite the fact that Katherine was completely ignoring his earlier order, Dominic was warmed by her statement. She wanted him to be proud. He couldn't remember the last time anyone considered what he wanted. Yet this woman who shared his last name, but who he knew very little else about, did.

"I'll be outside taking a stroll through the gardens if you require anything else, or if Mr. Mallory inquires about me."

Dominic drew back. It was freezing outside and the snow had only let up an hour before, yet she wanted to take a walk? She did love winter—that was one thing he had learned about her since they met. But it was a single glimpse, and nowhere near enough to satisfy this unforeseen curiosity he felt for her.

He doubled his step, but when he reached the

foyer, she was already gone. He climbed back up the stairs two by two and hurried down the hall to the parlor where they argued earlier. It had the best view of the estate grounds. Sure enough, he saw Kat in the distance, wearing a red coat with a fur-lined collar, trudging through the snow at a leisurely pace.

Immediately, he made plans to buy her at least two other outfits in that startling shade. It brought out the soft pink in her skin and the dark midnight of her hair. Perhaps a nightgown in red. Red satin that he could peel off her shoulders . . .

His body clenched with need as hot blood moved to the most uncomfortable places. She inspired such strong reactions in him. Such outrageous desires. Here it was, not even three, and he was already counting the moments before he would have her in his bed.

And why couldn't that moment be right now? They were newlyweds after all. A late afternoon tryst might be just the thing to calm his nerves. If he was lucky, he might even get her to open up a bit.

He'd all but made up his mind when his wife crouched down and made a snowball. With a small grin, she tossed it into a flock of birds, scattering them across the sky in a squawking mass.

The majority of the desire that pumped through him faded, replaced by a much more tender, warm feeling. Yes, he still wanted Katherine. But more importantly, he wanted to be near her. He wanted to laugh with her. He wanted to join her in the snow in the hopes that he might feel some of the joy reflected on her face.

"Matthews!" he called as he hurried away from the window. "Bring me my coat and gloves."

Katherine's aim with a snowball was already wicked, but it never hurt to keep it up. Not that the skill had any practical use, but she was still upset from her earlier encounter with Dominic and throwing something helped.

The man was so stubborn. Bullheaded. Even so, she felt a nagging need to comfort him. Sadness was buried in his stormy eyes, no matter how both of them pretended it wasn't. It only seemed to deepen the longer they stayed at Lansing Square. Whether or not he admitted it, the house he wanted so desperately to get rid of meant something to him. And whatever "business" he had there had something to do with his strange searching.

What could he be looking for?

She found herself bundling a second ball of packed snow into her fist. She took aim at a tree branch a fair distance away and let loose, pretending it was her husband's head as a target. It hit squarely and she couldn't help but smile.

"You've a good arm. Perhaps you'd like to practice on a better enemy."

Katherine spun around with a start to find Dominic crossing the lawn toward her with arms outstretched as if offering his broad, muscular chest as a mark. She blushed. She'd been caught. Thank goodness he couldn't read her thoughts.

"You want me to throw a snowball at you?" she asked with a giggle she couldn't suppress.

He gave her that half-grin that melted her every time. "The birds are easy marks, my lady. And anyone could have hit that tree branch. I am simply offering you a challenge."

Yes, he certainly did that. A challenge to her resolve.

He stooped and scooped up a handful of wet snow. With flourish, he rubbed a target on the breast of his dark woolen greatcoat, then stood back. "There, now I've made it even easier for you."

She couldn't hold back another burst of laughter. "Just remember *you* asked for this."

She wound up and was pleased when she hit him squarely in the middle of the chest, despite his last-minute sidestep.

He smiled. "Decent."

"Decent? I hit you full on!" she said in mock outrage before she balled up another snowball and threw again.

But he was just as quick and she found herself dodging as much as throwing. His aim was as good as hers and more of his missiles hit her than missed. As she straightened up for one last throw, she was pleased to see his coat was dotted with white marks.

At the exact moment she let loose, he stood up and the snowball connected squarely with his face.

She squealed in delight as he sputtered and wiped snow away from his eyes. Eyes that came up to meet hers with playfully murderous intent.

"Oh, you liked that, did you?" he asked as he dug into his pocket for a hopelessly damp handkerchief.

"I-I'm s-so sorry," she managed between giggles.

"Hmmm. It doesn't sound like it." He grinned. "But you will be."

With that, he dove toward her. She let out a small scream as she scurried away. Laughing, she ran across the snow with him hard on her heels. Just when she thought she would escape, he jumped. They both went down on the soft snow in a heap of red coat and laughter.

"Now you're going to get it," Dominic chuckled as he shifted his weight to pin her laughing, struggling form. "Now you're mine."

Something in his voice shifted and Katherine stopped fidgeting to look up into stormy gray eyes. Eyes that pulled her in bit by bit until laughter was forgotten, snowball fights were forgotten, everything was forgotten except how much she wanted him.

How much these moments together made her *like* him, despite how treacherous that attraction was.

His face swayed ever closer and her vision blurred

just as his mouth came down on hers. The kiss was gentle. Tasting and teasing, with the playfulness their snowball fight possessed. But behind all that was a passion that could haul her over an edge. Make her do things she shouldn't do . . . shouldn't want to do.

She had set a boundary a few nights before. A promise to herself to allow for physical closeness at night, but when the morning came to separate herself. Now that boundary was being crossed and she felt dangerously close to simply allowing it to happen.

With a sigh, she pressed her hands against Dominic's chest and pushed. He grunted his surprise, but rolled off. Scrambling to her feet, she took a few steps away and some short breaths to calm her pounding heart.

He pursed his lips as he rose to his full height. "Still angry with me about earlier?"

She arched an eyebrow at his sharp voice. "No, of course not. You made yourself clear, and so did I. We're at an impasse."

She hoped her voice wasn't trembling as much as her hands.

"I suppose we are." His face softened. "But I shouldn't have . . . snapped at you."

He shifted. This was a man unused to apologizing, that was clear. Yet he was offering her one.

"Why did you?" she asked, venturing a step closer. "Despite what you claim, it's evident something in this place is important to you. Why don't you want anything to do with the estate's upkeep?"

He clenched his jaw and averted his gaze as if ashamed. "This house wasn't given freely. I wanted to win, I didn't care about the prize."

"Whom did you win it from?" she asked.

"My brother." His eyes lifted to hers again, but this time in challenge.

She sucked in her breath between her teeth. Once again, she had stumbled into the middle of a feud between the two brothers. "I didn't realize this place came from your family. I thought it was a recent addition to your holdings."

He shifted uncomfortably as he brushed wet snow from his coat. "It is, but Cole didn't want to give anything to me, whether he had a rightful claim to it or not."

Her eyes narrowed. The jovial, teasing light in Dominic's eyes had gone out the instant Colden came into the discussion. His resentment for his older brother was evident from everything physical in him. From the way he stood, to the fire in his stare, it was clear he truly despised Cole.

Katherine still liked Cole, had once liked him enough to marry him, though she couldn't picture that future anymore. Dominic had seared those dreams away with his hot touch. But she couldn't understand why Dominic would hold such animosity toward him. Beyond that, it made his reasons for marrying her all the more confusing.

"You really hate him." She tipped her head to examine her husband's hard face. "And you feel very little for the rest of your family."

He flinched and for a brief moment she saw a flash of raw hurt streak across his gaze before he masked it. "I care a great deal for Julia. And I wouldn't want to see my mother come to any harm."

"But that still doesn't explain . . ." she trailed off, not sure if she dared go further. Already Dominic looked angry. Aside from that, digging into his history wasn't a good idea. It was counter to her promise to remain distant.

"Explain what?" he snapped as he turned away with clenched fists. He held himself stiff. If she touched him, she feared he would shatter.

"It doesn't signify," she said with a dismissive wave of her hand. She was too close already.

Spinning back on his heel, he narrowed his gaze. "But it obviously does. You have something to ask, some point to make. Please, do make it. I'm on tenterhooks."

His anger should have served as the warning he obviously meant it to be, but instead of fearing him or disliking him for this sudden shift, she felt something far different.

Empathy.

Because inside the fury that boiled in his eyes and darkened his skin, there was a twinge of something else. The kind of loneliness she herself often felt throughout the years after the loss of her parents.

"Very well," she said softly. "I only wanted to ask why you married me? At the time, you claimed it was to save your family from shame, but it's very clear you aren't the kind of man who would protect the family who rejected you. So why did you carry through with our nuptials?" She took an involuntary step in his direction and just barely resisted the urge to take his rigid arm. "Why did you save them? Save me?"

His eyes widened as if that was the last thing he expected her to say. "I—I . . ." He struggled for words for a moment. "Everyone has problems when it comes to their family. My God, don't you?"

A wave of nausea hit Katherine square in the stomach before it spread through her body. Her family. In her attempt to decipher what kind of man Dominic was, she'd once again forgotten just why she couldn't allow herself too close to him.

Pulling her damp coat closer around her neck, she turned away. "My parents died when I was very young. I have no 'problems,' as you put it. Now, I'm getting cold. I'll go in."

But before she could escape, Dominic caught her arm in a gentle, but binding grip. He turned her slowly and stared down at her with eyes that no longer expressed anger, but a softer emotion.

"I'm sorry. I shouldn't have snapped," he said softly. "I don't want to argue."

"What do you want?" she asked, though with

every word she cursed herself. She was opening the door to far too many options that she shouldn't pursue.

His eyes darkened, but he mercifully ignored all the seductive doors she opened with her question.

"A few days ago, I told you I invited my friend, Baron Malleville, to stay with us for a while. He sent word he'll be arriving week's end to meet my new bride and see the estate. We won't have much time alone together for the fortnight he'll be our guest."

Katherine should have felt relief at that statement, instead she felt a curious disappointment.

"I'll make sure a guest chamber is ready for his arrival," she said as she extracted herself from Dominic's distracting grip. It was hard to think when he touched her.

With a shake of his head, he said, "I appreciate that, but I merely wanted to ask you if we could take some time before his arrival. I have been told the lake on the property is perfect for ice skating. And if we don't do it now, we may be too late when it begins to thaw. Will you come out with me tomorrow?"

She shut her eyes with a shivering sigh. This was her chance to push him away. To tell him she had no interest in spending any extra time in his presence.

To lie.

"I—I don't have skates," was all she could think to say.

He smiled. "Matthews tells me there are several pairs about the estate."

She held back a groan. "I've never skated."

His smile broadened. "I'll help you."

"Very well." She was out of excuses, and out of energy to fight something she found herself desperately wanting. "Tomorrow afternoon."

The hard angles of his face softened with the excitement of a child on Christmas morning, and her heart softened with it.

"Then allow me to escort you back to the house where you can warm yourself and I can return to my . . . my duties."

She hesitated as she looked at the strong arm he extended to her. Touching him was always a gamble. Would her knees go weak or not?

And when she did and her legs turned to warm jam, she let out a sigh. Every moment with Dominic was such a risk.

She was courting disaster, but perhaps having a visitor *would* help. In fact, perhaps she needed to arrange for more than one visitor. She sighed as they entered the foyer and a rush of warm air made her skin tingle.

Yes, she could bring another person into this strange, confusing situation. Someone who would distract Dominic, and perhaps help her figure out what she wanted, and what she could afford to take.

Chapter 9

Dominic Mallory was a large man. Not just in size, where he towered above Katherine by more than a head, but in his presence. Any room he entered belonged to him. Katherine had no doubt this was the way in London, too. People noticed him, they were drawn to him . . . even feared him.

But at the moment, sitting on the floor amongst a pile of mismatched boxes, he looked more like a lost little boy to Katherine than a man who inspired terror in his enemies. He wasn't moving, simply stared at a stack of papers.

When he told her about leaving his family in the carriage the day of their wedding, he pretended that he didn't care about the loss. But being alone at such a young age couldn't have been easy, even for someone as strong as Dominic. Was this how he'd looked so many years ago? A frightened schoolboy with no family to reach out to, no place to call home? She winced at the image of her husband so isolated.

Even if he cut himself off from the Mallorys in anger, that separation from his family and the only life he ever knew must have changed him irrevocably.

She hazarded a step closer as familiar empathy brought unshed tears to her eyes and a twinge of pain to her heart. "Did you forget about me?"

He started at the sound of her voice and clambered to his feet, just barely avoiding a collision with a hanging mobile in the process. He pushed the dangling toy aside with a scowl.

"What are you doing up here?" he snapped. His vulnerability flew, replaced by the harder edge he presented to the world.

"We were to go ice skating today, were we not?" she asked.

Why was she pressing? Skating with her husband was a terrible idea for so many reasons. Time alone with him would only test her resolve and make her want things she would never have. She'd spent most of the morning finding ways to avoid it, but here she was, bringing it up. Forcing both their hands.

He seemed surprised. "I'm sorry, I lost track of time." Holding out his arm, he motioned to the stairway with his head. "Come, we'll go now."

She sidestepped his touch to look around the

room. The attic was cluttered with years, maybe centuries, of collecting. There were artifacts from so many generations that the place was a hodge-podge of old clothing, books, and letters.

"How many generations of Mallorys lived here?" she asked with a small smile as she fingered the worn edging of a moth-bitten gown on a dress-maker's mannequin.

He watched her for a long moment, long enough that she felt his stare through her clothes and skin to her very soul. But she refused to turn back and face those eyes and the heat that burned within.

"None," he said in a low, unreadable voice. When she dared a peek at him, his face was just as stoic. "This home was in my mother's family, not my father's."

"And what was her last name before marriage?"

"Emson."

"How many generations of *Emsons* lived here?" she corrected herself with the smallest of smiles.

"I'm not sure. Five or six. It was a secondary home, not a main dwelling." He tilted his head and she thought his lips twitched with a brief grin.

"And what deep, dark secret are you searching for in your family tree?" she teased with a laugh.

Any flash of humor was gone as quickly as it came, replaced by his scowl. Then he turned away to shut her out completely, leaving her chilled by his sudden change of attitude.

"We should go skate now if we're going to go at

all. The weather will turn in a few hours and Adrian is to arrive tomorrow."

With that, he stalked down the stairs, leaving her staring at his back in shock. But as she followed him, she knew she had uncovered something important.

Dominic's business at this house was personal, and he didn't want her to know a thing about it.

Why hadn't he come up with some vapid, pithy response to Katherine's questions about his family secrets?

Dominic glanced up from the skate he was lacing around Katherine's boot and explored her face. She'd been very quiet since they left the attic. Not angry, but contemplative.

He had a sneaking suspicion her distraction had everything to do with his near admission that he *did* have secrets to keep—ones about his past, ones about their marriage . . . ones that would horrify her if she ever uncovered them.

"What are you looking at so intently?" she asked, her voice a mere whisper on the brisk wind.

He started and returned his attention to the skate laces. "It's been a while since I tied these," he lied. "I need to make sure they're tight so you don't slip and fall."

When he glanced back up to see if she believed his excuse, her eyes were focused on him. Soft, as if pained. He broke away from that seeing stare and rose to his feet to offer her a hand.

"Ready?" he asked with false brightness.

She frowned. "I'm not sure I'll ever be ready."

But she stood nonetheless and caught the arm he offered. He hated to admit it, even to himself, but he felt her touch all the way to his core. Even to the dark places he'd forgotten existed over the many years he spent alone. Places he'd sworn weren't possible to reach.

"Just put one foot in front of the other," he advised as she stepped shakily onto the ice.

Nodding, she stared at her feet as she glided with jerky movements toward the middle of the lake. "Oh, this isn't so ba-ad!" she squealed as she slipped sideways.

The only thing that kept her from going down in a heap was his support, and she nearly took him down with her.

"Just take your time," he said as she clawed her way back up his arm to a standing position. "It takes a while to get used to the feeling."

She darted a disbelieving glance at him, but he was happy to see her eyes twinkled. His tormented, tangled emotions eased as he let himself enjoy the shared experience.

"That's easy for you to say. You already know how to do th-i-is!"

Again, she flopped to her right as her skate slid too far out from her body. When she managed to pull herself back to her feet, she was laughing.

"I didn't know I stretched that way," she giggled.

"Neither did I," he said, leaning a fraction closer to her ear and taking a subtle whiff of her floral-scented skin. "Perhaps we can utilize this talent later."

Her laughter increased, even as her cheeks darkened to the most appealing shade of pink he'd ever seen. "If I didn't think I'd fall right on my . . . my posterior, I'd slap you for that cheeky remark, Dominic Mallory."

He shrugged as he guided her in a long circle around the perimeter of the lake. "I'm only trying to put your mind on things other than skating. If you aren't concentrating so hard, you'll learn faster."

She arched an eyebrow as she clutched his arm to keep her balance. "Trust me, Dominic. The kind of discussion you were offering would *not* increase my balance. What else can I think about?"

He grinned. Two could play at the question-and-answer game. "Tell me more about yourself, then."

Her face went from pink to white in just a few seconds. "I-I'm not particularly interesting."

"Of course you are. What about your parents? Aside from the fact they were taken from you far too early, I know very little about them," he said as his own laughter faded.

Why had she suddenly changed from the wildflower who subtly teased about their lovemaking to a skittish rabbit who barely met his eyes?

She released his arm and pushed off, but as

quickly as she did so, she went down on the ice on her rear end with enough force that she winced. "I think I've had enough skating for the afternoon."

He watched her attempt to slide to her feet for a moment before he reached down to help her up. As he pulled her against his chest, he whispered, "Why are you so afraid?"

She blanched further, but was smart enough not to deposit herself back on the ice by pushing him away. "I-I'm not afraid. It's not a terribly interesting story and—"

"You're lying." He shook his head as he tried to meet her eyes. She ducked from his gaze. "What are you hiding from?"

She took a few short breaths while she stared down at her feet. Finally, her gaze came back up, dark and painfully green. "It is an upsetting subject. And it's personal."

No one understood that better than he did. Talking about family hurts was dangerous, but he found himself wanting to hear her story. And maybe even tell her some of his. Perhaps they could find solace together.

He jerked back at that notion. What was he thinking? He hardly knew this woman. Getting close to her was a ridiculous idea. He'd learned long ago how trust and emotion only made a man weak.

He let her go. She managed to stay on her feet by righting her balance with her arms outstretched.

"I think you're ready to go it alone for a few turns," he said, skating a few feet away.

Her eyes widened as she watched him go. "But I—I thought you were going to help me."

He shook his head, pushing away the twinge of guilt he felt from seeing the hurt on her face. "No, Katherine. I think you can take care of yourself."

Katherine stared at him for a long moment with a strangely emotionless expression. Then she nodded as if she understood completely and skated off on wobbly ankles toward the edge of the lake.

Away from him.

As much as that should have pleased him, it did not.

Katherine ran her hands over an old silk flower arrangement one more time, hoping to make it more presentable. It didn't help much. She was torn between worry that her houseguest wouldn't like Dominic's home and annoyance that her husband hadn't given her what she needed to make Lansing Square fit to be seen. If Baron Adrian Malleville thought the place wretched, it was Dominic's own fault.

She turned from the flowers with a sharp sigh. Why did her husband's lack of interest in his estate bother her so much? It wasn't as if she planned a life with him when they wed. Quite the contrary. Since the moment she agreed to Dominic and Cole's marriage switch, she had been trying to find ways to steer her husband's interest *away* from her. And being cooped up in an isolated estate certainly didn't do that.

If they returned to London, Dominic would probably fall back into the life he led before their marriage. And she could return to her own. No more heated arguments. No more uncomfortable avoidance of her past. If he found a new mistress, as she was sure he would, despite his vows to the contrary, no more passionate nights.

She groaned in dismay at the last.

"I must say, I am impressed."

Katherine looked up to see the object of her musings leaning against the banister leading into the foyer. Dominic looked as good as a long, hot bath after a day in the cold. With a crisp cravat and pressed jacket, she could almost forget what a devil he was. He'd even eliminated his ever-present stubble and smelled of shaving soap and male deliciousness.

She shook off her unwanted physical reaction to pretend a bright smile. "Impressed?"

"By what you've done." He straightened up and came a few steps closer. She fought the urge to lean into him when he passed by. "The foyer looks wonderful, and I noticed you moved things in the sitting room."

She scowled. How dare he compliment her even

as he refused to give her what she wanted? She folded her arms. "Well, you *should* be impressed considering what I have to work with."

He turned to give her a placating smile that raised her ire even further. "Kat, I have no desire to argue."

Kat. He only called her Kat when he wanted something. Or to drive her mad. And when in bed. She shivered.

"Then don't," she answered, trying hard to maintain focus and not think about how dark his eyes were. Or how focused they were on her. "Give me what I want to renovate. I promise you won't be sorry."

She held her breath as his look changed to one of annoyance.

"We already went through this. I've no interest—"

Stepping closer, she reached out to grab his hand. He seemed like he might give in if she just pushed a little further. Yet the moment their skin touched, her rational mind went fuzzy.

"Pl-Please, consider it an investment. If you put just a small amount into the project, you could sell the estate for much more, or even give it away if that pleases you," she said, trying hard not to look at their entwined fingers.

His eyes narrowed as he pulled his hand away. "Why are you so interested in this? Why is it so blasted important?"

She stumbled back at the sudden anger in his voice. "I don't know. I just like to . . . to fix things."

The anger in his stare faded, replaced by a brief flash of long-buried pain. Then it was gone, but there was no ignoring what she'd seen.

"Some things aren't fixable, Katherine," he said with a shake of his head. The jingle of bells outside drifted into the foyer. "That's Adrian's carriage. I'm going out to say hello."

Pushing the door open, he walked away. As much as she told herself it was best not to explore reasons for her husband's gruff exterior, Katherine found herself desperate to do just that. Even if it meant risking an attachment to Dominic that would never cause her anything but grief. Even if it meant risking her heart.

Katherine couldn't be a more perfect wife and hostess. Dominic leaned back and took a moment to enjoy the way she laughed at one of Adrian's bad jokes while she poured him a cup of tea. She even remembered the way his best friend liked it. Already she had the other man wrapped around her pretty little finger.

A swell of pride expanded his chest. There were few men in the world Dominic cared to impress, but Adrian was one of them. In the fifteen years he'd known him, he had often looked to the Baron as a father figure. He certainly felt more affection from his friend than he ever had from Harrison Mallory.

"Well, I'm sure you gentlemen have some catching up to do, so I shall excuse myself," she said as she rose to her feet and smoothed her dress. Both men got up as she went to the door.

"Are you sure you must leave us, Mrs. Mallory?" Adrian asked with a rakish wink, which Dominic knew he reserved only for women he truly liked. "I don't know if I can bear to be left alone with your husband, especially after your most pleasant company."

She laughed. "I'm sure you'll manage, my lord. I do somehow." She gave Dominic a saucy wink, then slipped away.

As she shut the door behind her, Dominic settled back into his chair with a grin. Later he would have her pay for her cheek. Already he was thinking of several pleasant ways. But those were plans for another time. For now, he had a friend to entertain.

"Would you like something stronger than tea?" he asked, getting up to motion to the bar.

"Sherry," Adrian said with a nod.

As he poured two glasses, Dominic felt his friend's eyes boring into his back. "Say whatever it is that's on the tip of your tongue, Adrian."

A deep laugh was his friend's answer. "Ah, you still know me well. I wonder if I can say the same about you."

"Why is that?" he asked as he held out the crystal tumbler.

Adrian took it with a smile and used it to motion to the doorway. "She's a beautiful young woman, Dominic. And what a spitfire. I often worried you would get yourself trapped into an arrangement with some simpering London twit. But Katherine is far from that. I like her."

"Thank you." Dominic settled back into his chair with a sigh. He didn't trust the gleam in his friend's brown eyes. He had a feeling he was about to get an earful, and not just regarding the wife he'd sprung on the Baron.

"In fact, I'd be a bit jealous you found such a wife since I've had my own difficulties in that arena, if . . ."

Dominic arched an eyebrow. He never knew Adrian was looking for a wife. He assumed his friend simply enjoyed his bachelorhood. "If?"

"If I thought for one moment that you were being genuine." Adrian leaned forward. "What the hell are you doing?"

Dominic sighed. He had known the man across from him since he was sixteen. Of all the people who assisted him, Adrian was the most consistent. The one he trusted more than anyone else. Adrian knew the truth about Dominic's parentage, as well as what Lansing Square really meant to him.

Hell, the Baron had been the one who hired the investigator that delivered the information about where Dominic was conceived. His friend had kept all his secrets without fail or question for well over a decade.

Considering the troubles Dominic was having, the feelings he was trying so hard to fight, perhaps he needed his friend's counsel one more time.

"What am I doing?" he repeated, staring into his glass without seeing. "Something I thought would be much, much easier, Adrian."

The Baron nodded slowly, then leaned back in his chair. "Start from the beginning."

Adrian downed his drink in one gulp, then slammed the glass down on the side table. Dominic watched his friend pace around the room a few times before Adrian ran a hand through his graying hair.

"I hoped you would tell me you'd fallen in love with this woman. That you finally realized you can't live your life in such anger. But this . . ."

Dominic squirmed in shame. "You don't have to make the situation any harder for me than it already is."

The Baron let out a burst of ugly laughter. "Why should I make it any easier? You used Katherine to get a *house*. A house, man! And not even one you intend to use."

Rising to his feet, Dominic held out his arms for understanding. "Not for a house. For my future."

Adrian stopped pacing and looked at his friend

with a mixture of exasperation and pity. "No," he sighed heavily. "This estate isn't about your future. It's about your past, about who your real father is."

Dominic winced. After he revealed his secret, they had rarely spoken of it. It was Adrian's tacit way of telling Dominic he respected him, bastard or not. That his friend would bring it up now only accentuated how upset he was by Dominic's story. And there was no use denying what the Baron already knew.

Dominic turned away to stare into the fire. "Of course that's what this is about. I wouldn't go through all this trouble, hurt all these people, if it wasn't so important. What could be more important than knowing who you are?"

"You know who you are!" Adrian said in exasperation. "I don't think I've ever met a man more sure of himself. But what about who you could be?"

Dominic shook his head. "I don't take your meaning."

"What about what you could be with her?" Adrian motioned to the doorway Katherine had departed from half an hour before.

Clenching a fist, Dominic turned his back on Adrian and the disturbing comments that tore through his very soul. "Adrian—"

"Leave what's been done behind you. It can't be changed. *She* could be your future, if you let her be. I saw the way you looked at each other. There's more to this marriage than a cold business deal."

He nodded. "I don't deny there is a spark between us. But it's desire. And God knows, that fades with time. It's nothing more."

"How do you know this will?"

Dominic started. "B-Because it always has in the past. I've never seen what I would judge a happy union amongst my friends or colleagues. And I've never felt any need to press a romantic entanglement of my own beyond a few enjoyable encounters."

Arching an eyebrow, Adrian said, "And have you ever felt for a woman the way you feel for Katherine?"

He swallowed as he considered that comment. He wasn't sure how to answer. After all, he had tried very hard to classify his reactions to his wife as desire driven. Nothing more. Even when he felt something deeper, he pushed it aside.

Adrian stared down his nose with a look of skepticism. "I think not." He waved away Dominic's interruption. "Please, don't argue any further. Continue to tell yourself it's only passion that drives you to this woman. It certainly doesn't hurt me. It only causes you pain, whether you want to believe it or not. Now I think I'd like a bath before my supper."

Before Dominic found the words to answer, Adrian gave him a curt nod and left the room.

Cursing, Dominic downed the remainder of his drink in one gulp. But even though he tried to drown his friend's words out with more liquor, they echoed in his head and haunted him.

Chapter 10

Katherine took a few steps into the dining room before she was distracted by a crooked painting. As she turned it to her satisfaction, she muttered, "If the stubborn ox would let me, I could make everything as perfect as this is now."

"Good evening, Mrs. Mallory."

She spun around to face the amused voice behind her and was surprised to see Adrian Malleville sitting in a side chair reading a wrinkled paper. He had a crooked grin on his face that made him look significantly younger than she knew him to be. From their first meeting, Katherine had been stricken by how handsome the Baron was. His graying temples only made him more distinguished and his brown eyes were sharp as a hunting hawk's, but much kinder.

"I'm so sorry, Baron, I didn't realize you were here," she said. Of course her husband's best friend *would* catch her muttering her frustrations to herself. She probably appeared both daft and shrewish.

"I should be the one apologizing," he said as he rose to his feet and offered her an arm. "I shouldn't have roamed about the house. But when I passed by the dining room and saw that painting you just adjusted, I had to stop for a second glance."

"There are some lovely things in the estate," Katherine said with a smile. She motioned to the more comfortable sitting room. Immediately, Adrian led them in that direction. "Which is why I'm all the more surprised by Dominic's lack of interest in the future of Lansing Square."

"Hmmm," he said as he escorted her to a worn chair in front of her favorite picture window. "I'm not sure I'm the best one to talk to about Dominic's interests or lack thereof. I've known him for a long time, but even I cannot understand his motives much of the time."

He searched her face for a long moment. She tilted her head with worry. Why did he look at her that way? As if he pitied her.

"I'm actually a bit surprised not to find you and my husband together, my lord," she said. "He was so thrilled by your arrival."

"I've known Dominic since he was little more than a boy," Adrian said with a faraway smile. "He's been like a son to me in some ways. Part of being his mentor is that I tell him things he knows are true, which doesn't mean he always likes them."

She arched an eyebrow at his cryptic remark, but still found herself liking the older man. Unlike Dominic's family, he obviously had a great deal of both respect and love for her husband. Whatever they had disagreed about was certainly something that could be fixed.

"I'm sorry to hear that. But then again, I do understand he can be a bit bullheaded at times." She frowned as she thought of Dominic's refusal of her request for funds to renovate. "And sometimes downright unreasonable."

Adrian laughed at her assessment. "Yes, that is most definitely true. But I can tell by the way you two interact that you know there is much more to Dominic than those often entertaining, albeit frustrating qualities."

She stayed quiet, even as she admitted to herself that Adrian was right. As much as Dominic tried to portray an image to the world of the cold, unemotional man, that was only the surface. He had never been cruel to her. In fact, he'd been gentle. Even tender.

How many times had she woken in the middle of the night to find he'd covered her with a blanket?

He'd already mentioned a *modiste* would be at her beck and call in London.

But it was more than just those material things. She'd seen the vulnerability he tried to hide. She'd seen it when she found him searching the attic. Or when they spoke about his life as a child and after he divorced himself from his family. Sometimes she even thought she saw it when her husband touched her.

But that was probably wishful thinking.

Cautiously she met Adrian's eyes. He seemed to be waiting for her to ask more, and oh, how she wanted to. But it didn't seem right. She didn't know this stranger well enough to question him about her husband.

As if he could read her mind, he said, "Perhaps you would like to know more about the man you married? If I know Dominic, I'm sure he hasn't been as open as he could have been. He isn't quick to share his past, even with those who care for him."

She swallowed with a slow nod. The Baron could see through her. He knew she cared for Dominic. Was she so obvious to her husband, too?

But still, caring for him wasn't the same as loving him or being obsessed by him. She cared for many people. Caring could still be safe.

Adrian said, "When I met Dominic, he was angry. He was so embittered by . . . by the past. But I saw something in him. I knew he needed a friend, guidance, although he refused to accept either my friendship or my advice for almost a full year."

His expression saddened as if remembering those times was difficult for him. Her regard for the Baron rose again.

"Why . . . ?" she hesitated. It almost felt like a betrayal to talk about her husband behind his back. Especially when her confidante was his best friend.

"Go ahead. What do you want to know, Mrs. Mallory?" he asked, leaning forward to rest his elbows on his knees.

"I'm not sure if I should talk about him like this. You know how private he is. I wouldn't want to damage your relationship with him," she admitted with a shake of her head.

He laughed. "Don't worry. Dominic and I have already suffered through too many wars of words to even remember. And I think you have a right to know—" This time it was Adrian who cut himself off. "Well, I think you have a right to know a great many things, but we'll take them one step at a time. So ask your questions and I shall do my best to give you the answers I feel comfortable with."

Drawing in a deep breath, she whispered, "Why was Dominic so angry when you met him all those years ago?"

He pursed his lips into a thin line. "Unfortunately, that is one of the secrets that isn't mine to tell. However, I will tell you Harrison Mallory wasn't kind to him, and his brother was little better."

She drew back at this newest revelation. "Cole?"

Adrian nodded with an even stare for her. "People wear masks, Mrs. Mallory. Surely you know that. Colden Mallory may be able to present a certain face to the world, but it isn't necessarily the truth."

"I—I suppose," she stammered.

She'd always questioned why Dominic hated Cole, but she never really considered the possibility that it could have been a situation of Cole's making. Could she have been wrong about the man she once planned to marry? As blind to his true character as she feared she would become to Dominic's?

Adrian leaned closer. "Dominic may wear a mask, too. One well worth pushing aside."

Her breath came short as a dozen questions swirled in her brain. None of them would help her keep the distance she fought to maintain between Dominic and herself. *All* of them required she break down her own walls even as she tore down the ones Adrian claimed protected her husband's heart.

Dominic's sharp voice tore her from her disquieting musings. "Adrian."

She looked up at him in surprise. His face was dark with displeasure and his stormy eyes were focused on his friend with undeniable anger. If that was his mask, what did he hide beneath it?

And why did that dangerous question spark both a physical and emotional response in her?

She rose to her feet. "Since my husband has

found you, I shall excuse myself to do some last minute checking on the progress of our supper." Her mouth was curiously dry as she slid past Dominic, and grew even dryer when he pinioned her with a sharp glance.

"Of course," Adrian said. She noticed he was on his feet, though she hadn't remembered him rising. It was disconcerting how Dominic's presence made her less aware of anything in her surroundings but him.

She hurried away. As Dominic closed the parlor door, she heard him snap, "I don't need you to fight my battles."

Adrian laughed. "I don't think you know what you need."

As the door muffled their remaining argument, Katherine paused to lean back on the wall. For some reason her hands trembled and her heart fluttered. In the back of her mind, a nagging voice told her she didn't know what she needed any more than Adrian Malleville claimed her husband did.

"What did you tell her?" Dominic asked, just barely keeping his anger in check. If he reminded himself that this man was the best friend he ever had, he could just do it.

"Nothing she hadn't already guessed." Adrian sat back down with a sigh and watched Dominic pace. "What are you so afraid of?"

Though he didn't acknowledge the question to his friend, it was the same one Dominic had been asking himself. It shouldn't matter what Katherine knew or how she felt. Not unless he cared for her. Which he did not, at least, not beyond the overpowering desire that throbbed through him whenever she passed by.

Anything more than that was sentimental rubbish. His body playing tricks on his mind.

"You had no right to pry," he said. "Did you tell her about my father? About my bargain with Colden?"

He couldn't imagine either of those things had come up. Knowing she married a bastard would have left her shocked enough, but if Katherine had discovered he married her for the sake of a trade, he doubted she would have left the room as calmly as she did.

Adrian stared at him and his eyes reflected the anger Dominic felt for a brief moment. It was rare for Adrian to show such volatile emotions, and he stopped pacing in surprise.

"What do you take me for, Dominic? Have you forgotten I'm on your side?" his friend asked in a low, dangerous voice. "I do believe your wife has a right to know about your disgusting deal, and the reasons behind it, but I think she should hear the truth from you. I want you to come to your senses before it's too late, but I would never betray you by telling her."

Dominic sank into a chair with a mixture of relief and guilt. "No, of course not. I'm sorry." He put his hands over his eyes. "I don't know what's wrong with me. It's this damn search."

"If you say so."

He uncovered one eye to glare at his friend. "What *did* you tell her?"

"Why don't you ask her?" Adrian sighed.

Dominic let out an exasperated curse.

Adrian shrugged. "I told her you were very angry when I met you. I told her your family wasn't always kind to you. Both facts I believe she guessed herself or heard from your own lips."

He nodded. Yes, Katherine did know those two things already. But having Adrian tell her made him uncomfortable.

"I don't want her pity," he murmured, more to himself than to his friend.

The Baron tilted his head in surprise. "What do you want?"

Conflicting desires raced through Dominic's head. He wanted to know the truth. He wanted things to go back to the simplicity he'd enjoyed before his wild Kat had fallen into his life. And yet, despite those things, he wanted her to stay with him even more, even though he knew desire ultimately faded.

"I don't know," he finally admitted.

Adrian was quiet for a long moment before he said, "Perhaps that's part of the problem." Then he stood to clap Dominic on the back. "One way or another, I doubt you're going to find the answer any time this evening. It's almost time for supper. You'll give yourself indigestion worrying over this. There will be plenty of time for your brooding later."

Yes, if there was one thing Dominic knew about himself, he could always make time for brooding.

Katherine didn't want to be the cause of any more strife between her husband and his best friend, and she was determined not to be. This supper would be pleasant and without controversy.

Of course, Dominic seemed to create controversy wherever he went, but she was going to do her damndest.

Her heart throbbed with nervousness as she approached Dominic's office, where Matthews said the two men were having a drink. She didn't know what to expect. Judging from the way she left them earlier, she could possibly find them at blows over what Adrian had or had not confided in her.

With caution, she tapped the door open and was surprised to be greeted by a roar. Not one of anger or frustration, but one of laughter. Both men leaned on the mantelpiece, bent over in loud, raucous laughter.

She'd never seen her husband look as he did at that moment. Certainly, he had laughed with her, but he'd never completely let down his guard. With Adrian, it was different. The caution was gone from his gray eyes, the worry. He seemed younger, more carefree, and utterly at peace, just for a flash of a moment.

She found herself wishing she could make him laugh like that. That he would trust her enough to be as open in her presence as he was in his friend's.

Shaking away the thoughts of things she shouldn't desire, she entered the room with a quiet clearing of her throat.

"I'm sorry to bother you, gentlemen," she said with an apologetic nod of her head.

Dominic stopped laughing and turned to face her. Though his smile remained, the guard returned. She was foolishly disappointed.

"Kat," he drawled. "You should have come earlier. Though some of Adrian's tales probably weren't fit for a lady's ears."

"I'm sorry," she said. "But supper is ready now and I would love to hear unladylike tales over our venison."

Adrian barked out a laugh as he came to her side to offer her his arm. She took it without hesitation and let him lead her to the dining room. She threw only one glance over her shoulder at Dominic, who was following behind them with a grin warming his usually hard, handsome features.

With her heart throbbing, she took her seat and motioned for the servants to begin bringing their supper.

"I'm sure you and my husband have many tales I will never hear," she teased with a wink for Dominic.

Adrian smiled. "Not too many, I assure you. Dominic and I were more often entangled in business than we were in pleasurable pursuits. Don't let this man fool you. He isn't the rogue he would lead you to believe."

Her heart fluttered. Much of her continuing resistance to Dominic was based on an imagined reputation—on her acquired knowledge of rakes and her belief that they could never change. Was Adrian being genuine in his denial? Or was he only trying to make up for his earlier conversation with her?

Darting her gaze between the two men, she couldn't be sure. Forcing a laugh, she said, "And here I thought I was reforming a rake."

"You are," Dominic said from the head of the table, his tone full of laughter even as his intense gaze gave her no doubt what he'd rather be doing at the moment. And it had nothing to do with light supper banter or his soup.

She turned away in order to maintain some level of decorum. How was it that just one look from the man could leave her a senseless, blithering idiot?

"Dominic never told me if you were married, my lord?" she said, searching for any topic that would be safer than her husband's suspect reputation.

Adrian cast a look in the other man's direction. "Honestly, did you tell her nothing? I'm surprised she knew of my existence at all." With a playful frown, he returned his attention to her. "No, Mrs. Mallory, I've not had the pleasure of married life as of yet."

She cocked her head. Surely this handsome, witty man could have had his pick of lasses in the marriage mart. She wondered why he'd entered his middle age without choosing one.

"Adrian prefers giving advice rather than taking it," Dominic chuckled.

Katherine shook her head with a laugh at the way the two friends played off of each other.

Suddenly, Adrian grew more serious. "I still believe in love, whether I've found it myself or not. And when I do meet the right woman, I think it will sweep me off my feet like a thunderbolt."

Katherine smiled at the Baron's sweet description of his hopes for love at first sight. But even as the conversation drifted into more boring topics, she couldn't help but steal a glance down the table at Dominic. From the first moment she met him, he captured her attention and her desire.

But was there really such a thing as love that lasted? Love that didn't destroy?

Dominic pulled a messy knot in his robe tie and folded his arms as he looked out the bedroom window over the estate. He was happy to be alone. At least, that was what he'd been trying to convince himself since Katherine sent word she would be staying in her own chambers rather than the master bed.

No matter how much his pride stung, it was better this way. He needed to think. Adrian put too many questions in his head. Confusing comments about emotion versus desire. And now Dominic had to decide if he should tell Katherine the truth or not.

He let out his breath in a low groan. He could only imagine her reaction when he explained what he'd done. She would be furious. The light that sometimes glimmered in her eyes when she looked at him would be forever extinguished. And right or wrong, he wasn't sure he wanted to face that possibility.

He jumped when the door behind him creaked open. Pivoting, he was surprised to see his wife standing in the opening between her chamber and his. She seemed as unsure as he was as to why she was there.

"Katherine?" he whispered, unwilling to ruin the moment by speaking any louder.

And he didn't want to spoil this moment. Not when her ebony hair spilled around her bare shoulders. Not when he could see the faintest outline of her dark nipples beneath the thin sheath of her nightdress. Not when her eyes were glazed with just a hint of desire.

But was desire enough? He'd never seen a relationship survive past lust. His mother and Harrison Mallory always had a miserable marriage. One that had been forced, much like his own to Katherine.

Larissa had turned to another, a man she claimed to love, but even their love hadn't survived.

He and Katherine had no benefit of emotion or love to bring them together. She had wanted his brother, but settled for him when it was clear she had no choice. That she desired him now was only pure luck.

And for his part? He was lying to her every day.

Adrian said Katherine was his future, if only he surrendered to the spark that danced between them. But was *anyone* capable of taking a spark of desire and making it into a lifelong flame?

"Dominic," she said softly.

He stiffened. Pleasure rushed through him when she said his name. He cleared his throat. "I thought you were going to sleep in your chamber tonight. Isn't that the message you sent me?"

"My room was empty," she said softly as she passed the threshold of the door and entered his room completely. Silently, she pulled the door shut behind her. "Cold."

He met her eyes and a sudden, terrible thought occurred to him. Earlier he overheard Adrian telling Katherine about his past. Was this overture of hers because of pity?

"Don't come here because of some distressing story Adrian told you." He turned away because he could barely stand to look at her without touching her. "I don't want your consolation."

"I'm not here to console you," she said. Her hand curled around his bicep and all his nerves shot electricity at once. The reaction nearly brought him to his knees.

"Then why are you here?"

He turned around to look into her face. He wanted to see her expression when she answered. Her eyes were clear as newly cut jade, pure and full of so much emotion and desire that it hurt him to look at her.

"I'm here because I—I want you." She blushed with her admission.

He shut his eyes. *Want. Desire.* Nothing more.

Adrian was just putting romantic notions in his head that more was possible. That the warmth which filled him when he looked at Katherine was love.

She stepped closer. With trembling fingers, she worked his robe tie open and slipped her hands inside to play along his bare chest. He hissed out an incoherent sound of pleasure before he regained control. Her hands were hot on his skin, hotter than the fire he'd been examining moments before. Hotter than anything he felt before. And he wanted her to burn him, to brand him as he had branded her so many times.

"I want you, too," he whispered.

Katherine rose to her tiptoes and kissed him with such passion that his knees nearly buckled. Her nails raked across his chest. He arched against her touch and the skilled tongue tracing his jawline, then his throat, to his collarbone.

"Kat," he breathed before he yanked her up against him.

To his surprise, she pushed back with a small smile and a tiny shake of her head.

"Not this time, Dominic," she admonished in a low, husky whisper designed to drive him mad. "This time I'm going to make love to you."

He wouldn't have admitted it, not even under torture, but for a brief moment he thought he might actually swoon with desire. Hot blood pumped to his ever-increasing erection and she hadn't touched him in any way beyond a tease. It was her voice.

"I want to make you call out *my* name," she continued, her words like honey as she pulled his robe down his shoulders. Her smile grew wicked as she realized not only was he naked beneath the thin silk, but at complete attention. "I want you."

He had a pithy reply on the tip of his tongue, but she never allowed him to say it. Before he could, she surged back up and claimed his lips again. Tasting, teasing, she nibbled at his lower lip, then plunged her tongue into the cavern of his mouth. Her kiss was merciless and claiming, as he knew his own had been so many times.

But this time he was at her command, and he wouldn't refuse anything she asked. He couldn't. If need was all they were capable of sharing, he would enjoy each and every moment like it was the last. He'd seen enough to know it very well could be.

Katherine's head was swimming with desire and newfound power. She liked being the one to control their lovemaking. Even more, she liked the way Dominic let out a low, deep growl when she thrust her tongue in and out of his mouth, mimicking the way their bodies joined. It seemed he was no more immune than she to the sensual tension created by each touch.

Carefully, *she* guided him to their large bed, until his muscular, defined thighs knocked against the edge. Then she extracted herself from his embrace and gave him what she hoped was a wicked, teasing smile.

"Lay down," she ordered, though her voice trembled a bit more than she would have liked.

He stared at her for a long moment before he did as she asked. Her hands trembled as she slipped her chemise straps down over her elbows and let her nightdress pool at her feet. For some inexplicable reason, she felt nervous. Almost like she had on her wedding night.

It was ridiculous. They had made love before; she knew what she needed to do. Except she didn't. She had never taken control. She'd never made love to *him*. And now she wanted to. Not for pity or consolation, as he had charged. But because she wanted to spark the same need in him that he always sparked in her. And because she desperately hoped to find some way to regain control over her body and wavering emotions.

"My God, you're beautiful in this light," he murmured just above a whisper.

She blushed as she took a glance at the firelight behind her. It did outline her perfectly, though it wasn't by design. Perhaps it was a sign that fate wanted her to give him this night of pleasure.

"You should see yourself in it," she whispered as she slid her naked body across the sheets.

He reached out for her, but she kept just out of his grasp. "No, no, no," she admonished. "Lie back."

Arching an eyebrow, he said, "And what if I don't want to be a passive partner in your game, my little Kat?"

She placed a hand against the wiry hair of his calf and gently stroked her way up to his knee. He sucked in air with a loud hiss and she smiled.

"Oh, Dominic. There's no way you're going to be passive."

She petted her way up the outside of his thigh to his hip, then trailed her fingers to the inside. He strained toward her, but she pointedly refused to touch his erection. Not yet.

"In fact, I'm going to insure you are an active and willing participant," she whispered with more seductive flare than she would have imagined she possessed.

Dominic groaned as she leaned forward a few inches. Her long, lush hair tickled his hip, coming dangerously close to his manhood before it trailed up his chest. He reached out instinctively to take her into his embrace, but instead of falling into his arms, Katherine smiled, then grabbed his wrists and pressed them above his head.

"You already know the answer to your unspoken question is no."

Her face was only inches from his now. Her breath smelled sweet, like strawberries. It mingled with the flowery scent of her hair to create a heaven he could lose himself in forever.

Then she kissed him and he decided losing himself in her taste would be much closer to perfection. Funny how he'd never noticed a woman's flavor before, but Kat was like no woman he'd ever known. Her lips were like wine and her skin cream. He had no doubt he could feast on her body for days before he needed other sustenance. A wicked part of him wanted to test that theory.

She pulled back, but he could tell by the glaze of her eyes that a bit of her control had cracked with the kiss. Still, she pressed down on his wrists as a gentle warning before she let go to lightly play her fingers along his chest.

"I love to kiss you," she whispered as she traced a line down the apex of his body. She swirled one curved nail around his nipple and an arch of heat went straight to the thrust of muscle between his legs.

"Then do it again," he ordered. His voice was rough with naked need, but he didn't care. It was obvious she already knew how weak to her he was.

She laughed. "Very well."

Inch by inch she lowered her mouth, but not to his lips. Instead, she placed a hot, wet kiss on the nipple she'd been playing with a moment before. He groaned before he could check his reaction. She smiled against his skin, then flicked just the tip of her tongue against the ridge a second time. His erection actually twitched in response.

"Mmm, I think I found something you like," she whispered with a wicked glance up at him. He stared back at her with wide, desire-filled eyes. She edged her mouth lower, lapping at the muscles of his stomach, but this time she let her hand drop down and just brush his manhood.

He moaned as she took him firmly in hand, reveling in the weight of his need, the hardness. Something she had done to him with just a few well-placed caresses. Something she could ease with a few more.

Finally her lips and hand met. It seemed natural to kiss him in the most intimate way, the same way he had kissed her so many times. So she did, catching the moist tip of him between her lips and rubbing her tongue across the sensitive skin there.

Dominic nearly spent himself right then and there. Her mouth was so hot and unexpected against him. There was nothing shy about her touch. And if he hadn't known better, he wouldn't have believed there was anything innocent about it, either. She kissed him like a woman who knew exactly where to press her tongue, when to suck ever so gently. When to speed up and when to slow her pace until he wanted to beg for more.

But it wasn't experience that made her so skilled at this new art of seduction. To his surprise and delight it was the fact that she knew him. In the weeks they'd been wed, she had obviously paid attention when they made love, to the moments that pleased him. Now she was using each one of his weaknesses to bring him to the very brink of oblivion.

"Oh, God, Kat, I need you now," he ground out, clutching the bedclothes in two fists. He was surprised he didn't rend the delicate fabric in two as he twisted it and tried to keep himself from taking his pleasure too soon. "Please."

She glanced up to meet his eyes. Then she nodded. "Yes."

Slowly, she crawled back up the bed and straddled him. He felt her ready heat when she eased just the tip of him against the cleft between her thighs. Then she shifted her hips forward a fraction and he found himself buried to the hilt in her warm, welcoming body. Home.

He started at that thought. Home? Could something fueled by desire be called home?

She shifted her hips and pleasure rocked him, dulling his thoughts as he put a hand on each of her hips.

Katherine shivered with the feeling of being joined. It amazed her each and every time how perfectly they fit. Like his body had been built for no other purpose than to give her pleasure. To give her comfort.

The thought made her rock forward. Her sentiments were lost in a wave of pleasure so intense she nearly climaxed right away. As she slowly rode him, Dominic leaned up and drew one nipple between his lips. When he sucked ever so gently, an orgasm rippled through her with the power of a wild storm.

She thrashed out a harder rhythm as she let out a wail of pleasure and emotion and need for more. He didn't disappoint as he grasped her hips and helped her grind against him. She rolled her head back over her shoulders as his fingers pressed into the flesh of her backside, guiding her toward another chance at rapture.

"Say my name," she begged, wanting him to let go this time as she had lost control so many times before. "Say it, please."

He pumped into her harder, taking her to the edge she craved so much. She danced along its precipice for only a moment before she could no longer contain her scream of delight. He joined her a brief second later, calling her name while he pulsed hot into her and dragged her down for a possessing kiss.

She lay limp for a long time, liking how solid and warm his body was beneath hers. Finally, he pulled her to his side and gathered her into his arms.

"You know," he whispered, laughter in his voice. "I think I like it when my Kat has claws."

Digging her nails playfully into the unyielding

plane of his back, she answered, "You haven't seen my claws yet."

He laughed as his mouth came down on hers for a long, passionate kiss. But he was more serious when he said, "And I hope I never will."

Chapter 11

At the time, Katherine would have invited Napoleon's army into her home if it would have helped her distance herself from her husband. Instead, she'd chosen Julia.

Dominic's sister was the perfect answer. Julia would both distract her husband, and give Katherine someone to spend time with. In the past year, Julia had given her sound counsel innumerable times.

But now things were different. The past few nights, she and Dominic made love on much more equal ground. He didn't just pleasure her, she took control, too. It made her a partner in their lovemaking, not just a willing party.

Even more, it made her feel like a partner in their

marriage. For the first time, she felt less afraid. Less like she was teetering on the edge of losing control over her emotions and her reason.

"Exactly why you need the distraction as much as he does," she muttered as she inspected the guest room the servants had been trying so hard to make presentable.

"Beg your pardon, madam?" the girl in the dressing chamber asked as she poked her head into the bedroom reserved for Julia.

Katherine flushed. "Nothing, Marie. Just woolgathering."

As the girl returned to her work, Katherine stifled a curse. This newfound feeling of comfort was no blessing. It was exactly what she feared most. Dominic was weaving a spell around her. Already she was dropping her guard. It was too familiar a scenario. First she had given in to his seduction. Then she resigned herself to letting him have her at night, but keeping her sanity during the day.

Now *that* plan was eroding, too. Chipped away by long kisses in corridors and playful caresses when they were sure no one watched. Her days were becoming as focused on the man as her wanton nights. So perhaps it was *she* who needed the distraction of a friend, not Dominic.

After all, she was the one who couldn't seem to keep control over her mind or her heart.

"Excuse me, Mrs. Mallory," Matthews asked as he came into the room.

Katherine turned to smile at the butler. "Yes?"

"Mr. Mallory has returned early from his outing with Lord Malleville. He's wondering why the household is in such an uproar." The man's lip twitched. "What should I tell him?"

She smothered a smile. Matthews, and truth be told, the rest of the staff, remained terrified of Dominic. Not that her husband helped matters by making clear his intentions to rid himself of the estate. Each and every day, Katherine saw the fear in the servants' eyes, the worry they would be set out in the street with nowhere to go and no reference for another position.

She patted the elderly butler's hand. "I'll speak to Mr. Mallory. Where is he now?"

Matthews' face relaxed when it was clear he wouldn't be forced to face Dominic. "In his private office, madam."

"Is he alone?"

"Yes, Lord Malleville retired to refresh himself after their cold ride." Matthews bowed as he finished.

"Thank you."

She turned to give Marie a few more instructions, then hurried down the stairs. At Dominic's office door, she paused. There was no way to gauge her husband's reaction to her unexpected houseguest. He hated surprises, she had learned, but he adored his sister. He was entirely capable of either roaring like a bear at her announcement or accepting her surprise with pleasure. With a deep breath, she pushed the door open.

He didn't seem to hear her, for he didn't glance up from the pile of papers at his desk. She took the opportunity to stare openly in awe of just how handsome he was. The crisp winter breeze had ruffled his thick hair and the sun had darkened his skin just a bit so his pale eyes stood out like a stormy sea. He had a strangely savage look about him. One that sent a familiar shiver through her.

"I wonder if you plan to say anything, or did you just come in here to enjoy the view?" he asked without looking up.

She grinned. "I always enjoy the view. But I did come to say something."

He looked her way and she saw laughter in his eyes. And desire. But then, that was always present when he looked at her. An emotion she craved and feared with equal measure.

"You mean to explain why the servants are in an uproar?" he asked, reaching out to catch her wrist as she came closer to the desk. He placed a warm kiss against it. How was she to concentrate with him doing that? "Matthews wouldn't tell me a thing. He's much more loyal to you than he is afraid of me."

Slowly she extracted her hand from his in the hopes she could regain some equilibrium. "You shouldn't want them to be afraid of you at all. If you gave them some assurance about their positions . . ."

He scowled and shook his head, the teasing light fading from his eyes. "Katherine."

Normally, she would have pressed the subject, but she decided against it. Telling him about Julia might irritate him enough. There was no use pushing him to that state any earlier than was absolutely necessary.

Raising her hands in surrender, she said, "Very well, we won't talk about the house for the moment. You wanted to know why the servants are in an uproar."

He nodded as he leaned back against his desk with folded arms. She suddenly felt like she was facing a firing squad.

"The staff is preparing the house for the arrival of another houseguest," she said, biting her lip as she awaited his response.

He straightened up to attention. "What?"

"I wrote your sister asking her to pay us a visit," she admitted. "And she should be arriving today."

"Julia?" he asked with wide eyes. "You invited her here without my permission?"

His tone and demeanor irked her. Katherine glared at him. "I was under the impression this was my home, too. I thought I would be as welcome to have a guest as you are."

"This *isn't* our home," he said through clenched teeth before he drew a long breath. "Of course you're welcome to invite people to visit you. I simply would have expected you to inform me. Especially when it's my own family who will be walking through the door."

"I thought you'd be pleased. Julia is the only family member you seem to have any regard for," she said with a frown.

"I *will* be pleased to see Julia. But my family is very complicated." He hesitated, searching her face as if he wanted to determine her thoughts and feelings. She shifted under the close scrutiny. "Katherine, there are things you don't know about me. About my family."

"I'm aware of that," she said with a tilt of her head. "Perhaps I would understand better if you told me."

She had no doubt there were many things she didn't know. Like why Dominic had run away from the Mallorys at such a young age. Or why he and his brother had such an abiding dislike for each other. Sarah's implication of some kind of impropriety with Dominic still stung, and had never been confirmed or denied. Katherine hadn't the courage to ask. What if it was true? She couldn't bear the thought.

Dominic paused as if struggling for words, and Katherine's heart leapt at the intent, yet resigned expression on his face. Perhaps she was about to learn the answers to those questions.

There was a light rap at the door before he could say anything. Matthews opened it, and with an apologetic frown, he said, "Excuse me, but Lady Julia is here, Mrs. Mallory."

She silently cursed the untimely interruption and continued to stare at her husband for a moment before she answered, "Thank you, Matthews. We'll be out to greet her in a moment." When the butler departed, she said, "Dominic, what do you want to tell me?"

"Not now. We need more time than this." He shook his head. Her own frustration was mirrored in his frown. "So much more time. You greet my sister, while I fetch Adrian. He's never met her."

Disappointment shook her. She hadn't realized just how much she wanted a glimpse of Dominic's heart. His past. No matter the folly in that, or how the desire to know him better was at odds with promises she'd made to herself.

With a shake of her head, she crossed the room to the door, but there she paused. "Dominic?" she said softly.

He glanced up at her with a forced smile. "Yes?"

She searched his face for answers, for clues, until she realized just how lost she already was in his eyes. In his life. That wouldn't do.

"Nothing. I'll escort Julia to the parlor."

"Julia." Katherine entered the foyer just as Matthews closed the door behind her sister-in-law. She held out her arms and enjoyed the comforting warmth of her friend's embrace. She hadn't realized how much she missed Julia until that moment.

"Katherine, I'm so pleased to see you with a smile upon your face," Julia said as she pulled back to look Katherine up and down. "With all the turmoil that surrounded your engagement to one of my brothers and then your marriage to the other, I've been worried about you."

"You're thoughtful," Katherine replied with a blush as she took Julia's arm and led her to the parlor. "But as I told you in my letters, there's no need to worry about me."

As she settled into a chair by the fire and accepted Katherine's offering of tea, Julia cocked her head. "Where is Dominic?"

"I'm afraid I sprung your visit on him as a surprise," Katherine admitted. "He has a houseguest of his own, so he went up to prepare and inform his friend of your arrival."

Her sister-in-law pulled a face. "Oh, my brother doesn't like surprises. Was he very angry?"

Katherine couldn't help but flash to the surprise she'd given him by making love to him a few days before. It seemed Dominic didn't mind *some* shocking things.

When she caught Julia's eye, she blushed. How could she be thinking such a thing with company in the room? Had she no self-control at all? The thought sobered her immediately.

"D-Dominic was very pleased at the news of your arrival."

Julia's eyes narrowed. "Are you certain everything is going well for you? You're acting a bit strangely."

Katherine jumped. "What are you talking about?"

"You actually blushed when I mentioned Dominic. And you haven't asked about Colden or Sarah yet. I thought that would be one of your first questions." She cocked her head. "I can see your mind turning, but I have no idea what it could be that troubles you so."

Where was she to start? With the fact that her feelings for Dominic were growing with each passing day? Or perhaps that her obsession with him was mounting at a much faster rate? And that didn't even begin to touch on the secrets she knew he was keeping. Or the ones she held close to her own heart.

"Katherine?"

She stared at Julia for a long moment. Throughout her yearlong courtship with Cole, she'd grown close to his sister. She'd looked to Julia for counsel and laughter. Now, more than ever, she needed her friend's good advice.

"Oh, Julia," she said softly, "I don't know how to begin."

Her friend covered her hand. "You can talk to me. I promise you, I'll keep any confidence you share."

Katherine drew in a long breath, but before she could speak there was a tap on the door. When it opened, Adrian Malleville stood on the other side. He smiled sheepishly.

"I beg your pardon, Mrs. Mallory. Dominic told me another guest has arrived. We intended to enter together, but he was waylaid by an important message from London. I hope you'll forgive my . . ."

He trailed off with suddenly wide eyes. Katherine followed his line of vision to see he was staring at Julia. Even more shocking was that her normally staid sister-in-law was staring back with a sparkle in her eyes Katherine had never seen before. She rose to her feet in surprise.

With effort, she composed herself. "Of course we don't mind, Baron. Please, come in."

He stood still as stone for a few moments too long, then seemed to remember where he was and took a few shaky steps into the room.

When neither of her two guests spoke, just continued to stare at each other, Katherine cleared her throat. "Dominic tells me you two haven't met. Allow me to introduce you. Julia, this is Baron Adrian Malleville, a good friend of Dominic's. And Baron, may I present—"

He stepped forward to take Julia's fingertips and press a kiss to her gloved hand. Julia jolted at the contact as if she'd been shocked, but the small smile on her lips made it clear she didn't mind.

"Lady Julia Mallory," Adrian said in a near whisper. "Of course. Your brother has spoken of you many, many times, but I fear he never mentioned just how lovely you are."

Though Katherine never would have believed it if

she hadn't seen it with her own eyes, Julia blushed and then she tittered. Julia Mallory, who Katherine had always known as a sensible spinster, giggled like a schoolgirl with her first crush.

"Oh, my lord, you are too kind." She withdrew her hand, but only to raise it to her heart. "My brother has spoken of you, as well. I'm very pleased to finally make your acquaintance."

"As I am to make yours."

Katherine stared at the pair. It was plain she could have stripped down to her chemise and danced a jig on the window seat and neither one would have paid her the least bit of attention. At present, they only had eyes for each other.

It was the loveliest thing she'd ever seen.

There had always been a sense of loneliness about Julia Mallory, a faded desire to find someone to care for her, no matter how unlikely that was with each passing year. But watching the other woman unfold like a rose in late bloom while Katherine was so torn about her own heart was difficult. It only magnified the trouble of her situation all the more.

Julia laughed at something Adrian said. Her eyes never left his. Katherine sank back onto the settee with a sigh. There would have to be another time to confide in her friend.

"I'm so sorry," Dominic said as he came into the room. "I needed to read that message. I hope Katherine introduced . . . you . . . to . . ."

He slowed down and came to a stop when only
Katherine seemed to notice his entry. His eyes narrowed as he looked from his sister to his friend.

"Yes," she said, hurrying to her feet in the hopes
of distracting him. Although she, too, was surprised by the obviously instant attraction between
their two houseguests, the last thing she wanted
was for Dominic to cause some kind of a scene. "I
did introduce Julia to the Baron."

"Very good." He looked at his sister with wariness. "Julia, how good to see you. I trust your trip
wasn't too difficult."

Julia nodded, but her gaze remained firmly fixed
on Adrian, as his did on her. "Yes."

Dominic arched a brow. "Yes, it was difficult, or
yes, it was not?"

His sister shook her head as if she was waking
from a dream. Finally, she cast her gaze on her
brother. "Dominic, there you are."

As she crossed the room to hug him, Dominic
looked at Adrian. His stare darkened.

"Yes, I've been here for some time," he murmured.

Julia blushed as she pulled away. "Of course.
Katherine was just introducing me to your friend,
Baron Malleville."

Her voice softened when she said Adrian's name.
Katherine couldn't smother a smile, though Dominic's deepening glower troubled her. Like Katherine, Dominic had obviously noticed the immediate
attraction between his friend and his sister.

Unlike her, he seemed less than pleased with the development.

"Please, Lady Julia," Adrian said with a dashing wink. "Your brother and I have been friends for an age. I insist you call me Adrian."

Katherine's eyes widened. It was a forward request, though not entirely scandalous if the familiarity was limited to private situations.

Julia blushed. "I don't know, my lord—"

Dominic clenched a fist. "It is entirely improper, Adrian, and you know it. I forbid such intimacy between my maiden sister and a known rake."

Adrian drew back. It was clear he hadn't expected such a strong reaction, even to a bold request. Katherine grasped Dominic's forearm in an attempt to soothe his sudden anger.

"Dominic—"

Adrian laughed, though it was a brittle attempt to ease the growing tension in the room. "Suddenly my friend is all respectability."

Julia smiled, though her gaze flitted nervously between the two men.

Adrian stepped closer to her. "I suggest we call each other by our given names only when he isn't present." He winked conspiratorially. "What he doesn't know couldn't hurt him."

The comment was clearly meant as a jest, but Dominic shrugged away from Katherine's hand and took a menacing step forward. "That will be enough, Malleville. If you cannot control yourself with my sister, I will ask you to leave. I won't have you taking advantage of her advanced years and loneliness to amuse yourself."

Julia gasped as humiliated color filled her cheeks. "Dominic!"

Adrian rocked back on his heels in surprise. Katherine couldn't blame him. Adrian was flirtatious, but he'd never given any indication he would take advantage of any woman. Let alone the sister of a friend . . . or former friend if the confrontation continued as it was.

Katherine rushed forward to keep Dominic from causing any more damage.

"That's enough." She turned to Adrian and Julia. "I'm sorry, Dominic is obviously not himself. I'm sure he doesn't intend—"

"You don't have to explain me to anyone." Dominic turned his angry gaze on her. "I'm perfectly capable of saying exactly what I mean and don't mean."

"I think you had better reconsider your words and your tone." Adrian straightened to his full height with the disdain only a true aristocrat could manage dripping from every syllable. "You owe me, your wife and especially your sister an apology for your shocking lack of decorum. You have been acquainted with me long enough to know that nothing unsavory was happening here. If I was shocked and charmed by your sister's beauty, that is certainly not any reason to accuse me of such lowly intent."

Julia looked up at her brother with tears sparkling in her eyes. She shook her head as she struggled with words she couldn't seem to find.

Dominic shifted as if some of Adrian's response pierced his overly protective instincts, but he folded his arms defensively. "When I come into my parlor to find my best friend staring at my maiden sister with lust in his eyes, I will react to protect her. I have no intention of apologizing."

With a cold nod, Dominic turned on his heel and stormed out of the room. Katherine helplessly watched him go. Why had he reacted so strongly to the attraction between his sister and his friend?

She turned back to find Adrian pale and Julia only just holding back tears.

"I'm so sorry. I have no excuse for Dominic's behavior. He has been under some strain of late. I don't know what work he's doing here at Lansing Square, but it seems to consume him. I'll speak to him. I'm sure when he calms himself and regains his reason, he will have sincerest apologies for you both." She sighed when both looked at her incredulously. "Please, have some tea while I find him."

She hurried from the room without waiting to see her guests' reactions. The damage to Dominic's relationships had been done. She didn't need to watch their faces to see that. But perhaps if she could make her husband see how foolishly he was behaving, he could salvage his friendships with both people. Because it was obvious they each filled a void in him.

She turned toward the stairs and climbed up first one flight, then two, and finally up to the attic. If Dominic spent his days searching here, he might come here to disappear as well.

From the sound of cursing when she shut the door behind her, she was correct in her assumption. Dominic stood by the far wall, his hands clenched at his sides. He drew in a deep breath, but it didn't seem to reduce his frustration.

Katherine hesitated, wondering at the intelligence of approaching a bear when he was angry. But when her husband dropped his hands to his sides, she knew she had to press forward and alert him to her presence. It was clear he needed her.

"What are you doing, Dominic?" she asked softly.

He spun at her intrusion and his skin darkened when he realized she'd witnessed his outburst.

"Go downstairs, Katherine." His voice was dangerously low. "Go downstairs before I do any more harm."

She sighed in relief. Already, he was aware of the folly of his extreme behavior. Keeping her voice gentle, she said, "Tell me why you reacted as you did."

He dipped his head, but she tilted her own, trying to chase his expression down.

"You can't tell me you didn't see the way Adrian was looking at my sister," he snapped.

She felt her expression soften yet she tried to stay detached. "And you can't tell me you didn't see your sister return that gaze. It was as evident to you as it was to me that the two of them had an instant connection. An immediate attraction. But that doesn't answer my question. Why would you behave as if they'd broken some law? Done something wrong because of some harmless flirtation? Why assume Adrian's attentions were dishonorable?"

He clenched his fists open and shut at his sides as he shifted his weight. "He was being forward."

She cocked her head. "Perhaps a bit. He was being playful. He was being Adrian. My goodness, the afternoon I met him he joked with me in a similar fashion. You weren't angry then."

Dominic shrugged. "He shouldn't behave in such a manner toward a spinster."

Katherine pursed her lips in exasperation. "Your sister has been alone for a very long time. Why would you want to deny her a chance at some happiness? Especially with a man who you've told me again and again that you respect and, dare I say, love."

He hesitated before he paced away. "Inviting him to our home was a mistake. He says things that only upset everyone. And now you've gotten involved and he has completely jumbled your mind."

She folded her arms. So this outburst was more

about Adrian's interference and advice than his attraction to Julia.

"*My* mind is completely clear. I think it is your mind that's jumbled. If Adrian said things that upset you, I'm sure he only said them for your own good. The fact that you don't like them gives you no right to behave in such an ugly fashion to a friend you've held dear for half your life."

She could tell by the way his face pinched in frustration that her words were sinking in. And yet he still fought them.

"I never asked for your opinion, Katherine. I can handle my so-called friend in my own way and my own time."

The thin control Katherine had been trying to maintain over her temper snapped. "I never thought you would be so disloyal to a friend. And to think that I was starting to . . ."

She stopped abruptly because the next few words out of her mouth were going to be a confession that she was beginning to care for him. Telling him that was the worst mistake she could make. Feeling it was even more terrifying.

His eyes narrowed. "Starting to what, Kat?"

She didn't fail to notice his shift to her nickname, or the way her body softened when he used it.

"N-Nothing," she stammered as she turned away. She couldn't let him see the emotions she couldn't seem to control.

"You have no idea what I'm trying to do here." His voice was suddenly tired.

"And why is that?" she asked, daring to face him again. "Don't pretend the secrecy between us is entirely my fault, Dominic. You've shut me out. You refuse to tell me what you're looking for. Is it because it's illegal? Immoral? Dangerous?"

He shook his head. "None of those things. And I would be wary of accusing others of keeping secrets, my little Kat. You are no better in that regard. You hide yourself away as much as I do."

Katherine actually felt the blood drain from her face in a slow slide. "I do not."

He moved closer and his body heat and presence hit her like a wall. "Then tell me about your parents. How did they die? Tell me about your childhood. Tell me anything of importance about yourself and your past."

She opened her mouth as she tried to find words. He had no idea just how tempting his angry demand was. In her heart, she knew Dominic was the one person who would understand the pain of being alone. And if he took her into his arms, she also knew she would find comfort there.

But that would mean telling him more than her past. It would mean admitting how much she'd come to care for him, despite her battle to keep that from happening. He could take away the power she so desperately needed to keep her demons at bay. As much as she desired it, she could never allow him into her soul as she dared to allow him in physically.

"My parents died. That's all there is to say."

Sudden tears stung the back of her eyes, threatening to rush to the surface if she kept looking into her husband's face. In a desperate bid for self-protection, she turned away. But not before she saw his disappointment.

"Well, then we are at an impasse, aren't we?" he said softly, no heat left in his voice. "As it always seems to be between us."

"I suppose so," she said as she turned to leave the room. At the door, she paused. "But you know as well as I do that your troubles have nothing to do with Adrian and Julia. And you owe them both the courtesy of an apology."

Before he could answer or argue, she fled the attic and hurried downstairs. She had to get away from the enticement Dominic presented to much more than just her body. The temptation he put on her heart was far more dangerous.

Chapter 12

Katherine wrung her trembling hands one last time as she approached the sitting room door. If her husband refused to make peace with his sister and the Baron, she would have to do it for him.

Was the door closed? Nearly, though she didn't remember shutting it behind herself when she slipped away to follow Dominic to his hiding place upstairs. She frowned. Technically, Julia and Adrian shouldn't have been alone with the door ajar only the tiniest crack, but if Julia had been crying, she could understand why her sister-in-law might desire privacy from prying eyes.

With a shake of her head, she gently tapped it open. Adrian and Julia stood facing each other in front of the fire. The Baron had one of Julia's hands in his own and he murmured words too soft for Katherine to hear. But they made Julia smile and blush as she broke eye contact.

Yanking the door back to its original position before the pair saw her, Katherine drew in a ragged breath. Apparently the ugliness of Dominic's outburst hadn't changed the attraction between Julia and Adrian. In fact, it seemed to have brought them closer.

She could only hope Dominic would recover his senses and accept it if the two took their relationship beyond a brief touch of the hand and a whisper.

She cleared her throat loudly and coughed several times, then opened the door again. As she expected, the two immediately separated. Julia returned to the settee, eyes shining and cheeks pink with pleasure, while Adrian fiddled with the items on the mantel. Both looked as guilty as children caught laughing at Sunday services.

"Did you find Dominic?" Julia asked as she smoothed her skirt uncomfortably.

Katherine nodded. "Yes. Though I doubt he'll come down. Whatever he thinks he saw between you distressed him. I think he needs some time to gather his thoughts."

Adrian frowned. "Dominic has always been volatile."

"Always," Julia agreed with a small smile for the Baron. "But he's fair underneath it all. I'm sure he'll calm down soon enough and we will be able to discuss this with civility."

"Any brother might behave in such a fashion if he felt his sister were in danger of being ill-used. Especially by a friend." She focused a long, pointed stare from one to the other. Both were unable to hold her eyes for more than a moment.

Adrian cleared his throat uncomfortably. "I see what you mean, Mrs. Mallory. And I intend to talk to Dominic as soon as I believe he won't engage in fisticuffs with me upon sight. But I wonder if there might be more to his anger than just a normal brotherly protectiveness?"

Katherine tilted her head. "Such as?"

It was Adrian's gaze that pinned her this time. "Perhaps he's upset because he feels he has little control over his own heart."

Katherine started as she realized Adrian was referring to the relationship she and Dominic shared. To the confusing emotions that lapped beneath the surface whenever they came in contact with each other.

"Men rarely feel those tender emotions, Baron," Katherine said as she turned away to face the fire. "They don't love, they possess. And when they grow bored, they abandon."

Julia drew in a sharp breath at Katherine's bitter rendition of romance. "Perhaps some men," Julia said. "But not Dominic. No matter what he's"—she paused and her eyes darted to Adrian—"done, he would not do that. He knows what it's like to be alone. To be deserted." Julia returned her dark gaze to Katherine. "Like you do, I'd wager."

Again, her friend's words cut Katherine as deeply as a knife. With a little gasp, she paced away from the couple. Her marriage had not been a subject she intended to broach when she returned to the parlor. How had this discussion turned so quickly out of her control?

"You two must excuse me," she said, ignoring the tears that stung her eyes. "My head is beginning to ache and I think I shall retire early. Julia, ring for Matthews when you're ready to retire. He will show you to your chambers." She gave the two a brief nod. "Good evening, Julia, Baron."

Before either of them could respond, she gathered up her skirt and hurried away. Flying upstairs, she closed herself into her chamber and leaned back against the doorway as she took a few panting breaths.

Julia and Adrian had given a voice to the thoughts that had plagued Katherine for the past few weeks. That Dominic Mallory wasn't much different than she. That he could understand her pain, her loneliness, in a way she didn't dare contemplate.

She found herself standing by the door that adjoined her private chambers to the bedroom she shared with her husband. Slowly, she pushed the door open and looked at her husband's bed.

Their bed.

With a sigh, she slipped inside. She drew his pillow up to her face and breathed in the faint smell of his skin that lingered on the linen.

It took all her strength to fight her own growing feelings. If Adrian and Julia were right, and Dominic was beginning to have those same emotions for her, she had no idea how she could keep up the walls she'd erected between them.

Or if she even wanted to anymore.

Dominic looked into the sitting room as he drew in a few short breaths to calm himself. His sister was perched on the edge of the settee, stitching on a piece of needlework. Though she appeared to be concentrating on her stitches, he could tell by the way she jabbed the needle through the fabric that she was still highly emotional. His initial reaction was to leave her to fret a bit longer. Anything to avoid a confrontation with the only family member with whom he still had any semblance of a relationship.

But if he hid, that relationship could be irreversibly damaged. No, he had to swallow his cowardice and do something he hated to do. Admit he'd been wrong.

He came into the room and with no precursor mumbled, "I'm sorry."

Julia glanced up from her needlepoint with a surprised gasp, but when she saw it was he who had interrupted her sewing, her eyes narrowed. She gathered her composure by pressing the needle through the material and set it to the side. She was silent as she did so, letting him stand in the doorway like an idiot as he waited for her acceptance or denial of his apology.

"Sit down," she finally said as she motioned to a chair beside her. Her voice was unreadable.

With a short nod, he did as she requested, though the chair felt uncomfortable beneath the weight of his regret.

Julia's voice was free of emotions, but her eyes were filled with pain. It put him to mind of the long, hurtful days of his childhood, before he put weaker emotions away. His sister had often been the one to comfort him when he faced off with his brother or Harrison Mallory.

Today he rewarded her loyalty and care with unkindness and an overreaction that had little to do with her and everything to do with his own situation with Katherine.

"I think you need to take a good look at why you reacted so strongly this afternoon," his sister said as she folded her arms and stared evenly at him. It was as if she read his tangled thoughts all too well.

He shifted under her gaze.

Clearing his throat, he said, "I haven't been sleeping well lately."

Her eyes and demeanor softened a fraction. "You never did. Even as a child, there were so many evenings I heard you pacing the floors. All night sometimes."

He frowned. As a young man, he'd spent sleepless nights wondering if Colden told him the truth about his parentage. Wondering when the day would come when the man he called father would confirm or deny the ugly words his brother had spoken. And wishing for those words to be true in some way. Longing for a father who didn't speak to him in hatred or touch him in violence.

Now it was different. His sleepless nights were filled with Katherine. For the hours she was in his arms, he could forget that he still couldn't find the answers to his pressing questions. So he took those hours greedily, hungrily, letting her fill the empty spaces of his heart.

Until the morning when reality hardened him again. Though lately, reality hadn't troubled him as much. Another bit of Katherine's doing.

"This is more than sleeplessness," Julia whispered, searching his face. "You've never been so angry, and over nothing." She blushed. "Nearly nothing."

Dominic couldn't let her statement pass unanswered. "It was more than nothing. You and Adrian were staring at each other with such obvious . . ." He shifted uncomfortably. "Desire . . . attraction. It surprised me, and I overreacted. That's why I'm apologizing."

Her mouth thinned into a pressed line. "You should be apologizing for your selfishness. I realize Adrian has been your close friend for years, and I have been little more than an afterthought of a life you ran from. But *I* couldn't run, Dominic. I was trapped because of my sex. Now I want my happiness, too. You shouldn't begrudge me a chance at it."

Drawing back in surprise, he murmured, "You think I reacted as I did because I was *jealous*? Of you taking Adrian from me if this situation develops further?"

"No, you reacted as you did because you're jealous of us finding a feeling you fear with every breath."

She rose to her feet and paced away, then suddenly spun back to face him with fire flashing in her eyes.

"Love, Dominic. You're terrified of letting anyone love you, or of loving them in return. That's why you cannot sleep. Because you hold a woman in your arms you're starting to love and it terrifies you. Especially when you know you married her under false pretences and hurt her with your lies of omission every day."

Dominic stumbled to his feet and backed away. Why did her ridiculous accusations prick him like the truth when they were nothing but sentimental rubbish? He cared for Katherine, he had accepted that. He hated that he lied to her, yes. But *love* her?

No, he didn't believe that was possible.

She continued, but her voice and face had softened. "Go ahead and look at me like I'm daft, but I know you. Sometimes better than you know yourself."

"Don't be ridiculous," he whispered.

She frowned. "I realize it's difficult that you only know half your parentage. Even more so because Cole used it to maim for so many years, and Mother refuses to share any details with you. Were you hoping to find some answers here?"

Dominic stepped back, too stunned to deny what she said. "Yes. I have viable information that I was conceived in this house. I hoped to find some evidence of my father's identity." He paused. "I wasn't aware you knew of my—my being a . . . bastard."

Julia laughed humorlessly. "You must take me for a fool. Your arguments with Cole and later with Father could have brought the house down. I wasn't a child when you left and I wasn't deaf. I knew." She reached out a hand to cover his. "And I never loved you one bit less, or saw you as any less my brother."

His jaw twitched at her words of familial love. They cut through the thick layer of anger that had cloaked him so long and touched a part of his heart he long believed was dead.

"I'm so sorry, Julia," he whispered as he drew her into a hug. "I never should have said those things about you being a spinster. I never should have implied there was something untoward between you and Adrian."

She smiled. "Thank you. In honesty, I don't know if what you saw today will lead anywhere." Her expression took on a faraway look. "Adrian claims to believe in love at first sight and has vowed to honorably pursue me with that in mind, but I have been out in society long enough to be more practical. All I know for sure is that I have never felt something like this before for any man."

He hesitated as he flashed to the first moment he saw Katherine on the terrace. He'd certainly felt a strong draw to her in that instant. Lust. And something more. Something *he* had never felt before.

He shifted his focus to Julia. "You deserve happiness. Whether it's Adrian's notion of love at first sight or something that develops over time. If you find that with my best friend, I will be pleased. And I shall tell him that as well, when I apologize to *him* later tonight."

Her eyes softened. "Thank you, Dominic." She leaned up to kiss his cheek. "May I offer you some advice?"

He sighed. "I doubt my saying no will keep you from doing so."

Her laugh was full of humor this time. "You're probably right. *Please* don't make the mistake of keeping Katherine out of your life and your heart just because you made a bargain to take her." She tilted her head. "I'd be a fool if I didn't see your marriage is more than a bargain now, isn't it?"

He opened his mouth to deny her claim, but couldn't seem to find the words. Not when he knew they were true. What he felt for Katherine had changed, shifted over the past few weeks of their marriage. Now he didn't know what it was. More than lust, yes, but was *more* truly possible? He'd told himself so long that it wasn't. Now it was hard to change that view.

"Perhaps." He shook his head. "I don't know."

"You know," she said softly, "you simply do not want to see it."

With a sigh, she turned to the door. "I'm exhausted. It's been a long, trying day for all of us. But think about what I said, will you? I watched you go through hell at home. I would hate to watch you create a hell for yourself now that you have a chance to be truly happy." Her smile was sad. "Good night."

"Good night," he said as she slipped from the room and closed the door behind her.

Once he was alone, he sank into the closest chair with a groan. His rubbed his fingers over his throbbing temples. When the hell had life become so complicated? So out of control?

Not only did he wake every morning yearning for more than just his wife's body, but he was so tangled up in her that he'd hurt his sister, endangered a life-long friendship with Adrian, and had been entirely distracted from his search for his real father. Why?

Julia's pointed questions forced him to face what he'd been trying to deny. He was getting used to having Kat in his life. Not just his bed or his house, but in his life. His mind. Even some small part of his heart.

Only there were so many half-truths between them. As much as he dreaded it, the time had come to tell her about his devil's bargain. It was the only way to protect the future he was beginning to long for. Only after she knew the truth could he analyze what that future was. And how to make it a reality.

Dominic sighed as he entered his chamber and stripped off his shirt. A long conversation with Adrian left him feeling much better. Not only had his friend forgiven his earlier outburst, but had reassured him he was completely serious about Julia, no matter how sudden their attraction.

The crisp linen hit the floor with a swish and Dominic went to work pushing one boot off with the toe of the other before he sat down in a chair by the foot of his bed to finish undressing. He had no desire for a valet tonight. He wanted to be alone with his thoughts. Or better yet, sink into the dark oblivion of sleep.

"Mmmph."

Dominic slowly turned to the bed. In the glow of the firelight, he saw a lump beneath the blankets. A shapely lump. A lump that resembled his wife.

What was Katherine doing there? She had been so furious when she left him in the attic earlier in the day. He was sure she'd finally make good on her vow to sleep in her own chambers. Yet there she lay, dark hair spread across the pillows and her arm draped across his side of the bed, as if she'd reached out for him some time during the night.

Frozen by her beauty and the surprise of her presence, Dominic stared at her. He was overwhelmed by a feeling of tenderness toward this woman he'd not known just a few months before.

Slowly, he rose and removed the rest of his clothing. The bed was warmed by her as he slipped between the sheets. He rolled over and gently gathered her to his side. She didn't wake, but made a low sound of contentment and snuggled her smooth cheek into the crook of his arm.

She muttered something unintelligible against his skin. The only word he understood was his name, whisper-soft as her breath caressed him.

Katherine was the first good thing that had happened to him in a long time. And though their marriage had come about as part of an ugly deal, somehow she wasn't tainted by that association. In fact, she was the one thing in his life that had none of the torment of his past.

He could keep it that way. At least until their tender emotions faded over time. If he first made amends for all he'd done and then admitted the truth, he might be able to keep her at his side.

Now he truly understood how much he wanted that. And how much he was willing to risk to have it.

Chapter 13

Katherine was utterly and completely confused. She frowned as she pretended to measure her chamber windows for curtains, though she doubted anyone who walked in would believe her show. She certainly didn't. What did decorating matter when things had changed so much?

For days Dominic hadn't continued his seemingly endless search of Lansing Square. Not since the ugly scene with his sister and Adrian. Instead he was sequestered in his office. The one time she gained entry, she found him hunched over his desk, writing madly on a document. He hid it the moment she cleared her throat. Their conversation had been curt, to say the least.

He only appeared for meals and the occasional outing with their houseguests. Even then, he was distracted. And though he'd made apologies to everyone, including her, about his stunning lack of manners, he still seemed unable to concentrate on anything for more than a few moments.

Not that Adrian and Julia seemed to mind. The two of them took full advantage of their host's state of mind. They were constantly together, whether it was ice skating on the frozen pond, going to the village nearby, or taking sleigh rides through the countryside, Katherine could see their immediate attraction blossoming into a much deeper connection.

She would have been happy if she wasn't so . . . so . . . envious.

Yes, she could admit she was envious, though it stung her to do so. Julia and Adrian were living a dream she'd long ago let die. They were falling in love right before her very eyes, and no matter how she tried to convince herself that love was dangerous, it was also beautiful. Seeing them growing so close stoked the ache she felt whenever she dared take a side-glance at her husband.

But he obviously didn't feel those same tugs of emotion. The last night they slept in the same room was the night of their most recent argument. Even then, Dominic hadn't tried to seduce her as he had every night before. He'd just let her sleep, and had slipped away before dawn. If she hadn't woken in the night to find herself in his arms, she wouldn't have known he'd been there at all.

Her private chambers were beginning to feel very big and lonely. In the deepest recesses of her heart, she missed sharing a bed with her husband. Missed feeling his warm arms around her. She missed *him*.

"This is what you wanted," she reminded herself quietly as she sunk into a chair and covered her eyes.

She'd repeated that statement innumerable times over the past few days, yet she still didn't believe it. In truth, she ached for Dominic's company, and was disappointed he didn't ache for hers. Somehow she'd expected him to come to her room, or court her back to his. The emptiness of his disregard was shocking, no matter that she'd predicted it would happen.

"Excuse me, madam."

With a start, she uncovered her hot face and turned to the door. Matthews stood in the entryway, uncomfortable in the face of her pain. She smoothed it away with an embarrassed blush and said shakily, "Yes, what is it?"

"A package has arrived for you. Shall I bring it in or have it placed elsewhere?"

She cocked her head. Nothing she ordered should have arrived for weeks. To save money, she'd specified nothing was to be shipped with expedience.

"Bring it in, Matthews. I have no idea what it could be."

In a few moments, the butler reappeared with three packages, all long and thick, wrapped in plain brown paper. Though the label was addressed to her, she didn't recognize the shop name stenciled across the back.

With a curious shrug, she cut the string with the scissors Matthews had handed her. Peeling back the paper, she gasped. Inside was the exact fabric she'd envisioned for her parlor furniture. Deep, rich blue, with just the faintest design. It was obviously expensive, much more than her meager budget would allow.

"And I was instructed to give this to you once you opened the package."

Matthews held out an envelope. She took it with trembling hands as he smiled and bowed out of the room. Barely keeping herself from ripping it open, she slid a finger beneath the seal, pulled out a thick, rich piece of paper, and read the missive inside.

It was from Dominic's solicitor, increasing her pin money and informing her of the establishment of a special fund for renovation of the estate. When she saw the amount that had been deposited into said fund, her jaw dropped. Not only would she be able to finish every room in the house, but do some maintenance on the grounds when spring came.

Why had Dominic done this? Especially now when he seemed to have lost interest in her?

Her eyes widened with sudden, shaken understanding. Perhaps that *was* the reason! He no longer wanted her, so he offered her the estate as some kind of consolation. Something to occupy her mind, to help her forget him and the time they'd shared together.

Despite how many times she told herself being thrown over was inevitable, believing it would happen was far less painful than actually experiencing it. She had to find Dominic. To look into his eyes and see for certain that he no longer desired her.

Stuffing the letter into her pocket and sweeping a ream of the extravagant fabric into her arms, she opened the adjoining door to his room. He wasn't there. With a sigh, she hurried down the stairs into the foyer.

"Matthews?" she called out, peeking through doors and around corners, but the butler was just as absent as her husband seemed to be. Dominic wasn't in his office, and she hadn't heard him in the attic, either.

Then she heard voices coming from the last place she would have expected them. Dominic's rich baritone was coming from the parlor she had chosen, the one she longed to decorate.

"Matthews, I don't want you to worry about that," he said. "I realize it's been weighing on the minds of the staff, but no matter what happens, I will make sure you and the rest of the servants are taken care of."

"I appreciate that, Mr. Mallory." Matthews sounded more relaxed than he had in weeks. "And I will be sure to pass along your reassurances to the others in your employ."

"Very good. Now, did Mrs. Mallory's package arrive?"

She stiffened as her hand curled around the doorjamb.

"Yes, sir."

"Did she—" he hesitated. "Did she like it?"

As Matthews drew in a breath to answer, Katherine walked through the door. "Why don't you ask her yourself?"

Dominic's eyes darkened and she felt a swell of irrational triumph to her very core. There was still sharp desire in the endless gray of his stare, even if it hadn't been demonstrated in a few days. Perhaps his gifts weren't given to apologize for a lack of interest.

"Matthews, that will be all," he said quietly, never taking his eyes from her as the butler left. He only looked away when the quiet click of the door indicated they were alone. "I didn't think eavesdropping was your manner, Kat. Did you hear anything of interest?"

His tone was nonchalant, even playful, but that was at odds with the tension she saw around his eyes and in his stance. For some reason, he was intensely interested in what she'd heard. And how she had reacted to his gifts and his words.

"I overheard," she corrected softly, keeping her distance though it was difficult. "That isn't the same as eavesdropping. And in answer to your question, I did hear several interesting things."

She set her armful of fabric on a rickety side table so she could focus entirely on him.

His gaze darted to her face. "Which were?"

"You reassured Matthews that the staff shouldn't worry about their futures."

She finally gave in to her wish to come nearer, though she only allowed herself a half-step. It was enough to feel his body heat. Immediately her muscles tensed with longing. What was wrong with her? They hadn't even touched.

She took a breath and continued speaking, "It was a kind thing to do. But why did you do it? I've been asking you to do so for weeks and you refused."

He shrugged uncomfortably. "I thought if I gave the staff some guarantees, they might not be so terrified of me. Perhaps they'll do their jobs more efficiently."

"I thought you didn't care if they were frightened of you," she whispered, watching unnamed emotions play across his face as he patently avoided her gaze. "In fact, my impression was that you didn't really care what they thought of you at all."

"It could be I was wrong." He shifted his weight. "Perhaps you were right. Either way, it makes little difference."

But it did to her. And he knew that. Was that why he'd given Matthews his promise? For her? No, it couldn't be. Still, the idea gave her a pleasure so powerful that her knees trembled.

With shaking hands, she picked up the parcel and held it out. "You arranged for the fabric I wanted for the chairs in this room. Why?"

His face hardened, but she could see he forced the expression. It was a barrier, but not to deter her, to protect himself. Why hadn't she seen that before, during all the times he'd been cynical or distant?

"What do the reasons matter? Do you like the material? The color? It can easily be replaced within a few days if you don't." He moved to turn away, but she caught his arm. The muscles flexed beneath her hand and his face tightened.

"It matters to me," she whispered. "The fabric came with this letter." She held the note up beneath his nose. "You've increased my pin money and given me a stipend for renovations. I want to know why, Dominic."

Gently, he extracted himself from her grip and paced over to the fire. He looked trapped, like a caged beast wanting to be free of her inquiries. Yet she couldn't let him be until she understood his motives.

Not that she understood her own. A sane woman would have simply taken the money and left it at that. A woman who knew she was weak to her husband wouldn't have pursued him, cornered him, pressed him for answers.

But here she was, standing in the parlor, which felt like it was shrinking, waiting for him to explain.

"Why did you give me these things, Dominic?" she asked, gentling her tone. "I thought you wanted nothing to do with this house."

"Do you want me to send them back?" he asked, turning from the mantel with a frown.

"No. I'm just baffled by this change. By you."

Wasn't that the truth? She'd been confused by Dominic Mallory from the first moment she saw him on the terrace and he admitted he didn't believe in love. Since then, she'd expended an inordinate amount of energy trying to solve the riddle of the man before her. Even though it was counterproductive to care so very much.

He shrugged. "I—I thought about what you told me when we first arrived here. If I do decide to sell Lansing Square, I want it to be in the best condition it can be. And if I decide to keep it—"

She dropped the fabric in shock. "You're thinking of keeping the estate?"

The muscle in his jaw worked as he stared at her with a promise of passion in his eyes. But behind the desire she saw more there. Emotions she was too terrified to face in herself, let alone admit he might feel for her. Yet seeing naked need in his eyes softened her to him.

"It's so important to you, Kat. I'm beginning to find I like watching you make this house a home." His voice was soft and gentler than she'd ever heard it before. Immediately, he shook that off and said gruffly, "It's an investment."

Tears pricked her eyes as she came across the room to stand before him. He wanted to give her a gift. He wanted to give her a home, even though it was an obvious sacrifice for him to do so.

"Thank you," she said as she leaned up to press a kiss on his rough cheek.

She gripped his arms to steady herself as warmth stirred low in her belly. His presence seemed to surround her even though this kiss was the most chaste they ever shared. But somehow it still meant something. Just as every touch meant something.

With a finger, he tilted her face up to his and her knees turned to water. He was so close. From this distance there was no mistaking how much he wanted her. And she wanted him, in every part of her, including her heart.

Their lips were mere inches apart, but instead of kissing her, Dominic said, "I want you to understand, Kat. I want to explain so much."

She gripped his arms tighter. What could he want to say at a time like this?

"Then explain," she murmured, even as she lifted her lips closer and prepared for the kiss she knew would send her over the edge of reason.

Just as their lips touched, the door behind them opened. Matthews stepped inside. "I'm very sorry to interrupt."

Dominic jerked his head back as if he'd been awakened from a dream. His eyes were hazy, as cloudy as she wagered her own gaze was.

"What is it?" he asked as he took a step back and ran a hand through his hair.

"I tried to explain to the gentleman that you were not in residence," Matthews said with an apologetic shake of his head. "But his footmen were already unloading the carriage. He shoved me aside and . . ."

"Who?" Dominic said impatiently.

Matthews let out a long, beleaguered sigh and a terrible sense of premonition filled Katherine. "Your brother and his wife are waiting for you in the foyer, sir."

Dominic staggered back and found himself leaning against the mantelpiece, the fire hot against his back. Colden was here? That was just typical. The very moment Dominic got up the nerve to reveal the truth to Katherine and his brother showed up to ruin it all.

Frustration and anger coursed through him, but a deeper, underlying emotion was more troubling. For the first time since he left Harrison Mallory's house so many years ago, a niggling of fear quickened his heartbeat.

He took a sidelong glance at his wife. Katherine's mouth was still open in shock, one hand covering her rounded lips. What if seeing Cole brought back those feelings she once felt for her former fiancé? For weeks Dominic had tried to make her forget, he knew in some ways he had. But a few stolen moments and all that could be for nothing. Then the truth would be meaningless.

He drew in a long, calming breath and ground out, "I'm sure you did your best to restrain my brother and his wife, Matthews. Please, show them in."

The butler nodded. Dominic turned to Katherine. He had to say something before Cole came in, something to remind her of all the pleasure they'd shared. But no words came. She seemed just as lost as she stared at the parlor door, waiting for a man she'd once planned to marry. The one she'd chosen.

Dominic's stomach churned.

"Lord and Lady Harborough," Matthews announced as he held the door open wide for Dominic's brother and sister-in-law to enter.

Sarah immediately released Cole's arm and scanned the room the moment she came in. Her cold, hard eyes skimmed over every stick of furniture, every line in the wall hangings. Then, before any welcomes had been said, she giggled. Dominic cringed at the harsh, cruel sound. How could he have ever found that harridan attractive in any way?

Katherine stiffened at his side, and for a brief moment her jade eyes were icy. Then, to his surprise, she smiled and the face of a hostess replaced her anger.

"Colden, Sarah, good afternoon," she gushed, motioning to two chairs beside the fire. Despite that, no one in the room sat. "What a surprise to see you!"

Cole shot a harsh look in Dominic's direction. "I assumed since my sister was invited that Sarah and I would be welcome as well."

Dominic set his jaw. There were so many things he wanted to say to his sibling, but when he opened his mouth to speak them, Katherine placed a soft hand on his elbow. The gesture was calming, as well as silencing.

"Of course you are. Dominic's family is always welcome in our home. Did you bring your mother?" She smiled, but behind the friendly expression, Dominic thought he could see a glimmer of her own upset. It gave him hope.

"No," Sarah said, but didn't even do Katherine the courtesy of looking her way. Instead, she slid a bit closer to Dominic. "How are you, Dominic? How do you find married life?"

Katherine's hand tightened on his arm, though her face never did so much as twitch. He gave his sister-in-law a cold smile. "Perfect."

His wife's hand relaxed before she slowly let him go. She nodded to the group. "I'll fetch Julia. I'm sure she will want to see you all."

Dominic jolted at the idea of being left alone with their uninvited guests. "Are you sure you don't want me to find her?"

"No." She shook her head and the message in her

eyes was clear. She wanted to get away from Sarah for a moment, not that he could blame her. Their unexpected arrival was unsettling to say the least. "I want to give some directions to the servants since we'll have more guests tonight for supper."

"You mean you *have* servants here?" Sarah laughed. "It's so rustic, I never would have guessed."

Again Katherine's mouth thinned into a hard line, but she said nothing. Dominic swelled with pride at her utter control. He knew how much the estate meant to her, and how much Sarah's digs about its condition must have hurt. That she was able to keep her tongue was a testament to his wife's elegance and grace.

With a nod, Katherine turned to go, but Cole stepped forward before she could safely escape. Dominic's pride turned to worry at the determined look on his brother's face. Cole seemed to be impressed by Katherine's reaction, too. Uncontrollable jealousy sluiced through him.

"Why don't we all go together, Katherine?" he asked as he slowly advanced on her to offer her an arm. "I'm sure my wife and I would both like a tour of your *estate*."

Katherine hesitated for just a fraction of a second before she took the arm Cole offered. Dominic couldn't read her reaction, pleased or otherwise. With a frown, he turned to offer his own arm to

Sarah. Instead of taking it, she sank down on the settee with a flirtatious smile.

"Oh, I think I'll cry off on a tour just now. I'm so very tired from our journey." Her smile widened. "I'm sure Dominic wouldn't mind keeping me company while you two are gone. Would you?"

"No, of course not," Dominic murmured reluctantly.

His gaze stole to Katherine. Her eyes had grown wide and all the emotions she'd been able to keep in check since their guests' arrival were clear. Still, he couldn't tell if she was happy for her time alone with Cole or jealous that Dominic would be spending a few unaccompanied moments with Sarah.

"Very well," Katherine said softly as she turned and let Cole lead her from the room.

The instant the door closed behind them, Dominic sank into a chair with a muted groan. God, how he hated the fact that his wife had left on his brother's arm.

Not so very long ago he'd caught Katherine wishing on stars on the terrace. Just a few short weeks before she considered his brother perfection. She'd said as much the first night they met. If she were reminded of that perfection now . . . No, he couldn't bear to think about it.

"Would you like a drink, Sarah?" he asked in a hoarse voice. He certainly needed one.

"Yes. I'm sure you remember how much I like

brandy." She gave him a feline smile as he rose to pour them each one. "You look better than I expected."

He stiffened as he turned to face her. Again he was struck by how much he disliked her. She wasn't even beautiful to him anymore, especially when compared to Katherine's warmth and light.

"What did you expect?" he asked as he held out the drink.

She rose to her feet and took a step closer. "Katherine seems very cold," she whispered as she ran a long fingernail down his shirtfront. He stiffened under the touch, but not out of pleasure. "You must be bored. But now that I'm here, I promise I could help you remember what it's like to have your blood boil."

His nostrils flared in distaste. "I don't think so, Sarah. Not anymore."

"You wanted me once." She slid the glasses from his hand and put them on the table behind him. "I came to your bed in London and you took just a moment too long to push me away. Even then, it was duty to your brother that kept you from taking me. But now I think you don't feel anything toward your brother. So perhaps you'll give me a taste of what I've been missing. If I ask very, very nicely."

With a smile of satisfaction, she leaned up to press her lips against his. Unlike years ago when the same scenario played out in his town house in

London, Dominic felt nothing. Not even a stir of desire moved him. In fact, he found himself comparing her touch to his wife's, and Sarah was lacking in each and every department.

Grasping her wrists gently, he pushed her back. "No, Sarah. I am more than satisfied in my current situation. I don't want you. If you stay here, it won't be in my bed, and if you expect me to knock on your door, you will be sorely disappointed."

Her eyes widened, first in disbelief and then in pure, unadulterated rage. "You—you can't be serious."

He nodded. "I am."

"B-but you wanted me," she sputtered in disbelief.

He cocked his head. How typical of Sarah to look to be the center of attention. To want to cause strife and rifts for her own twisted pleasure and need for control. Only now Dominic had no interest. Now he had Katherine.

He started. Cole had wished to marry Katherine, too. Instead of the two men desiring Sarah, they both wanted Katherine. Not being the one in the middle had to bother Sarah. For once, she wasn't the cause of emotional upheaval. She wasn't the woman everyone craved.

"I don't deny I once desired you, Sarah. But we both knew it never could have come to anything, even then. Whatever my feelings toward Colden, I wouldn't betray him with his own wife. And I'm with Katherine now. I certainly wouldn't bring her that kind of pain, even if I did desire you."

Suddenly, understanding flashed across her face. "You love the little twit, don't you?" she said with a malicious hiss.

Dominic jolted at the accusation, but made no attempt to refute it.

Her eyes narrowed. "I can make her hate you. I can make sure she runs screaming as far away from you as is humanly possible."

Fury filled him at the thought of Sarah or anyone else ruining his life with his wife. Driven by irrational jealousy or not, he wouldn't allow her to damage his already shaky union. He caught his sister-in-law's shoulders and gave her a small shake.

"Don't you threaten me, Sarah. If I ever catch you near my wife whispering your vicious lies and innuendos into her ear, I won't be responsible for what I do. Don't push me." His voice was deceptively low, but he could tell by the flash of fear in her eyes that she understood him perfectly.

She shook out of his grip with a cry, then made a show of straightening her hair and gown. When she looked at him again, it was with eyes filled with smug hatred.

"No, I won't have to destroy your marriage, Dominic. If you're fool enough to love her, you'll ruin yourself in the end, bastard that you are. Cole and I can just sit back and watch you destroy everything on your own."

With that, she spun on her heel and stomped from the room in the direction in which Cole and Katherine had gone.

Chapter 14

When Katherine was forced to marry Dominic, she assumed she would make comparisons between the two brothers. It was only natural to do so. What she hadn't anticipated was that Cole would come out the loser so consistently and completely.

As she nodded at something he said, she considered all the things that had once drawn her to Cole. Safety had been a main one. Just being at his side had once made her feel content and at ease.

Now as they strolled through the hallways of Lansing Square, the touch of Cole's hand on her arm brought her no peace. In fact, she resented it. Just as she resented his presence in general.

Dominic was so close to sharing a secret with her. Better yet, he'd been ready to kiss her, claim her as he hadn't for what felt like forever. She hadn't ever wanted anything more, but Colden's intrusion put a swift end to that.

She shot a glance at her former fiancé. They had been friends once, but no easy companionship existed between them anymore. Each time he said something in subtle deprecation of Dominic, she liked Cole less.

Was he still talking?

"And this is Dominic's office," she said as she stifled a yawn. Instead of looking in and passing by as he had during the rest of her tour, Cole entered his brother's private room and peered around with a malicious smile.

When he turned back to her, the ugliness was gone, leaving her to wonder if she only imagined it. Perhaps she was influenced by Dominic's hatred for his brother. Even if she didn't feel anything toward Cole, that didn't mean she had to dislike him. She and Cole simply had to redefine their relationship. Perhaps, over time, she could even be a bridge between the two brothers and help them forge a stronger bond.

Cole released her arm, and she found him staring at her. She turned away from his close scrutiny. Without warning, it was as if she were walking a tightrope between being polite and drawing boundaries.

"Are you ever sorry, Katherine?" he asked softly as he gave the door behind them a gentle push.

Her eyes darted to the tiny crack that now separated them from the hallway. It was entirely inappropriate to be alone with a man who wasn't her husband. Especially one who was looking at her in that pointed manner. But it had to be her imagination. Cole never showed her inordinate physical affection when they were engaged. Why would he do so now?

"S-sorry?" she repeated as she swallowed hard and backed away. "Sorry about what?"

His smile turned condescending. "That we couldn't wed as we planned, of course." He moved closer, invading her personal space enough that she knew he did so purposefully.

"Things happened," she said as she tried to skirt away from him. "It all worked out for the best in the end, I suppose."

"*I'm* sorry," he murmured as he reached out to cup her face. "We could have been so good together."

And then he was dipping his head toward her. Katherine let out a gasp and pushed him away as hard as she could. He was going to *kiss* her! Another man's wife. His *brother's* wife!

Her hands shook as she yanked the door open to keep them from being alone. "Colden, our marriage would have been one of friendship, not passion. You seem to have forgotten that, though I don't understand why!"

His mouth thinned into an unpleasant frown, but he bobbed out a curt nod. "Of course. Forgive me."

"I do miss being your friend," she said, softening her tone as the shock of his actions began to wear off. "But as I said, things have worked out for the best. You belong with your wife, and I seem to belong with Dominic." She couldn't help but picture her husband with a soft smile. "He's much different than I feared he would be all those months ago."

For a brief moment, potent rage flashed across Cole's face. She could almost feel it vibrate through her. Then it was gone, and he gave her a sad frown that irked her to her core.

"Perhaps he isn't so different," he said with a falsely distressed shake of his head. "Katherine, I'm afraid I misled you about the purpose of my arrival. Yes, it was to pay a visit, but part of why I came here was to ensure your welfare."

"Oh, for heaven's sake, Cole," she said, unable to keep her growing annoyance out of her voice.

She was still shaken by his aborted kiss, and now anger was added to her turbulent emotions.

"You have absolutely no reason to fear for my welfare. I'm perfectly fine—"

Clearing his throat, he interrupted her, "And to assuage my own guilt at putting you in this untenable situation."

His growing contempt for Dominic brought out the protector in her. "Well, I free you from your guilt. I'm very happy here."

The moment the words fell from her lips, she was filled with a sense of how very true they were. She was happy in Lansing Square. And more importantly, she was happy with Dominic. Despite her attempts to push him away, despite his secrets and searching, she enjoyed her husband's company. She longed for his touch. And she couldn't imagine her life without him in it.

For a moment, Cole's face fell. Then a look of contemplation filled his eyes and he suddenly gave her a triumphant smile. Katherine's stomach flipped. Why did he look so . . . so smug?

"I feel no guilt over that, Katherine. No, my guilt comes from the bargain I struck with my brother." He let his words sink in silently.

"Bargain?" she repeated softly. Trepidation tingled through her every nerve as that one little word slipped from her lips. "What are you talking about?"

Cole clucked his tongue in disapproval. "I knew he wouldn't be man enough to tell you the truth. Though I hoped, for your sake, he would reveal everything. To let you choose your own fate rather than to hold you under false pretenses."

"Stop talking in riddles," she snapped. "And tell me what you mean."

Cole started at her harsh tone, but immediately his cold smile was back. Almost like he was enjoying each and every moment of this uncomfortable game.

"The night of our engagement party when you first met Dominic, do you know why he was there?" he asked, sitting down at his brother's desk as if he owned the room.

"No," she said shakily. "I assumed he was there to wish you well."

Cole laughed. "Dominic, wish me well? Not bloody likely. No, he was there because he wanted something. Some place, actually." He leaned forward for effect. "He wanted Lansing Square."

"Now I know you're mistaken," she said with a renewed sense of relief. "Dominic doesn't care one way or another about this place."

"Oh, but he does, though I don't know why." Cole smiled. It was a humorless expression, devoid of all kindness and filled with only anger and ugliness. "And he was willing to trade in order to acquire it."

"Trade?" she whispered past suddenly dry lips.

"Yes. I needed someone to marry you in order to reduce the scandal on my name. And to save you from a life of whispers, of course. And Dominic wanted this house badly enough that he was willing to take *you* as part of the bargain." He leaned forward with a gleam of satisfaction in his eyes. "Although he did protest long and hard, I finally convinced him that the only way he would ever get his hands on this estate was if he married you. So he did."

Katherine sank into a chair as a wave of nausea almost undid her. "I—I don't believe you."

But that denial was a lie.

Cole statement made perfect sense to her. Dominic's claim that he'd married her to save his family from scandal never rang true to her. Not when her few glimpses into his past revealed a man neglected and abandoned by his so-called family.

But marrying her in order to acquire the estate made perfect sense. Even though Dominic claimed to despise the place, he'd been obsessed with searching it. Whatever secrets he looked for there were more important to him than anything. And valuable enough that he would marry a woman, any woman, to find them.

But did that mean everything between them was a lie? Was the passion they shared just part of some game?

Cole reached across the desk to take her hand. She flinched back, not wanting his touch after seeing him take so much pleasure in telling her this . . . this story.

"You may not want to believe it, Katherine, but I swear it's the truth. Can you ever forgive me for my part in this deception? Please know it was done with only the intent to protect you from society. At least, on my part. Dominic had other motives." He finished with a slow shake of his head.

Tears stung her eyes, but she refused to give in to the pain in front of Cole. Instead, she did her best to focus on the anger building in the pit of her stomach. Still, she couldn't seem to formulate any words. She was too afraid that when she spoke, she would scream out her anguish and reveal too much of her heart to Cole, and to herself.

If only she'd stayed true to her original plan and kept herself separate from Dominic, his deception wouldn't hurt so much. But no, she had come to care for her husband. To grow closer to him with every kiss, with every kind word. But now she knew everything had been an act designed to obtain a piece of *property*. Perhaps some of the façade was genuine, but it had been a means to an end.

"Katherine?" Cole asked with a concerned frown.

"Why?" she croaked out as she stared at him. "Why would you come all the way here to tell me this? Evidently, you wish to destroy your brother and whatever life we have built together, but I don't understand it."

Cole's face darkened and hardened in a way she hadn't seen before. "He has always taken what wasn't his. He lived in a house he had no right to, with a name he had no right to bear."

She cocked her head as confusion mixed with sickening anger and hurt. "You're talking nonsense. I don't understand—"

Before she could finish, Katherine heard Dominic and Sarah's angry voices in the hallway, then the two entered together. Using all her remaining strength, she rose to her feet and turned to face her husband with what she hoped was an expression of utter disdain and not total devastation.

He didn't seem to notice as he snapped, "Cole, you and your wife will leave. You were not invited and you are no longer welcome in my house."

Katherine's eyes narrowed as she clenched her shaking hands behind her back. Was he trying to hurry his brother and sister-in-law away before they revealed the truth? Was this more of the same deception that had gone on so long?

"Why in such a hurry, Dominic? Are you afraid Sarah and Cole will tell your secrets?" she asked, lashing out at him in a tone designed to cut him as deeply as she had been cut.

The color drained from Dominic's cheeks as he turned his attention on her. For a brief moment, she saw all his emotions flash through his eyes. Desperation was there. Horror. And also resignation, like he'd been waiting for this moment to come.

Everything Cole said was true. Dominic had been hiding the truth from her from the first moment they were joined as man and wife.

Her heart shattered. She wanted to go down on her knees and weep and pound the floor at what a fool she'd been. All her nightmares, all her fears had come true. She'd become so wrapped up in Dominic that she'd been blind to his lies. Just as she knew she would be if she let him into her heart. Why? Why hadn't she kept her distance and prevented this agony that wracked her now?

Sarah broke the silence in the room with a low laugh. "Oh, Dominic, looks like I'm too late to destroy anything for you. Cole, darling, did you tell the Ice Princess about Dominic and me?"

Cole came around the desk with a glare for his wife. "Sarah!"

Katherine stared at her husband in disbelief. Sarah's ugliness had only been limited to innuendo before, but now it was practically an admission of an affair. And judging from Dominic's inability to meet her eyes, it was an admission he couldn't deny.

"What did you tell my wife?" he asked low and dangerous.

Cole's eyes widened and his smile faltered in the face of his brother's quiet rage, but he managed to remain confident when he said, "Only the truth. Only what she deserved to know. That you took her in trade. That you have lied to her every day of your marriage."

"Oh, Cole!"

Katherine pivoted to see Julia and Adrian at the door. Julia's face was pale, but she looked anything but surprised by her older brother's statement.

"How could you tell her? Why would you do that?" Julia asked with a disgusted shake of her head.

Katherine gasped. A new round of embarrassment and shock raced through her. The tears she'd been struggling to quell now filled her eyes. She blinked them back with ferocity.

"Oh God, you knew, too? You knew what Dominic and Cole had done and you didn't tell me? You were supposed to be my friend."

Julia shifted uncomfortably. "Katherine—"

She turned away before Julia could finish. It wasn't enough humiliation that she had been traded like chattel, but the entire family was privy to the arrangement? And judging from Adrian's pitying face, he too. It seemed she was the only one who hadn't been in on their little joke.

Dominic had remained strangely stoic, but he stepped forward with a clenched fist. There was resignation on his face. Almost a relief that Katherine didn't understand.

"If you're here to make confessions on my behalf, Colden, why stop with this one?" He moved closer and Cole skittered back with fear in his eyes. "Or perhaps I should take responsibility for my own lies and you should claim yours. You have as many as I do."

Cole drew away, his face paling as he shot a glance at Sarah. Dominic spun away from them to face Katherine. His expression softened as he reached for her hand. She dodged his touch and he nodded as if he understood.

"Katherine, I wanted to tell you so many things for so long. I've tried, but something always interrupts, whether it's uninvited houseguests"—he shot a glare over his shoulder at his brother—"or my own cowardice. I'm sorry this had to be revealed in this manner. More sorry than you'll ever know, but I want you to hear everything from my lips, not my brother's poison ones."

Katherine struggled to remain composed when she wanted to scream. Somehow she managed to keep her emotions at bay and her gaze fixed on Dominic.

He shifted under her scrutiny, but never broke his stare away from hers. "What my brother says is true. I made the agreement to marry you in trade for this house."

She turned her face with a stifled moan. Hurt exploded in her chest and seeped through her bloodstream. "Why?"

He straightened his shoulders and lifted his chin. "Harrison Mallory was not my father."

With a jolt at his sudden announcement, she looked up at him. Was this true? Pain and anger flashed across his angled face as he nodded.

"I am a bastard, Katherine."

Sarah let out a burst of laughter, but Dominic ignored her cackle and the way Cole grinned. "I believe there is evidence to the identity of my true father hidden somewhere in this house. Cole refused me access to the estate unless I married you."

She cast a glance over her shoulder at Cole. At least he had the decency to stop grinning and put a falsely apologetic expression on his face. Still, his eyes sparkled with glee. Nausea and fury rushed through her in equal measure.

"And that leads us to Julia's question," Dominic said, breaking eye contact with her finally to stare at Cole. "She asked why our brother would do this.

Why he would come here to tell you these things and ruin whatever we shared in the last few months. It's because his father taught him to hate me, taught him that I deserved nothing. Cole can't stand it that I have something he once desired. That I have you."

"A bastard doesn't deserve a lady," Cole said as he folded his arms. "He certainly doesn't deserve the lady *I* was meant to marry. I thought Katherine would never grow close to you, but when I found her letters to Julia that expressed only her contentment, I knew I couldn't let that go on. I couldn't let you have what you didn't deserve. To protect my name, I may not be able to tell the world you are a bastard, but I'll be damned if I will see you be treated as my equal if there is anything I can do to prevent that from occurring. Now your wife knows the truth of what you are."

Katherine stared at the man she once planned to marry. Cole's pettiness, his childish jealousy and cruelty shocked her nearly as much as Dominic's lies. Being a bastard in name was something her husband had no control over. Being a bastard in action was something Cole apparently thrived on.

"So all this pain you caused, you did it out of some old childhood grudge?" she murmured in disbelief to Cole.

"I thought you should know the true character of the man you married," Cole said, the kindness returning to his eyes. Only now Katherine could see how false that was. How pretended. She had been blind to his true character.

"And what of the man she would have married had Sarah not returned when she did?" Dominic asked. "What of the secrets you kept? The cruel lies you told her and everyone else?"

Cole blanched. "Dominic . . ."

Katherine shook her head. If there was more to be told, she wanted to hear it. Now that she was aware of how in the dark she had been, she wanted to come into the light. She wanted to know it all.

"Tell me," she whispered.

Dominic looked at her. He didn't flinch away from her emotions. He only gave her what she needed, though she had no doubt it wasn't easy for him to reveal what he'd fought so hard to keep secret.

"Cole required your fortune after a long series of bad investments and nights of gambling. And he desired the property you inherited from your father. Your guardians were to receive a special stipend if you were married before you were twenty-one, so my brother used their knowledge to transform himself into the man of your dreams."

Katherine choked on a strangled cry. Eustacia and Stephan, the ones who were supposed to protect her, had been a part of this deceit as well? And all for money. The pieces of the painful puzzle snapped together one by one, leaving her ever more alone and feeling foolish and heartbroken.

Dominic swallowed hard at her outburst. His

hand stirred, but he didn't raise it to touch her. She wasn't sure whether to be grateful he respected her need for distance or not.

When she managed to calm her breathing, he continued. "When Cole thought he had won your hand, he wagered away your property and spent your money before he had the right. That was why he needed me to take his place. To keep his fraud from being revealed and your fortune within the Mallory family."

She covered her mouth. Tremors rocked her from her head to her toes. She could hardly breathe. But she needed to know more. "Is that all?"

"I don't know." Dominic turned on his brother. "I believe there is more, but I have no proof."

Julia stepped forward. "Please, isn't this enough?"

The thin control Katherine had managed to keep on her emotions snapped. "No!" she cried. "It isn't. I want to know everything. I want to know every lie told. Now!"

Dominic flinched at her fury, but he kept his gaze on her face. Somehow, even knowing everything he'd done, it comforted her to see that he didn't back away. He didn't attempt to placate her or treat her like a child.

He sighed. "I think Cole knew Sarah was alive before that fact was revealed the night of your engagement soiree."

"No, that cannot be true," Julia said as she stumbled back. Adrian caught her arm to steady her.

"You think not?"

Now it was Sarah who spoke. For the first time she didn't look smug, she didn't look cold. She looked angry. Vengeful.

"Sarah, don't!" Cole snapped.

Sarah shook off the hand he placed on her arm. "Why, Cole? So you can play victim even more? I'm tired of being the one to blame. I want you to have your share." She smiled at Katherine with feline nastiness. "Of course my husband knew I was alive. He knew for years. In fact, it was because of Dominic that I was 'lost' in the first place."

Dominic reeled back. He had suspected Cole was aware of Sarah's survival at some point, but he hadn't realized his brother had known for so long. And he certainly had no idea he played some part in their cruel trick.

"Explain yourself!" he ordered as his anger threatened to overflow.

Cole grasped Sarah's arm, but she pushed him aside as she stepped closer. Dominic felt an urge to throw himself between Katherine and Sarah, but he resisted. From the utter betrayal and pain in his wife's eyes, he doubted she would appreciate his protection now. He'd certainly failed to protect her up until this point.

"Although we tried for several years, Cole and I never managed to produce any children, let alone a male child to inherit the Harborough title. My inability to produce brats was the only reason why I was allowed to have as much fun outside our marriage as Cole was."

Katherine flinched at the crude reference to Sarah's sexual escapades.

"Cole didn't care and neither did I. We didn't want any children interfering in our lives. But then you began to raise yourself up in the world, Dominic." Sarah smiled. "Women began to whisper about you at parties in our circles. Despite not having a title, you were becoming an eligible bachelor. And though you expressed no interest in marrying, Cole knew that could change if the right opportunity arose. He realized if he and I produced no children, but you had a son, that boy would inherit the title, the estate, and all the money in entail."

"The son of a bastard," Cole said, finally stepping forward. "Holding *my* father's title. I could not allow it. I thought of spreading the story of your true parentage, but I realized that would only put a blight on the Mallory name. I realized I would have to find a way to produce a legitimate child."

Sarah glared at him. "He told me he wanted me to go away. That he wouldn't divorce me in order to prevent another scandal, but if I disappeared for long enough, he would have me declared dead and marry again. Of course, I resisted. London is my home. All good society is here. Why would I leave just to satisfy his desire to keep his precious bloodline pure? But then he offered me money. He offered me freedom on the Continent. Freedom I would never be allowed here."

Julia uncovered her mouth. "Freedom?"

"To do whatever I desired," Sarah laughed. "You wouldn't understand, little spinster, what pleasures a woman desires. Cole promised me a fortune to hide away. By that time, we had very little love between us, so I agreed. The fact that the ship I was intended to travel on actually sank and I was immediately believed dead, rather than the years it would have taken by our plan, was a lucky coincidence. I wrote Cole upon my arrival and told him I expected my payments to arrive on time."

Dominic shook his head. Their deception went even deeper than he imagined. "If you had this devil's agreement, why did you ever come back?"

Her face twisted. "After a while, his 'on time' payments grew later and later. Eventually, they got smaller and smaller, too. I hired an investigator to see why and realized the damn fool was squandering away his fortune. And then I discovered his plan to marry *you*."

Katherine shook her head, but didn't turn away from Sarah's pointed glare. "My God."

"Why should he be allowed to marry again if he didn't hold up his bargain? When he ignored my demand for my latest payment, I boarded a ship and headed back to London. I made sure he knew about it when it was far too late to stop me." She smiled over her shoulder at her husband. "He never should have crossed me, and I will never make the mistake of entering such a bargain with him again. As Dominic just learned, Cole is loath to keep up his end of any agreement."

Cole glared miserably, but remained silent. Dominic shook his head.

"You did all this just to keep me from a title I never desired? From the children I never intended to have?" he asked. "You are pathetic. You told so many lies and caused so much pain. Well, I denounce any claim I have on your father's title, and I will do whatever is necessary to make that claim legal."

Cole's eyes lit up, but before he could say anything, Katherine whispered, "Cole isn't the only one who caused pain."

Dominic turned to her. His heart ached at the way she stared at him with such emptiness. He hadn't realized how alive her stare had been before. How attached he'd become to the glitter of desire and emotion in her eyes when she looked at him. That was gone now. Lost because of his betrayals.

"I know that," he began.

She waved him off. "I don't care. I don't want any more explanations. I've had enough." She turned to Cole and Sarah. "You are no longer welcome in my home. Please leave."

Cole drew back. "But—"

"Go!" she repeated a little louder. "Now."

He nodded as he took Sarah's arm and led her

away. Once they were gone, Katherine turned to the rest of them. "As for all of you, I have no words. Perhaps later I'll be able to find a few, but for now I'm going to my chamber. I do not wish to be disturbed. Good afternoon."

Turning on her heel, Katherine swept out of the room. Dominic watched her go helplessly. How he longed to run after her, to gather her into his arms and beg her forgiveness. He took a step toward her, but Adrian placed a hand on his arm.

"Not yet," he advised quietly. "Let her have a little time before you go to her."

"I don't think time is going to help," Dominic said as he covered his eyes. "I've lost my wife."

As he stared at the door, he realized if he lost his wife . . . he would lose everything.

Chapter 15

Katherine stared out her window. She was happy for the winter scene below. Its barren starkness was a perfect compliment to her empty heart. She didn't think she could bear it if there were singing birds or budding flowers to accompany her loss.

Lies. So many lies. They were layered one on top of the other, tangled like a web, until she could no longer discern the truth anymore.

She'd taken refuge in her chamber for over two hours, but she still hurt so much that it was unclear what pained her most. The people she trusted had used her.

Cole pretended to be her friend, pretended to

care for her when in reality he had only played at being everything she thought she wanted. That her guardians had played a part in his cruel deception only stung all the more. She never believed Eustacia and Stephan loved her, but she had been comfortable in the knowledge that they had her best interest at heart.

It seemed she could not judge anyone's character.

Certainly, if someone had come to her six months before and told her Cole arranged for his wife to disappear and pretend to be dead so he could illegally marry someone else and have a child with her, she would have laughed. It was preposterous. She would have said how truly grief stricken her fiancé was. She would have told them Cole wasn't capable of thinking such a thing, let alone putting the plan in action.

How could she have been so wrong?

But there was one hurt that stabbed at her worst of all. More than her guardians' falsehoods. More than Cole's deceptions and frauds. More than Julia's silent acquiescence to the plot between her brothers.

Dominic.

She winced when she thought of him. Shutting her eyes, she pictured his face. Over and over again, she thought of the acceptance in his expression when she heard he only took her as a wife in trade. He had expected the truth to come out at some point. Perhaps he was even relieved. Now he no longer had to pretend their marriage meant something.

She covered her eyes.

"Why?" she whispered. "Why couldn't I keep you from my heart?"

She heard the door in the adjoining chamber open and straightened to attention. From the heavy footfalls in the other room, she knew it was Dominic in the chamber they once shared. He strode to her door and hesitated on the other side. Her breath caught and she realized she was actually praying he would enter.

Even after all he'd done, she still had no self-control.

Hardening herself, she folded her arms and called out, "Come in if that's what you wish to do."

The door opened and Dominic stepped inside. Her heart thudded treacherously at the sight of him. Framed by the dying light of her fire, his face was dark and haggard. It was clear regret weighed heavily on his shoulders.

But was it regret over deceiving her, or being caught in his lies?

Did it even matter?

"Kat?" he said, his voice unsure and shaky from the distance he so wisely maintained.

The nickname he'd chosen for her warmed her even as she fought those foolishly tender feelings. She forced her anger and betrayal to the surface over her grief and disappointment. She wanted Dominic to see the damage he'd caused, not how easily he could sway her with a few tender words or a gentle touch.

She'd already given him far too much power as it was.

"Don't call me Kat." She broke his gaze. It was too hard to look at him. "Don't *ever* call me Kat again. The last thing I want are reminders of how you misled me into caring for you."

Dominic's eyes went wide and he gripped the back of the closest chair. Katherine started as she realized what she'd just said. She had admitted she'd come to care for her husband.

Well, she didn't anymore. His lies killed those feelings.

But she still couldn't manage to look him in the face.

"Please, let me talk to you," he said softly.

It was a tone she'd never heard from him before. Patient. Gentle. Her mind was jumbled with thoughts. Was this still part of some trick?

"I don't want to hear your explanations," she said with a tired sigh as she turned to the darkening sky outside. "I can't listen to any more lies."

"No more lies," he promised.

The anger she'd been looking for to protect herself bubbled up without her having to search for it. "How am I to believe you, Dominic? How can I believe anything you say?"

He dipped his head. "I don't know. But I swear to you, I'll tell you everything you want to know now, like I should have done weeks ago."

She stood up and paced to the fire. Folding her

arms as a shield across her heart, she turned back to him. "I don't want to talk."

His spine stiffened. "That's unfortunate, because I'm not leaving this room until we've resolved this."

Humorless laughter bubbled out of her. "You think there is resolution possible? You lied to me, you deceived me, you made me into the greatest fool. Nothing you say can change that."

"You're right." He frowned. "I did all those things. I hurt you, I know that. But what I said to you in front of Cole and Sarah, it was only the surface. I didn't want you to hear what I did from my brother, of all people. I wanted to tell you myself. But there is more, Katherine. More to it than just lies or a bargain."

Her hands trembled as his words and his pleading tone touched her. Dominic had always been strong, mysterious. Now he looked at her with nothing hidden. His emotions shone in his eyes, and it was clear he needed her. Needed to confess.

And she needed to hear him. Despite her anger.

"What more is there to say?" she whispered.

"I want you to understand why I struck that agreement with Cole." He winced. "It was stupid and cruel, but I was . . . Katherine, I was desperate and I'm not a desperate man."

She took an involuntary step closer. "Why?"

"I spent my life knowing I was different. Feeling

Harrison Mallory's disdain for me and my mother's coldness, but never understanding why. Then one night, Cole revealed the truth."

He hesitated and she heard him fighting to measure his breathing. Her heart went out to him. No matter what he'd done to change his fortunes, no matter how he struggled to become the strong man he was, remembering the pains of his childhood wasn't easy. He fought emotion with every part of himself, from the stiff way he held his body to the flat tone of his voice.

"I was only thirteen, Cole was eighteen. We argued frequently, but this time was different. He told me I was nothing but a bastard. I told him I didn't believe him, but it struck me as so true."

"Did you ask your father or your mother?" she asked, even as she cursed herself for wanting to know more. It would have been wiser just to push him out, but she needed his explanation. Needed him to tell her why he made her no more than a pawn.

He shook his head. "I wanted to, but I was young. When Harrison Mallory was angry, his reprisals were swift and unpleasant, I was too afraid to court them. For two years, I watched every movement around me, listened to each word spoken, hoping to catch someone in a lie, or learn some secret. Finally, plied by a little drink I snitched from the cellar, I got up the nerve to confront the man I'd called father for fifteen years." He shook his head as if to erase the memories.

He cleared his throat. "I asked him flat out if I was really a Mallory. He only stared at me for a long time, but then he admitted the truth. He told me I was the result of an affair my mother had. And that he couldn't stand the sight of me."

Katherine turned her face away as pain exploded in her chest. Pain for the boy her husband had been. No matter what he'd done to her, she didn't believe he deserved such little regard from the man who raised him. She couldn't believe someone could be so cold to a child who had no responsibility for how he had come to be in the world.

"What did Larissa say?" she asked in a choked voice.

Her mother-in-law had never been a warm person, but she hadn't been flatly unkind, either. She was distant and unemotional, but Katherine could hardly believe she would stand idly by while her husband and son abused Dominic.

He laughed humorlessly. "Throughout my life, my mother could hardly look at me. Perhaps I was a reminder of a mistake, I don't know. But when I asked her for the truth about my parentage, she pretended as if the question was never voiced. Denials became the only words we shared. Only once did I manage to get her to say anything about my real father. One night after she drank too much, she admitted she had loved the man. And implied that her arranged marriage to Mallory had kept her from him, whomever he was."

Katherine shook her head in disbelief. "But she never told you his name?"

"No, nor anything about his circumstances." It was a matter of fact answer. "I couldn't live there any longer with a 'father' who hated me and a mother who denied me my past. When I returned to school, I threw myself into my work and into my anger. I never came 'home' again. Not even when Harrison Mallory did the world a favor and died. Eventually, I realized I couldn't live my life trying to prove the man wrong about me. I had to shrug off his hold. But I couldn't forget I had a real father in the world somewhere. I wanted . . . and still want to know who he is."

She nodded. That, at least, she understood. "So you began inquiring?"

He looked into the fire, his eyes distant with memories. "I had resources of my own by that time and I put them into finding out the truth. That was when I discovered my mother had spent a great deal of time alone in this house around the time I was conceived." He sighed. "So I put my energy into gaining access. But Mother wouldn't hear of it, and Cole kept me out just for spite until . . ."

He trailed off with a shake of his head.

The blood drained from Katherine's face. Here was where the story involved her.

"He was desperate to rid himself of me and cover

his fraud." She swallowed hard. "So you made a trade with Colden. He offered you the house if you took me as your wife. The scandal was averted and you got what you wanted. Lansing Square."

"Yes."

Everything was becoming clearer now that she knew the truth. "You spend all your time here searching for clues to your father's identity. That's what you've been doing in the attic."

"Yes." He took a step closer and she stiffened. "I thought this was the only way."

She shook her head. "And you were willing to sacrifice me to get what you wanted. You were willing to lie to me, deceive me, even after you had experienced those same things in your own past. Even when you knew how deeply lies could cut."

His face fell. "I-I'm sorry, Katherine."

"So am I."

She turned away so he wouldn't see how much she wanted to touch him. Comfort him. His story moved her, although she hated that it ended with his betrayal. That he was more willing to chase the past than consider her and her future.

But what did she expect? Even while he told her lies about why they married, he had never gone so far as to say he cared for her. Or that he would put her needs above his own. She should have known he wouldn't. No man in her experience ever had.

"You must be relieved this charade is over," she said, shaking her emotions off. "Now you can stop pretending you plan to pursue a life with me in it. Now we can each choose our own path."

The breath he drew in was sharp and loud in the quiet room. She lifted her head to see him shaking his head.

"But—"

She held up a hand. "There's no need to pretend you ever wanted me now. The truth is out. You married me to obtain this property."

She shrugged, though she was anything but nonchalant about what he'd done. She wanted to put distance between them. She didn't want him to see how much power he still had over her.

Turning her back, she said, "I suppose in some ways, it's not much different than countless other marriages in society. Many people marry for political or financial gain." She flinched. "Most aren't deceived into doing so, but they manage nonetheless. We are married now and have consummated that union . . ."

She shivered as she thought of how much pleasure she'd taken in that consummation and how much her body still ached for his touch even now.

"What are you saying?" he asked.

His voice was harsh and when she turned he was staring at her with wide eyes.

Her heart flipped, but she crushed her weakness. "The marriage is legal and binding. But now that the true purpose behind it is in the open, there is no reason we cannot continue. I'm more than happy to help you search for the evidence you're seeking. I think you deserve to know who your father is."

Dominic stared at her as if she were speaking some foreign language. "And when we have found what I'm looking for, or if it becomes clear that it isn't here, what then?"

She shrugged. "You will return to London and find a mistress, as we talked about when we first married. And I shall stay here. I love this house." She looked around her room with a weak smile, then folded her arms. "I think it's only fair I should keep it since the home I inherited was given away without my permission, or even my knowledge."

Dominic swallowed, speechless for a long moment. He clenched his fists and shifted his weight. His voice was very low when he said, "Let me be sure I take your meaning. You wish to help me investigate who my father is, but when that investigation is over, you want me to return to London while you stay here. You want to live separate lives?"

Katherine wanted to give an immediate, strong answer in the affirmative. But looking at Dominic, knowing what his arms felt like wrapped around her. How his eyes lit up when he laughed. Remembering how heavenly it felt to give him her body and her heart, it was impossible to disregard him so easily.

She dipped her head. "Yes."

"No. Absolutely not."

* * *

It had been a long time since pain so powerful rushed through Dominic. Not since he departed his family and learned to support and depend on himself had he experienced such an empty agony.

Katherine didn't want him? She didn't want this marriage? It was no more than he deserved, but it brought him to his knees nonetheless. She had only just admitted a few moments ago that she cared.

Or at least . . . she had before. It wasn't something he expected or even desired when he took her as a bride. But knowing he'd lost whatever tender emotions she once had filled him with frustration and heartache, each surprisingly powerful.

"I beg your pardon," she said, folding her arms. "Did you just tell me you refuse to live separate lives?"

"I lied to you," he admitted, grasping for the protection of anger to mask his other troubling reactions. "And for that I am truly sorry. But I will not give up what we share."

Her nostrils flared delicately. "You mean, you still want me in your bed?"

Dominic clenched a fist. He wanted to bellow that he wanted her in his life, but now wasn't the time. Admitting that shocking desire would only open himself up to further rejection. Instead, he had to take a different tactic.

He needed to remind her that she still wanted to *be* in his bed. If he could woo her back there, he could slowly open her heart to him in a way he couldn't do by merely saying words. At present, she didn't believe a good portion of what he said.

Actions were key.

He stepped forward and closed some of the distance between them. She stiffened at the motion, refusing to back down even as her skin flushed at the reduced distance between them. Relief flooded him. At least she still wanted him. He saw that sparkle of need in her eyes along with the other conflicted emotions the truth caused.

"Are you saying you no longer desire me?" he asked, low and seductive.

"You lied to me," she burst out. "You cannot expect—"

"Desire often has very little to do with truth," he drawled, reaching out to stroke the back of his hand across her cheek. She flinched away. "And whatever lies were told, the fact that I desired you was never one of them."

She hesitated. Was that part of her resistance? She thought his desire was as false as his words? Well, he could easily relieve her of that false impression.

"You don't believe me?" he asked, chasing her gaze until she could no longer avoid it. "From the first moment I saw you on the terrace, long before I knew who you were, I wanted you. In fact, I was trying to devise a way to seduce you before your guardian interrupted us that night."

Her lips parted and a flicker of anger darkened her eyes from jade to emerald.

"Why should I believe anything you say?" Her voice trembled, wavering between disdain and hopefulness.

He cupped her chin and tilted her face up. "I can easily prove it to you."

Her eyes went wide just as he brought his mouth down on hers. At first she stiffened, trying to fight the anger she didn't want to release. But slowly, her resistance fell and she parted her lips. He delved into her mouth with gentle insistence. Each stroke of his tongue demanded her acquiescence, yet begged her forgiveness.

She responded with a sigh, gripping his forearms in her fists as she met his kisses with harder, more passionate ones of her own. It was a duel, a battle for control and surrender. He could give her neither. Not tonight.

Not if he ever hoped to regain her trust and rebuild her more tender emotions. And that was what he found he wanted more than anything, even though it was folly to want those feelings. They couldn't last. He simply wasn't ready to relinquish them yet.

He pulled her closer, cupping her against the hard planes of his body. She melted against him as her hands shifted to the buttons on his shirtwaist. One by one, she loosened them, then slid her hands into the warmth that had been trapped between the heavier fabric and his shirt.

Her fingertips skimmed his stomach as she unbuttoned his shirt next. Then skin met skin as she flattened her palms against his bare chest.

He hissed out a breath of pleasure that broke their kiss. Kat leaned away with confused, frustrated desire melding with the remaining emotions on her face. He watched her closely, waiting for her to pull from his arms, ready to continue pursuing her, even if it took weeks to woo her back to his bed and eventually back into his life.

Instead, she frowned. "Just this, Dominic," she said softly. "I can only give you this. Nothing else."

He nodded. Her body was all she could risk after everything. Though that should have been a victory, it seemed hollow. For the first time, he wanted far more than a woman's touch. But if this was all she could give, he would wait for the right moment to claim everything else.

"This is a gift," he murmured as his mouth came down again.

Katherine melted in her husband's arms, caught between the manifestation of her fears and the moment of her deepest desires. He offered her nothing but his touch. That should not have been enough. But it was all there was.

And she needed that comfort. For him to prove these moments they shared, at least, weren't a lie even if everything else had been.

He hadn't begun to touch her in those wicked ways that would make her melt. Instead, he seemed content to just kiss her, as if he wanted to memorize her taste. Still, it was enough to make her rock her hips against his in a slow rhythm that drove her as mad as she was trying to drive him.

With deft, careful steps, he guided her back across the room until her thighs hit the side of the bed. He cupped her backside and lifted her up until her feet dangled over the side. Pushing her legs open, he stepped into the space between. He was close enough that she could feel every hard inch of him through their clothes.

She murmured a plea, but was too drunk with desire to know what it was. It didn't matter, because he understood her incoherent request and responded by wrapping his arms around her to unbutton her gown. When it drooped around her back, he slid his hand inside, beneath her thin chemise.

She arched against his questing fingers, and let out a mewl of satisfaction when his thumb grazed the hard bud of one nipple. His hands were so hot. It seemed like she would combust if he continued to touch her. And she knew from wicked experience that she would. Everything in her world would burst into glorious, decadent flame when their bodies joined.

She pushed at the gown's silken sleeves, but he was faster. In a few blurry moments, her dress and under things sagged around her waist and his hands had free reign to roam and touch in all the ways she needed. He cupped her breasts, rolling her nipples between his fingers before his dark head came down and he drummed his tongue lightly over the taut flesh.

She dipped her head back with a throaty, "Yes."

Her womb contracted as he suckled while one hand crept slowly, purposefully, under her gown and up her smooth leg. A trail of fire and need was left in its wake. But just before he reached the core of her desire, she forced herself to push him away and struggle to her feet.

Dominic tensed as Katherine stood up. He thought he had succeeded in tapping into her desire, but now that she stood staring at him, that certainty fled. What if she pushed him away? Refused him.

She swallowed hard, then slowly pushed her gown down around her feet and stepped free. In a few deft movements, she removed her slippers and stockings and stood before him. The only article that hid her body in any way was the luscious length of her dark hair.

Relief flooded him as she reclaimed her spot on the edge of the bed. He scrambled to shed his own remaining clothing. Cupping her face, he kissed her deeply. He drank in her warmth and prayed he would have a chance at more than just this joining again.

He gasped when he felt her soft fingers grasp his erection. She stroked him once, twice, then guided him to her wet entrance. Cupping her hips, he thrust into her body and she enveloped him with a welcoming sigh.

For a long moment, he stayed as he was. Wrapped together, one body, it was easier to forget everything that stood between them. The moment was perfect and he didn't want it to end.

But his body's needs called, and Katherine arched beneath him with a whimper. Driving forward, he moaned when she flexed around him. Each stroke brought him closer to the edge, closer to her. She met him with equal passion, but also a hint of desperation he longed to erase.

It only took a few thrusts for her to wail out a long cry of release. But as she sagged against him, sated, he wouldn't let her go that easily. He continued to swirl his hips in slow, languid circles.

She shivered in release again and Dominic let himself go, pouring his seed into her as he couldn't pour his heart. And hoping she would someday forgive and accept him the way she had accepted his touch.

Katherine propped herself up on one elbow and watched Dominic sleep in the flickering firelight.

With trembling fingers, she reached out to trace the harsh lines of his jaw, softer in slumber than they were when he was awake. She trailed her hand down to his shoulders, his stomach, memorizing each and every curve and hollow.

She was in love with him.

When had she realized it? The thought didn't seem all that surprising. In fact, it was more like the emotion had been part of her forever, just another piece of her personality.

With a shiver, she rose from the bed to replace Dominic's warmth with that of the fire. She sank down on the footstool near the hearth and tucked her legs beneath her. The flames warmed her naked skin and helped her focus on reality.

Over the past few weeks, somehow she let what started as a spark of desire fan into love. No matter how hard she tried to stay separate from Dominic, the walls she built were far too weak. With passion, care and confession, he knocked down her defenses and made his way into her heart.

Each time she watched him when she didn't have to, her heart opened to him. Every laugh and smile they shared brought him closer to her soul. Bit by bit, she'd surrendered her love to him.

It was the worst time to accept the inevitable. The truth had finally come out and it was clear there was no chance Dominic returned her love. All those things that brought them together were part of some illusion. She was a means to getting what he wanted. Even tonight, when he asked for her understanding and forgiveness, he had pursued her with sex, not something deeper.

She sighed. She had promised to help him look for the truth about his father. He deserved that. But she had no intentions of returning to London with him when his business here was done. If she couldn't have a real marriage, a real life with him, she didn't want a shell in which only lust existed.

Dominic grunted again, but this time his eyes fluttered open slowly as he reached over to her side of the bed. His hand slid across the sheets, but when he realized she wasn't there, he sat up.

"Kat?" he asked, voice heavy with sleep and confusion.

"I'm here," she whispered, watching him with all the love in her heart swelling in her chest. "I'm here, Dominic."

He smiled and her heart melted at the sight of his tousled hair and bleary, but purposeful eyes. "Come back to bed."

Her eyes fluttered shut. Leaving this man, her life and her love, was going to be the hardest thing she'd ever done. And until she had to do it, she was going to savor every moment they shared. She was going to imprint him on her every fiber so she would never forget his taste, his smell, or his touch.

"Yes," she said as she stood up and slipped back between the sheets. His warm arms came around her.

She blocked out everything else as his hard, hot body moved to cover hers. When he kissed her with gentleness she never would have guessed he possessed, she clung to him and prayed she would have the will to do what she needed to do when the time finally came.

Chapter 16

Katherine covered her eyes. The world spun and a wave of nausea crashed over her. She cast a side-glance at Dominic from across the attic, but he was too caught up in a ledger to have noticed her sudden flash of illness. It was just as well. If she was coming down with something, she didn't want him to worry. They needed to focus their attention on finding out the truth about his father.

She flipped through the pile of letters in her hand as her dizziness subsided and her nausea faded to a faint bitterness in her mouth.

"These are very interesting accountings of the workings of society thirty years ago, but they tell me nothing."

She shoved a few loose strands of hair behind her ears and dared to rise from her sitting position on an old crate. Thankfully her knees held and her breakfast stayed in her stomach where it belonged. "Are you having any more luck?"

"Nothing." With a sigh, he rubbed his eyes, but the exhaustion in them wouldn't be pushed away so easily. "Damn it. This is fruitless. I'm never going to find anything in this blasted house."

Hurt stabbed through her, a compassionate response to his frustration. It was something she couldn't assuage. Even with the aid of Adrian and Julia, who were now searching Larissa Mallory's old library, they hadn't found any clues to his father's identity. With each passing day, Dominic slipped further and further into despair over the search.

"I'm sorry."

She longed to offer more to him than words as comfort, but since the day of their confrontation with Cole, she had forced herself not to. No more did she seek her husband out. Even at night, it was he who came to her chamber. She no longer passed through their adjoining door.

She couldn't when betrayal still stung her or when an equally powerful love for the man grew in her heart. That emotion gave her no pleasure when it was clear he had not ever felt the same, nor would he.

He hadn't even noticed the distance she put between them. Without the lies regarding their marriage hanging over his head, he seemed more than comfortable in their current arrangement.

And that broke her heart. She wanted so much more.

He stared at the pile of items they'd already gone through. They were stacked on one side of the attic, some on the piano and others all around it.

"Dominic," she said softly, finally bringing him back from wherever his reverie had taken him.

"Perhaps this is folly." He shook his head. "I have chased the truth for so long, maybe I didn't realize the time has come to let it go."

She shook her head. He'd pinned his hopes and his future on finding out the truth. He'd even married a woman he didn't love to find his heritage. If he gave up, she knew he would never find peace. If she wanted him to be happy, she couldn't allow him to disregard his need for answers. And she did wish for his peace and happiness, even though the resolution of his past would signal the end of their marriage.

She shook off the hurt accompanying that thought. "Perhaps we've been going about the search the wrong way. Searching the house from top to bottom is just too broad. If we were more specific—"

He turned away. "How can I be more specific when I don't know what the hell I'm looking for?"

With a growl, he kicked the nearest crate and sent it skidding across the floor. She heard the tinkle of breaking glass as it slammed against the opposite wall. For a long moment, he stood with his eyes shut, refusing to look at her or say anything.

Finally, he turned back with a sheepish shake of his head. "I'm sorry. This is just so frustrating."

"I know," she whispered, clenching a fist behind her back as she resisted the powerful urge to run to him and hold him. "I would do anything to make it easier, but I'm afraid things may become harder before we can find the solution to this riddle that is your parentage."

He frowned. "What do you mean?"

"There are two people in this world who know the truth without having to search through boxes and letters," she began with a tilt of her head. "And one of them is your mother."

Dominic raised a hand in protest. "No, Kat. That is out of the question. I can't—"

"When did you last attempt to speak to her about this?" she insisted.

"Probably five years ago," he said, stiffening at the memories the conversation obviously brought back.

"What did she say then?"

He was quiet, but eventually he said, "My mother refused to speak to me on the subject. Even when I pointed out that Harrison Mallory was long cold in his grave and could no longer bring her grief, she simply turned away from me."

"I don't understand how she can do that." Katherine sighed.

He shrugged. "Refusing me has become second nature to her, I doubt if any amount of questioning will ever change that."

He shook his head. It was clear the idea of going back home was as unpleasant as the thought of questioning his reticent mother. She couldn't blame him for his reluctance.

"I have no doubt it will be difficult." She sidled closer and finally dared to do what she had been avoiding for days. She took his hand. Awareness crackled through her, along with love. "But we could do it together."

He stared at their intertwined fingers for a long moment, then his gaze slid up to her face. "We?"

She nodded. "I told you I would help you and I meant it."

He considered that statement for a long moment, then sighed. "I'll tell Matthews to ready our things for travel as soon as possible. All I want to do is end this."

With a kiss on her knuckles, Dominic slipped from the room and down the stairs. After he'd gone, she sank down on the piano bench.

End this. Dominic meant his search, but for her it meant so much more. Every day she spent with him made her realize more and more that she couldn't live with the man she loved. Not when he didn't return her feelings.

And he didn't.

* * *

Dominic started when Katherine touched his hand. He glanced up from his spot on his mother's settee and looked at her.

"You're nervous," she said softly.

He shook his head. He could only hope his anxiety wouldn't be as apparent to his mother as it was to his wife. Nothing ever seemed to upset Larissa Mallory, so his desire was to appear just as calm and collected as she.

"Why do you say that?"

"Your foot." She smiled and cocked her head toward his boot. When he followed her gaze, he saw that his foot was twitching wildly. It took effort to slow its movement.

"I'm sorry," he said with a sheepish shrug.

She slowly withdrew her warm hand from his. He regretted the loss of her touch. It was a pleasure she gave him less and less since their argument a week before. The change was subtle, but as evident to him as if someone had cut off his air.

Katherine hadn't fought with him since their encounter when she learned the truth. In fact, she spoke kindly to him. She aided him in his search, as she promised she would. She even submitted willingly to his desires when he came to her in bed.

Despite all that, she was distant. It was as if she were carefully removing herself from his life. Or removing him from hers.

He didn't know how to heal the breach he'd caused. He only knew he wanted to. But he couldn't do it now. Until his past was fully resolved, he couldn't begin to approach the future.

Katherine stood up and walked to the window. She stared outside for a moment before she said, "I know this is difficult for you. I wish I could make it easier."

He stood and took a step toward her. She didn't turn, but the stiffening of her shoulders let him know she was aware of him.

"You help me simply by being here," he said softly. "It means everything to me that you accompanied me even though I know you're still hurt and angered by my regrettable actions and choices."

She did turn at that, eyes wide as if she were surprised he had even noticed her emotions.

"Dominic—" she began.

Before she could finish, the door to the parlor opened and Larissa Mallory entered. From the stiff way she held herself and the wariness in her eyes, it was clear she had guessed the reasons for their visit and wasn't looking forward to the confrontation any more than he was.

"Dominic, Katherine," she said.

When he stepped forward to kiss her hand, she waved him back. He frowned as he followed her silent order, refusing to let his mother's quiet disregard worry him.

"I didn't expect you. You should have sent word you were coming."

"Can't a son visit his mother?" he asked in an empty voice.

Her eyes narrowed. "Yes, of course. But perhaps next time you could write so I'd be prepared."

"With what?" he barked, clenching his fists as his control faltered. "More lies and denials?"

Katherine stepped closer to grasp his hand. One by one his fingers unclenched of their own accord and the tension in his body eased a fraction.

"Larissa, Dominic," Katherine said in a soothing tone meant to moderate. "I'm sure neither of you wants to say or do anything that will damage your relationship. But there must be a way to resolve this problem." She looked at his mother evenly. "You know why we're here."

Her nostrils flaring, Larissa nodded once. "To stir up a past that is better left unexplored."

Dominic barked out a bitter laugh. "Well, that's the closest you have ever come to admitting there *is* a past without a drink in your hand. I suppose that's progress in its own way."

Katherine opened her mouth to intervene a second time, but Larissa was quicker. "You shouldn't have come here, Dominic. And you shouldn't have pursued whatever drove you to take Lansing Square away from your brother."

"You know why I took it," Dominic growled. "I want to know who my father is."

His mother paled a shade at his directness. "I

was married to Harrison Mallory when you were conceived. In the eyes of the law, you are his son."

He surged to his feet as years of suppressed frustration overcame him. "And what about the eyes of God? Or my own eyes? Or is the law the only thing that matters to you, Mother?"

"What matters to me is protecting the people I love!" she cried.

Dominic shook his head. "Who do you love, Mother? Harrison Mallory? The man treated you with nothing but contempt. Colden? He is his father incarnate. Why do you wish to protect them over me?"

Larissa hesitated. Her gaze flitted up to his face and softened just a fraction. For a brief, powerful moment, he thought she might finally give him the answers he sought. But then she looked away. Her face hardened with ice.

"Leave this be, Dominic. The past is better left hidden."

He shut his eyes as he attempted to tame the anger and disappointment that closed his throat.

"Better for whom?" he asked when he was able. "I cannot leave the past hidden. It is everywhere. I cannot rest until I have the answer to one question. Just one, but you are the only person who can answer it. This is your last chance to do so. *Who is my father?*"

Katherine gasped, but other than that the room

was silent as he waited for his mother's reply. Larissa stared up at him with watery eyes and trembling hands. He almost pitied her. She must have suffered her own hell throughout her years as Harrison Mallory's wife. Enough that she sought comfort in the arms of another man.

"Knowing his name will bring you no peace," she whispered. "And it will certainly bring him nothing but heartache. Our lives are very different than they were thirty years ago. To pursue him would only cause pain. Even if Harrison can no longer harm him, it doesn't follow that no harm could be done by pursuing this." Larissa took a shaky breath. "I am sorry, Dominic. You've wasted your time coming all this way for answers I'll never be able to give you."

Katherine released his hand and stepped toward his mother. He saw a fire hidden deep in her stare. "Surely you aren't saying you'll never give Dominic the benefit of the truth? How can you let his pain continue if you care for him at all?"

Larissa winced. Color filled her face as she turned to Katherine. "*You* know nothing about it. It isn't your affair. I beg you to leave it be."

Dominic's jaw twitched. "Katherine is my wife, my past is most definitely her affair."

Katherine touched his arm. "Dominic, it's all right. Emotions are high and—"

He cut her off with a shake of his head. "No, it isn't all right. My mother has no right to dismiss us in this fashion. You are only trying to help, and I am only trying to determine information I believe is within my rights."

"Information she's wise not to share."

The group turned at the cold voice at the door. Colden stood in the doorway, his arms folded and a smug smile on his face. Dominic stiffened. As unpleasant as this confrontation had been so far, it was about to get much, much uglier.

Powerful, unsettling anger filled Katherine as she stared at the man she once planned to marry. A week ago she'd been too shocked to truly react to Cole's deceit. Now she'd had plenty of time to reflect on everything he'd done, both to her and to her husband. Her anger threatened to overflow. How dare he interfere? How dare he look so smug?

Cole straightened up with a laugh that cut through Katherine's body into her soul. "Go home, Dominic. Go run away and continue searching for a father you'll never find. My father didn't want you and neither does your own. Learn to live with it, By-blow."

Larissa stiffened at her eldest son's ugliness. "Colden, that's enough!"

Katherine stared at her mother-in-law. *That* was all she could say? Protective fury rushed through her. She hated Cole for causing the man she loved so much pain. Not just tonight, but for all the years he rubbed Dominic's parentage into his face, for the way he denied Dominic entry into Lansing Square until her husband had been forced to make a devil's bargain. For making the lines of Dominic's face hard with years of bitter disappointment.

"How dare you?" she heard herself utter in a low voice that pierced through the room nonetheless. "How *dare* you speak to Dominic in that fashion?"

Cole started as if he hadn't noticed her presence before. The smug smile faded, replaced by false sympathy. She reeled back as she once again saw how wrong she'd been about him.

All her life, Katherine believed love could blind her to a man's faults. To a husband's betrayals. That belief had driven her to look for a life devoid of love and passion.

In was ironic that her choice in a husband had been the very worst of men. Ultimately, she had been blinded, not by love, but by faith in the mask Cole wore. A mask of safety. Security.

But her true security had been with Dominic. It had been from the moment they said their marriage vows. Even with lies between them, Dominic had never manipulated her heart. He'd never tried to take advantage of her fears.

She stared at her husband as that realization took full effect.

Cole shook off his shock at her outburst and stepped forward. "Katherine, I'm sorry. Sorry about deceiving you and sorry I allowed you to be shackled to my brother. If I could but take back my actions . . ."

Katherine stiffened her spine and folded her arm into the crook of Dominic's. "If I could go back in time, I would change nothing," she said softly. "I thank the heavens every single day I didn't find myself shackled, as you put it, to you. Because *you* are the only bastard in this room. Dominic is just a victim of a family who never gave him a chance to find out the truth about himself." She shot Cole a hard look first, then Larissa.

But when her eyes drifted to Dominic, she found him staring down at her in shock. Then the shock faded to gratitude and tenderness, both true and real emotions she had no doubt he felt.

Just not love.

He hardened his jaw as he looked his brother and mother up and down. "I should have known I would find no peace here. I never have. And this will be the last time I'll look for it. Colden, enjoy what you earned by your lies and betrayals." He leaned closer and there was a clear message in his eyes. "Because I will not save you from yourself ever again. And mother"—he turned on her and his expression softened just a fraction—"you guard your secrets. I don't know why. But since you cannot seem to bear the sight of me, I won't trouble you again. Julia is my only family now." He smiled down at Katherine and her heart raced. "And my wife."

Larissa jolted as if she'd been slapped, but she remained motionless as Dominic led Katherine to the door.

"Wait," she said.

Dominic turned back and Katherine could feel the hope and anxiety in every fiber of his being.

"Yes?"

"I wish . . . If I thought giving you the answers you seek would come to any good—"

Dominic's shoulders relaxed with disappointment, but then he stiffened his posture. "Yes. So you've said."

Though his face was strong as he swept from the room with her on his arm, deep in the steely gray of his eyes, Katherine saw his loss. She'd never been more proud of another person in her life. He had left with dignity. She only wished he could have left with answers. With any kind of resolution.

As they settled into the carriage, Dominic sagged against the seat. For the first time, he looked defeated, as if the years of wondering about his past and worrying about his future had finally caught up with him in just the few short moments they spent in the sitting room.

In a way, she supposed they had. He had offered his mother one final chance to make the right choice. Katherine thought she would. She never guessed a mother would deny her child outright. Now Dominic believed his search would never come to an end. At least not the end he envisioned over all his years of looking and hoping.

With a sigh, she reached out to touch his cheek.

He smiled at the caress, but his eyes were curiously blank.

"Oh, Dominic, I'm so sorry," she whispered, wracking her brain for a way she could make this right. Only one came and it would require something she hadn't thought she could give. Her forgiveness. Her comfort.

Her heart.

Chapter 17

Katherine set down her spoonful of stew with a sigh. She couldn't bear to swallow even one more bite. Not when her stomach churned with nausea and her head spun.

It didn't seem like her husband was faring much better. He'd hardly spoken since they left his mother and brother after their ugly confrontation. In the carriage he was withdrawn, weighed down by emotions. Since their arrival at the inn, the same one where they spent their first night together as man and wife, he had been little better.

His anger was evident. Less evident, but just as present was his disappointment. His regret.

There was so much Katherine wanted to say to

him, but she kept her counsel for now. Until they were alone, she didn't dare broach the subject of what had happened today. And when she offered him comfort, she didn't want a chance of interruption. She wanted Dominic to lose himself in her completely. Until she helped him forget.

Dominic looked at her sharply, as if he suddenly recalled they sat together.

"You've hardly eaten," he said, his voice harsh in the stifling quiet of the room. Though there were other travelers at the inn, none were eating so late.

She smiled gently. "I'm not hungry. It's been an upsetting day."

His face twisted. "Yes. I'm sorry our time was wasted."

She itched to take his hand or smooth the wayward lock of hair from his forehead. To do anything to ease the memories of that afternoon and the uncertainty of the future. She fought the desire for a brief moment, but finally surrendered to it. She took his hand.

"I'm not sorry we tried," she said.

He was quiet, but for a long time simply looked at their entwined hands, then up to her face with an unreadable expression that still warmed her through her every fiber. He cleared his throat.

"We should go up. As you said, it has been a long and upsetting day. We both need our rest." His voice grew distant. "Tomorrow we return to Lansing Square, and then . . . I don't know . . ."

Slowly, she nodded, anticipating what she would offer him once they were alone. Her body as solace. Her heart, even if he didn't recognize that gift.

"Very well."

The innkeeper's wife, who remembered them from their wedding night stay, seemed to sense their mood, for she said very little as she led them upstairs. But she couldn't resist a smile when she opened the door to their room.

"I thought to put you in the same chamber as last time, Mr. and Mrs. Mallory. Like a second wedding trip for you."

Katherine blushed as she remembered her first wedding trip. Dominic seemed to hardly notice the room as he strode inside.

"Thank you very much," Katherine said, so the woman wouldn't be offended. "The room is as lovely as it was the first time. We're pleased to stay here a second night."

The innkeeper's wife gave Dominic a cautious glance, then whispered, "Will you be needing anything else, my dear?"

Katherine shook her head. "No, good night."

She shut the door and turned in time to see Dominic toss his jacket on the table and slump down in a chair by the bright fire. In the light, it was easy to see just how weary he was, both physically and emotionally.

She drew in a breath and finally gave in to her desires. The need to touch him. To hold him. To give him everything worth sharing.

Quietly, she slipped up behind him and began rubbing his shoulders. The muscles were tight as she worked each one with firm strokes of her hands. Rolling his head back against the chair, Dominic let out a low, satisfied groan.

"Good?" she said softly as she worked an especially tense muscle with her thumb.

"Mmmm," was his only reply.

She continued her massage in silence for what seemed like a long time. Slowly, Dominic's body relaxed and his breathing became heavy and regular. She was beginning to wonder if he'd fallen asleep in his chair when he said, "Kat?"

Without stopping her soothing touch, she answered, "Yes?"

"I am at a loss. You've seen the way my family works, but I know nothing about yours, even after all the time we've spent together." His voice was measured, but she sensed the real need behind his words.

She hesitated. Her plans for surrender tonight were all associated with the physical. Dominic was asking for an emotional gift, instead. One she found herself longing to give, even if she couldn't tell him everything.

"Let me ask you something first."

His neck worked under her fingers as he nodded

wordlessly. She drew in a deep breath. "Sarah implied more than once that you and she carried on an affair of some kind. Did you?"

She held her breath. Heavy silence filled the room and Katherine almost faltered in her continued massage as she waited for the inevitable answer.

He exhaled slowly. "When Cole first married Sarah I will confess I found her very beautiful. It was her greatest attribute . . . often the only thing to recommend her to others. She was accustomed to the attention. She knew the signs when a man found her attractive. I was no different. She flirted with me."

Katherine nodded begrudgingly. "There is no denying Sarah's beauty."

His shoulders tensed again. "I admit I returned the flirtation, though it was innocent and casual. Whatever I felt for Colden, I wouldn't have gone so far as to pursue his wife. Despite the growing problems between them, I never believed Sarah would turn to me, either. Until one night when she showed up in my bed in London. We kissed, just once. I realized I wanted nothing to do with the kind of woman who would marry one brother and play with the other."

She nodded as a sharp but brief flash of pain ripped through her. "What happened?"

"When I refused her advances and asked her to leave, she turned to her usual bitter diatribes as retaliation. I went to the door to go myself, but found Cole on the other side."

Katherine sucked in her breath. She could only imagine the scene that had followed. And Sarah Mallory had undoubtedly encouraged that ugliness.

Dominic nodded at her wordless comment. "I can tell you've guessed the rest. Cole believed the worst. Not that I blamed him. His wife was half-naked in his brother's bed. Worse, she didn't even seem surprised he discovered us. I immediately re-alized my instinct about her appearance in my home was correct. She arranged for Cole to find us together."

"Why?" Katherine said with a shudder. That level of cruelty was hard to fathom.

He shrugged. "I've thought about that over the years. At the time, I believed it was some petty act of vengeance. Some jealousy over one of Cole's own affairs. But now, knowing what we do about their plan to feign her death, I believe it might have been Sarah's twisted parting shot at my brother. Some fi-nal way to enrage him before she was no longer able."

Looking down at Dominic, Katherine allowed re-lief to wash over her. A kiss was all he'd shared with Sarah. One he hadn't even enjoyed. She hadn't realized just how much the thought of Sarah and Dominic together bothered her.

"You asked about my parents," she said softly.

He met her stare, nodding slowly.

She drew in a deep breath. She had not told anyone about her parents before. It was her secret. One she'd kept for so long she couldn't remember a time when it wasn't a part of her.

"It—it was an arranged marriage, but my mother loved my father since she was very young. She truly believed she could make him return that love. Even when he proved himself unworthy."

She stumbled over her words. The last thing she wanted was to heap some kind of guilt on Dominic.

"He wasn't able to return her love, I mean," she corrected herself. "I was their only child and I saw their unhappiness every day."

He reached up to slide his hand across her cheek. "You must have been lonely."

She nodded and the friction of his hand against her skin was almost too much for her. "A similarity between us," she murmured.

He caught her hand and slowly eased her around to sit on his lap. For a moment, they simply locked gazes, but then he caught her face in his hands and pulled her down until they nearly kissed. Her heart fluttered at the gentle play of his breath against her skin and the heat of his body as it cradled her.

"I'm not lonely now," he whispered before he kissed her.

She softened immediately, surrendering to this man who she had fallen in love with bit by bit each and every day they were together.

"Neither am I."

For now that statement was true. While she was in his arms, he filled her, body and soul. And she wasn't alone anymore. If only that joy could last past the dawn.

"Dominic," she murmured against his lips. He pulled back, eyes glazed with desire.

"Yes?"

"Before we go to bed, I want you to know something." Her voice broke. "I wish what was done had never happened, but I do understand your motives for lying to me. I also know you never intended to harm me. Cole didn't care if I was hurt. If it suited his purposes, he brought me pain without a second thought. But you, you were not like that. And I forgive you for your part in that deception."

His eyes widened and his fingers curled on her jawline. Deep, powerful emotions flashed across his face. Surprise. Relief. Even joy.

"Thank you," he whispered as he gathered her into his arms and carried her over to the bed where they first made love. The bed where she relinquished that first tiny piece of her love.

"Thank you, Katherine."

He lay down on the bed beside her and drew her up against him until the entire length of their bodies touched. And then he spent an eternity simply kissing her. She shut her eyes and forgot the world, forgot her past, forgot everything else and lost herself in the moment. She memorized his taste, the feel of him as if this would be the last time they made love.

Because she knew, in the recesses of her heart, that it very well could be. She could give him her love tonight, but tomorrow she would pay the price when reality returned. She couldn't picture herself doing this every night for the rest of her life. Giving him her heart when he held her, realizing he couldn't return his heart when morning came.

Loving and losing him every day would be too much.

But that didn't signify tonight.

Tonight she wanted to experience everything her husband could give. To feel him fill her. To be one with him.

She fiddled with the buttons of his shirt, setting each one free until she was able to bare his chest. Slowly, she kissed his collarbone. Then his throat, and then down to slide her tongue across one flat nipple. He let out a low groan—one of satisfaction and need all at once. Wanting more and yet being perfectly content with what he was given.

Her hands slid lower as she continued to kiss his chest. With a few swift motions, she unbuttoned his fly and slipped her hand inside to touch the long, hard length of him.

"Two can play at that game, you know," he said with the first laugh she'd heard from him in days. The sound filled her with joy.

As he rolled her on her back and covered her

body with the hard, lean weight of his own, she gazed up into eyes as dark as pewter. They locked on hers and held there.

"No, Dominic," she whispered. "No games tonight."

He slipped gentle fingers into her hair and pulled her up for a long, hot kiss. When he broke away, he said, "You are mine, Katherine. Mine forever."

She buried her face in his neck for a kiss, but also to hide the tears that suddenly filled her eyes. She would be his forever. He owned her heart, and no amount of distance would ever change that. But it was an unfair trade. His body for her heart. She needed more.

Then his touch washed away those last fleeting thoughts of the future. All that was left was him. His fingers that pulled her gown down her hips. The mouth that sucked one taut nipple even through the thin fabric of her chemise. The hard thighs that slowly eased her own apart until she was wide open for his touch, his kiss, his body, whatever he wanted.

And he took. Slowly testing her readiness with one thick finger. When he found her wet for him, he whispered, "I want to take my time. Later. But right now, I need you. I need to feel you around me. To know my entire world hasn't changed. That there's at least one place that remains the same."

She nodded breathlessly.

And then he was inside of her, filling her every

inch with pleasure and need and fulfillment. He kissed her as he began to stroke, and she felt herself approach a powerful climax almost immediately. He caught her cries with his mouth and offered her no respite from his continued thrusts, bringing her down and up, over and again until she was begging him. To stop. To keep going. To make her forget all the bad things that had happened that day, that would happen someday.

And with one final thrust, he obliged, sending them both careening over one last edge. And as she pulled his sweat-misted, hard body down on hers for an embrace, she reveled in the fleeting moment. She reveled in the feeling that she loved him.

No matter what happened in the future, nothing could take that away.

Katherine let out a long, low sigh, then she opened her eyes and looked a second time at the underthings she'd just removed. Still nothing. This was the seventh day she'd gone without her monthly courses and one thing was becoming alarmingly clear.

She was having a baby.

It was something she suspected from the first day her cycle had been late, but she explained it away by blaming it on the strain of finding out the truth about Dominic's deception or the hardship of her recent winter travel. Now those little lies caught up with her as she thought of casting up her accounts yet again that morning. Of the slight swelling of her breasts. Of her clean underthings.

Covering her eyes, she struggled to maintain calm. Part of her was deliriously happy at the prospect of a child that came from the love she felt for Dominic. The other part knew this pregnancy only advanced the inevitable. She would have to leave her husband.

Katherine had lived in a loveless household. She knew the tension a child felt as she watched her mother struggle for her husband's love. Or the horror when she realized her own father cared very little for his own family.

Dominic wouldn't be as unkind as her father had been, but he had already admitted he didn't believe in love. He certainly hadn't experienced that emotion from his own cold family. And he had told Cole outright before their marriage that he never intended to have children. She couldn't let her own son or daughter relive what she had experienced.

She couldn't ask Dominic to turn his life upside down for a family he never desired.

Somehow she gathered the strength to rise from the chair. She had friends a few days' journey from here. They would help her for a while if she asked. Perhaps she could go to America in the spring. The account Dominic created for her pin money was generous enough to start a new life.

She would have to begin her preparations to depart right away. Dominic had gone to the village for the day on some business. It would be best to leave now rather than after his return. If she didn't, he would argue with her. He wouldn't understand her reasons for going. He would feel guilty, compelled to ask her to stay. With a few kisses, he could easily convince her. But if she simply disappeared . . .

"Excuse me, madam?"

She turned toward Matthews' voice with what she hoped was a bland, unemotional expression. "Yes?"

"Madam, the servants have begun sorting through the attic as Mr. Mallory requested, but we have a question."

She'd all but forgotten Dominic had ordered the attic to be sorted and cleaned. It was a signal he was ready to move on, she supposed. Or that he knew the answers he sought wouldn't be found by searching endlessly through crates of history.

"What is it?"

"The piano, madam," Matthews replied. "It obviously doesn't belong in the garret, but it's far too fine to throw away. Not to mention that it is very heavy. What are your wishes?"

"Let me come up and examine what's been done so far. Perhaps I can be of some assistance." She was surprised how easily she was able to answer. As if nothing was amiss while her very world crumbled.

He smiled. "Thank you. We would appreciate that."

As she followed him through the hallways, Katherine looked around her and took in every detail of Lansing Square. She had fallen in love with the estate the moment she looked up at it in the snowy night. She'd looked forward to building it back up to its former glory. She had fought for that chance. Now it made her sad to know she would never get to follow through.

With a sigh, she said, "You know, I always found it odd that the piano was in the attic in the first place."

"Yes." Matthews nodded. "It *is* very odd."

"Moving it must have been a terrible, dangerous chore for the poor servants required to do so. Wouldn't it have made more sense to have it repaired or destroyed?" She cocked her head as he opened the attic door and motioned for her to enter first. "Whoever ordered it to be moved must have been very attached to it, indeed. And yet not attached enough to salvage it."

"The household staff has always found it unusual as well. However, no one is left from that time to give us the answers," Matthews said.

She looked around with wide eyes. Unlike just days before, the boxes were stacked and neatly labeled. Some were obviously trash, while others had been marked as family heirlooms. Still others had her name on them as items whose fate would be determined by her judgment.

Except, she would no longer be there.

With a shiver, she turned her attention to the piano. It wasn't a lady's pianoforte, but a grand piano more fitting a musical master. It was obviously an expensive piece and one that had been much loved until the recent past.

She sat down on the bench and laid her fingers on the keys. After she played a few bars of music, she was surprised the only obvious problem was that the instrument was out of tune. That was to be expected after so many years of neglect. Certainly, it wasn't a reason for banishment to the drafty attic.

"I'm not sure—" she began, but stopped when she pressed down on several keys and heard no notes in response. "Oh wait, the problem seems to be here."

She cocked her head. Why hadn't the person who sent this instrument upstairs simply had the chords repaired?

Her intuition and curiosity piqued, she stood up. "Matthews, could you have the piano lid opened, please?"

He nodded, then motioned to a footman. Between the two, they eased the piano lid open and propped it up. With an apologetic smile for the unladylike action she was about to do, she bent over the opening and looked inside.

She was surprised the piano chords were only dusty, not broken or worn. There was no reason for them not to play except . . .

She cocked her head in surprise. Letters. There was a yellowed pack of letters hidden in the piano.

"Matthews, press on one of the keys that didn't work," she ordered.

"Yes, madam," he said. She felt the piano quiver slightly as he sat. When he pressed the key, there was no sound and she saw why. The letters prevented it.

"Thank you," she said as she reached out and barely managed to grasp the grimy packet. She pulled herself back out of the piano and brushed dust from her gown and her hair. She held up the notes with a smile. "An odd hiding place, isn't it?"

The butler cocked his head. "Very."

"These must have been awfully important for someone to hide them so well," she murmured to herself. Then she shook her head. "Try playing the instrument now."

Matthews returned to the piano bench and fingered out a simple tune.

"Seems you've fixed the piano, madam," he said with a smile. "What should we do with it now?"

She shrugged. "I'm certainly not going to have you all kill yourselves trying to move it downstairs. Let me think about it for a while and mention it to Dominic. In the interim, continue to clean up around it."

"Yes, madam," he said to her retreating back.

She took a few steps out of the attic before she paused to lean back against the wall and look at the bundle of letters. Her hands trembled and her blood raced with premonition—feelings that proved wise when she untied the ribbon binding the papers and turned over the first envelope to see that it was addressed to Larissa Mallory.

She hurried to her chamber where she closed and locked the door. Opening the top missive, she began to read out loud.

"My darling Larissa, I wonder if you still play the piano. I sometimes dream of you sitting there, making beautiful music in the world we created. A world where your husband could not interfere or take you away from me."

Katherine's heart leapt. She had finally found the truth.

Chapter 18

The truth would set Dominic free. But that didn't change the facts of the situation. Katherine had to leave before he returned and discovered her plans. Now. Tonight.

In fact, setting things right for her husband only made her departure that much easier. The information she'd found in the piano would lead him straight to his father. He could be happy.

She sank down next to her half-packed bag and brushed her hand across her womb. Her heart soared with the knowledge that Dominic would finally know his father after all his years of searching. But it also sank at the thought of never seeing him again.

The door behind her flew open and Katherine surged to her feet to greet Julia. The other woman's dark eyes were bright with happiness and her skin was flushed. She looked as beautiful and young as any debutante.

"Oh, Katherine, I have news!" she burst out as she crossed the room and enveloped Katherine in a hard, fierce hug. "Adrian has asked me to be his wife!"

Katherine fell back in the closest chair with a thump as she stared up at her friend. For a moment, her own disappointment vanished, replaced with shock and intense joy.

"J-Julia," she stammered. "That—that's wonderful! When did he propose?"

"Just now," her friend gushed as she gave herself a giddy hug and danced around the room on a cloud. "He says he has no interest in waiting, but wants to take me to Gretna Green tonight."

Katherine's mouth dropped open. "Tonight? But don't you want a large wedding? Time for society to celebrate your engagement?"

Julia turned back and pulled a face more befitting a child than a woman in her thirties.

"Heavens, no. I've sat on the sidelines labeled an old maid for far too long. I know how the *ton* will react. I have no interest in accepting their false congratulations or overhearing their loud whispers about wallflowers and spinsters and the kind of reasons they marry." Her gaze softened. "I want Adrian. I want to be his wife now, to start a life together right away. I've known that from the moment our eyes met. He was meant to be my husband. Why wait to fulfill my destiny?"

Katherine blinked in surprise. The woman before her wasn't the sensible, staid spinster who opened her heart to Katherine and made her a part of the Mallory family no matter which brother she wed. This woman was wildly, passionately, and without apology in love. She had no doubt of the beautiful, romantic life she would have with the man she had chosen and had chosen her.

Katherine's heart twitched with sudden envy. Why couldn't her own marriage be so clear and simple? She turned away so Julia wouldn't see.

"I-I'm very happy for you," she murmured. "When do you leave?"

"We are only waiting for Dominic's return to tell him the news and then we'll be off."

The laughter in her voice faded and Katherine glanced over her shoulder. Julia looked around the room with a shocked expression.

"Wait. Why are you packing a valise? You and Dominic just returned. He never mentioned a second trip to me."

Katherine jolted to her feet. "I—I—"

Julia gasped and a wealth of understanding flooded her face. "*You're* leaving, aren't you? Just you, Katherine."

Katherine winced. "No, of course not," she lied. "Why would I go?"

Julia cocked her head. "Don't play me for a fool. You're packing a bag and it looks like you've another already brimming. The tears I see in your eyes are from anything but joy. You have been the biggest advocate of Adrian and me pursuing the attraction we felt, so I know you would be ecstatic if your own heart weren't breaking. Tell me the truth. Are you leaving my brother?"

Katherine drew in a shuddering breath. "Yes." She reached out to take her shocked friend's hands. "But you mustn't tell Dominic. Let me disappear without interfering."

Julia shook her head in utter disbelief. "Why in the world would you possibly want that?"

"It's complicated," she answered on a wail.

"How is it so complicated that you feel you must run away into the night like some kind of criminal?" Julia asked with wide eyes. "I know my brother and I know you. You two love each other."

The truth cut Katherine more than any knife. If she admitted she loved Dominic, Julia would tell him. That could only create more problems. Dominic's guilt might drive him to make promises he couldn't keep. Ones she wanted to believe with everything in her.

She forced herself to deny the words with a firm shake of her head. "No."

"You do!" Julia insisted. "And something is driving you to leave. What is it?"

Katherine shivered. How was she supposed to

explain to Julia that she loved Dominic, but he didn't return that sentiment? Didn't even believe it was possible. Or that she knew from personal experience that a woman couldn't force a man to love her? She couldn't bear to relive the heartache she experienced in childhood.

She couldn't expose her own baby to such emptiness.

"We simply don't belong together," she whispered.

Julia shook her head. "Perhaps I can help you. I could talk to my brother. Adrian and I could mediate any problem you're having. I'm sure if you just spoke to him—"

"No." Katherine's answer was firm and louder than she wanted it to be. Then her shoulders sagged in defeat. "Thank you for your kindness through all of this. You have been the best friend I could have. And now I need you to do just one more thing for me."

Julia opened her mouth to continue her protests, but Katherine didn't allow it. She grasped the bundle of letters by her bedside and the note of goodbye she'd penned to her husband. With trembling hands, she offered them to Julia, who took them with a frown.

"Please, let me go and don't say anything to your brother until he comes looking for me. He won't return until late evening and I'm leaving directions for him to be told I have a headache and have retired to my own chambers. Let me have the night to put some distance between us. In the morning, give him these."

"What are they?" Julia asked, examining the awkward bundle with a scowl.

"They're the answers he's been looking for," Katherine admitted with a sigh. "And I want him to have them."

"The answers . . ." Julia's eyes came up. "You mean about his father?"

Katherine nodded silently. What would Dominic do with the information she'd found? What would his expression be when he realized these letters told him everything he'd been looking for over the years? She would never know.

"My God, if you found the answers, why wouldn't you stay? This will be the most difficult time for him. Dominic will need you!"

Katherine shook her head. "It will all work out. One way or another, Dominic will know who he really is. You and Adrian will support him, just as you did long before I married him. I can't stay."

Julia set the bundle aside. She caught Katherine's hands and whispered, "Please, don't do this!"

Katherine shook off bitter tears. She couldn't shed them now. There would be plenty of time later. For the moment, she needed to focus on escape and convincing her friend to do this one favor for her.

"I must," she said. "There is no choice. And believe me, I've tried to find one over and over. We simply do not . . . suit. This is the only way."

Julia's hands dropped in a gesture of defeat. Katherine should have felt pleased she'd won, but didn't. In fact, disappointment raged through her. In some secret part of her heart, she'd hoped her friend would force her to stay. Then the decision would be removed from her hands.

Julia turned away. "I should have been a better friend to you in the beginning." She sighed heavily. "I should have told you what my brothers were planning. Perhaps all this pain and anger could have been avoided."

Katherine started. Julia thought she was leaving because Dominic deceived her. Letting her believe that was certainly easier than explaining her true motivations.

"We can't live on what might have been," she said with a gentle brush of her friend's shoulder. "And we can't go back in time. You did what you believed was best for everyone involved. I don't blame you. What I need is for you to be a better friend today, right now." She turned Julia back to face her. "Please."

Julia's face fell in response and she nodded slowly. "Go." Her hand tightened on Katherine's arm. "But please, take some of the time you spend alone to think about what you're doing and why. I lived without love for so very long, Katherine. I would hate to see you throw it away over a mistake made so long ago."

Katherine hesitated as she thought of all she would give up by leaving. Dominic's touch. His laughter. His kiss.

But she couldn't forget the pain that would plague her if she stayed.

"I have no other option."

With that, she gathered up her bags and hurried downstairs. Only a few servants knew of her departure, but the carriage was waiting for her. Once the door had closed and she was alone, she sank down into a prone position on the seat and sobbed. Leaving Dominic was like cutting a piece of herself away, like breaking her own heart.

But if that was what she had to do to protect herself and the child that grew within her, she would.

Dominic entered the house with his eyes firmly focused on the reports in his hand. His undercover man still had no hint of his father's identity or whereabouts. Dominic felt a strange peace about it, despite his long search.

Something had happened to him since he last confronted his mother and brother. Something in him changed that night. Katherine knew he was a bastard, but she still chose to share her life with him. Now he looked forward to the future. The one he was building with his wife.

After all his years of feeling empty, she somehow filled him up. Yes, he still wanted to find the man who sired him, but the search no longer consumed him.

He looked up and was surprised to see Julia and Adrian waited for him in the foyer. Both were pale and looked worried. Julia even appeared to have been crying. He lowered his papers with a skipping heart. He guessed what they were going to say. They were getting married, and were afraid of his reaction to their announcement after he'd been so irrational.

"I need to speak to you, *now*," his sister said as she came forward.

He glanced from his best friend to Julia, then back again. "Yes, I do want to talk to you, but first I need to see Katherine. When I arrived, the footman said she'd gone to bed with a headache, but I have a gift that might make her feel better."

He dipped his hand into his pocket and brushed his fingers against the velvety box hidden there. Inside was a ring. Not one that had been chosen by his brother, but by him. One that would tell Katherine she was his wife by choice. It would tell her how much he cared.

"This cannot wait," Julia interrupted with a frown. "It needs to be done immediately."

Dominic stared at her impatiently. "If this is about the two of you, I know you and Adrian have grown very close in the last few weeks. Despite my initial reaction, I'm very pleased you are growing serious in your intentions. I am more than happy to talk to you and give you my blessing for whatever your future together holds, but first—"

He turned to go up the stairs as he spoke, but Adrian's tense voice stopped him. "She's gone, Dominic."

Ice flooded his veins as he halted midstep. He must have misunderstood. Slowly, he turned back to the couple in the foyer. "What?"

His sister nodded with renewed tears sparkling in her eyes. "It's true. Katherine is gone. I walked in on her finishing her packing and confronted her." She shook her head. "I tried to keep her here, Dominic, but she insisted on leaving. And she wanted me to keep it a secret in the hopes you wouldn't follow her."

His mouth dropped open and all he could hear was the whoosh of blood in his veins. He felt no emotions, just an overwhelming numbness that threatened to take him to his knees. But behind it, the pain was coming. He just had to get all the facts before agony took over and he collapsed under its weight.

"Secret?" he repeated.

"That's why she told the servants she was going to bed with a headache," Julia explained.

She swayed toward him like she wanted to offer him comfort, but held back. It was just as well. He didn't know if he could bear her touch, or anyone else's if this was true.

Julia's voice broke. "She hoped her lie would

keep you away. Then you wouldn't discover she was missing until the morning. My walking in disrupted her plans."

Adrian nodded. "Julia knew keeping Katherine's departure a secret would be wrong, so she told me and we decided to inform you together."

The pain began surging through Dominic's veins. He shook his head. "No. She is not gone."

Turning on his heel, he rushed up the stairs and charged down the corridor to the chamber the two of them had shared since the first night they arrived. The chamber Katherine slowly personalized and made a home for them. Like everything else at Lansing Square.

She wasn't there. The chamber was empty and strangely quiet.

With a growl, he stormed into her adjoining chamber. He tore open her armoire only to find it bare. All evidence of his wife's existence, of the life they shared, was gone. Packed away and taken. Except for the soft floral smell of her skin that still clung to her pillow. Except for memories that threatened to overpower him as he stared at the vacant closet in shock and horror.

"Damn!" he howled as he slammed his hand against the wood. It did nothing but send a shot of pain through his fist and arm.

"I'm sorry, Dominic," Julia said from behind him.

He spun on his heel. He wouldn't give up so easily. "Where did she go?"

"That I don't know," she admitted softly. Then she held out a packet of papers with a frown. "All she left were these things. I was to give them to you tomorrow morning after you discovered she was missing. Perhaps they'll give you some clues to where she's gone and why she left."

Dominic took the bundle with trembling hands and stared at it blankly. Was *this* all he had left of his wife? All she could think to gift him with was a bundle of worthless papers? Not her laughter, or her touch, or her love for a lifetime. Just letters.

He almost laughed, but couldn't seem to muster the strength. In an empty voice, he muttered, "Go. I want to be alone with whatever it is she has to say."

Julia opened her mouth as if to protest, but Adrian caught her arm gently. With a short nod, he said, "Whatever you need, Dominic. We'll come back in a while to check on you."

Dominic nodded as he ushered them out of his chamber and shut the door. Then he turned to the pile of correspondence. The top one was in her handwriting. His name stared up at him, mocking him.

With a roar, he stormed over to the fire. He was tempted to throw the bundle in. To forget he ever met or married Katherine Fleming. To forget he'd fallen in love with her.

With a start, he pulled back from the flames. He was in love with her.

Of course he was. He had been for some time, he

had just been so obsessed with finding the truth, so convinced love didn't exist, so tangled up in lies that he hadn't recognized or accepted it.

But now that Katherine was gone, it slapped him across the cheek and woke him from his haze.

His gaze drifted back to the note she'd penned. No, he couldn't just throw away his wife's explanation. He had to find out why she'd gone. Why she chose to leave him with nothing but a pile of paper and a broken heart.

Dominic didn't even bother to look up when Adrian came back into the room an hour later. He sat on the floor, staring at the two letters in his hand, as he had been for the past quarter of an hour. One revealed his past, the other took his future and crushed it into powder. Both stabbed him like knives.

"Dominic?" his friend said softly.

He glanced up briefly, but didn't answer. How could this be? How?

Adrian stepped over the line of letters Dominic had spread out on the floor around him. "My God, what is this?"

He shook his head and forced himself to look at his friend for more than a moment. He had to concentrate, regroup.

"Uh, yes, the letters. They belong to my mother."

"Why did Katherine give them to you?" Adrian asked as patiently as Dominic guessed he could manage. It was obvious Dominic's quiet anguish frightened and worried his friend.

"Katherine gave them to me because they reveal who my father is. He wrote them."

Adrian stared at him with much the same look Dominic guessed he had himself when he realized the truth the slender packet of letters held. Shock, absolute disbelief.

"Wh-Who?" Adrian whispered as he sank down on his knees across from Dominic.

"His name is Charles Vidal."

The name rolled over his tongue. He somehow expected his father's name would feel different. Would make him tingle or give him some sense of who he was. It didn't.

Adrian wrinkled his brow. "I don't recognize the name."

Dominic shook his head. "You wouldn't. He isn't a peer. He isn't even a gentleman. He was a piano master my mother intended to hire when Julia showed a talent for music at a very young age."

Adrian's eyes went wide. "My God."

Dominic nodded. "According to the letters, the relationship blossomed very quickly. She interviewed with him in London, and was surprised when it turned out he was here in the shire teaching another gentleman's daughter music."

He thought of the beautiful words Vidal had written to Larissa. They were heartfelt admissions of true love and regret they were kept apart. He even expressed fear over her welfare in Harrison Mallory's home.

"My mother was very unhappy in her marriage," he said softly. "More miserable than I ever knew. This man brought her joy."

"Then why was she so indifferent toward you? Why did she keep his identity a secret for all these years?"

Dominic shrugged. "When she became pregnant, Mallory knew immediately the child could not be his. He went on a rampage, demanding to know the truth about who her lover was. To keep Vidal safe, she cut him off. Many of his letters beg her not to turn away. Ask her to run away with him. And plead for access to his child. To—to me."

He swallowed hard. Knowing Mallory as he had, he understood why Larissa turned from the man she loved. If Harrison discovered his wife's lover was without the protection of society or title, he would have destroyed him.

But despite that knowledge, an angry ache continued to burn his chest. He had been kept from a man who wanted him. Who begged Larissa for any small detail about his son. Who even wrote for several years after it was clear Larissa ceased answering, holding out hope he might have a glimpse of Dominic.

"What happened to him?" Adrian asked.

Dominic fingered the last letter in the pile. "This one is dated six years after my birth. It says Vidal had gained some reputation for his musical talent in London. He also mentions an engagement. He told my mother he loved her still, but knew they weren't meant to be together."

He stared at the missive. Even a quarter of a century later, the droplet stains on the paper were clearly from Larissa's tears.

Adrian stared at him. "What will you do? You know his name and that he lived in London. Surely you'll be able to find his whereabouts with this new information. You can go to him. He must know who you are. I'm sure you could—"

He lifted a hand to cut his friend off. "What does it matter now?" Dominic slowly rose to his feet and dropped the letter from his father. Now he only held Katherine's missive. "Katherine gave me the gift of this information, but only on her way to leaving me."

"Did she say why?" Adrian asked as he, too, got to his feet. He held himself stiffly, like he was unsure how to handle Dominic's tormented emotions.

Dominic held out the letter. "She says she tried to forgive my lies."

He thought of the night she gave him that beautiful gift of forgiveness. It had taken such weight from his shoulders. It had given him hope for a future even if he never discovered the truth about his past.

"But she says she can't forgive. She doesn't care for me and can no longer share my home."

"She lies."

Dominic turned to watch Julia enter with her mouth in a thin line and her eyes flashing.

"She loves you, Dominic. I don't understand why she felt compelled to leave, but it isn't for her lack of love. She was broken by her decision. And desperate to give you the truth about your mother and father. She wanted you to find peace. If she truly didn't care for you, she wouldn't have worried about whether you found out about your father or not."

A sharp jab of hope surfaced in Dominic's overwhelming despair, but quickly faded. "Even if that's true, what can I do? Sarah's disappearance and resurfacing is proof enough that a woman who doesn't want to be found won't be. Even if I can find her, it may be for nothing if she really doesn't care."

Julia stepped forward to place a hand on his forearm. "Dominic, it comes down to this. Do *you* love her?"

He didn't even hesitate before he nodded. "I love her with everything I am. Everything she saw in me."

Her face softened. "Then you must follow her. Don't let her resist. Don't allow her to go one more moment without being sure of your feelings. I, for one, am sure of hers. No woman runs away into the night unless her heart is involved."

He stared at his sister and the man he had called

friend for so many years he'd lost count. Hope overwhelmed him as he thought of Katherine. She might not have admitted her love to him, but she'd proven it more than once. Julia was right. Something else drove her away. And he knew he could overcome that 'something' if he found his wife.

Clearing his throat, he said, "You two have someplace to be. You should go."

Julia flushed in surprise. "What do you mean?"

He cocked his head with as much of a chuckle as he could manage under the circumstances. "Oh yes, I heard rumblings of your plan to go to Gretna Green. So, off with you. And don't return until you're a baroness."

She smiled, but the expression was fleeting. "I don't want to leave when you need us."

He reached out and drew his sister in for a brief hug. "I love you dearly for worrying. And for caring so much for me over the years." Pulling back he looked down into eyes that were nothing like his own, but still held a part of him. "But you can't help me anymore. I must do this alone."

With a sigh, Julia stepped back to stand beside Adrian. Dominic's friend put his arm around her and said, "And what *do* you plan to do, Dominic?"

He tilted his head with a determined smile. "I'm sending for my horse. I have a wife to find."

Chapter 19

Katherine strummed her fingers along the wooden table with a sigh. She knew she *needed* to eat the roasted pheasant, potatoes, and bread the kind innkeeper's wife set before her. For her child's sake, at least, she had to take a few bites. But she couldn't seem to bring herself to do it. She didn't want to eat. She didn't want to drink. She certainly didn't want to think.

She'd been on the run for two days now, heading for her friend's estate in Northern England with only a lady's maid for company, but her heartache wasn't growing less. If anything, her thoughts turned even more to Dominic.

She dreamed of him at night and when she

347

dozed in the carriage. At stops for rest and food, she had lost count of how many times she thought she saw him, only to have that vision turn out to be false.

By now, he had read her letter and its lies that she had not truly forgiven him and had left because she didn't care. Hopefully, he had read the letters from his father as well. She could only pray he was heading to London now. Perhaps already there if he'd ridden hard. With the name Charles Vidal and the missing details, she was sure it wouldn't take long to find the man.

She sighed. How she wished she knew how Dominic fared. But she'd made the right decision in leaving. The only choice for her sanity.

Oh, why couldn't she convince herself?

"Can I do anything for you, love?"

Katherine looked up to lock eyes with the woman who had been serving her since she sat down.

"Oh no, this is fine." Katherine took a bite of her food to reassure the woman. She hardly tasted it. "I'm just road weary."

"Beggin' your pardon, ma'am, but you look a bit life weary." With a smile, the woman sank down beside her uninvited. "Would you care to lighten your load by talking about it?"

Katherine flushed, uncomfortable sharing with this stranger, no matter how kind she seemed to be. "Thank you, but no." She forced a smile. "There's nothing to tell."

"It's a man, t'isn't it?" The woman pressed. When Katherine was silent, she said, "I'm Nell. I understand your not wanting to tell your tales to a person you don't even know. But I've been through my own trials of the heart. I won't ask you again, but if you change your mind, I'd be happy to listen."

Katherine worried her lip with her teeth. "What were your troubles?"

"See that man there?" Nell motioned toward the bar.

Katherine followed the other woman's gesture to the round, soft form of the innkeeper who was polishing glasses behind the bar. "Mr. Wilcox?"

"Yes." Nell smiled like a schoolgirl in love. "When I met him, I was married to a hard man. He used to beat me something awful. I knew from the moment I met Blaine Wilcox that I loved him, but it took two years and a runaway horse that finally kicked my Martin in the head before I could be with him. Still, I never gave up. I never lost hope, even in the darkest hours."

Katherine stared at the worn, heavyset woman across from her. She'd probably seen more in a year than Katherine would see in a lifetime. Saying her troubles out loud would at least relieve some of the pressure, and it wasn't as if the woman could spread the story.

"My husband," she stammered with heat filling her cheeks. "I love him, but we can't be together."

The woman cocked her head. It was clear she

didn't understand how that was possible. "Why not? Is he cruel to you?"

"No. Never," she whispered.

"Honey," Nell said before she pushed back to her feet. "If you love the man, you must find a way together. Don't throw love away over some foolishness."

As the innkeeper's wife moved off to get drinks for a family at a nearby table, Katherine rose to her feet and trudged upstairs.

She slipped into her chamber and stared into the roaring fire. Though she was pleased by its warmth and light, it offered her no comfort. There would be no peace or resolution for her. She'd done exactly what Nell had cautioned her against. Thrown love away.

And no matter how she reminded herself of the necessity of her actions, it still broke her heart and ate at her soul.

"Oh, Dominic," she whispered. "I do love you. If only there was a way—"

She was interrupted by a pounding at her door. She scrambled to her feet with a start.

"Mrs. Wilcox, I'm sorry I didn't finish my food," she said as she approached the door. "I just want to be alone and try to sleep."

"Let me in, Katherine! Please!"

Katherine took a step backward as the blood drained from her cheeks. Dominic. He was on the other side of the door, his voice filled with a desperation she'd never heard him possess, even throughout his entire search for his father. Even when she confronted him about his lies.

It was the voice of a man who was lost.

Why was he here? Her heart soared with brief hope that he loved her, but that hope subsided. Dominic cared for her, certainly, but not in that way. If anything, he'd come after her to keep up appearances.

She fumbled her way closer and somehow managed to get it open. Dominic framed the doorway, big and powerful, but with a gaunt face and a haunted look in his eyes that touched her to her very center. To that place that insisted on loving him.

"Is it all right, madam?"

She finally noticed the red-faced innkeeper. Nell stood behind her husband close by. Though he had the stance of a man ready to fight, she could see by his look that Mr. Wilcox wouldn't challenge Dominic. The innkeeper knew he wouldn't win.

Just like Katherine knew she wouldn't, either.

"Y-yes," she stammered. "He's my husband."

Dominic slowly turned to glare at the innkeeper. The man's eyes widened, but Nell didn't look as frightened as her husband did. Instead, she gave Katherine a bold wink and walked away.

"Yes, ma'am. Good night to you both." The innkeeper followed his wife, scrambling away as fast as his pudgy legs could carry him, leaving Katherine alone with Dominic.

His presence was as powerful to her as it had been the first night they spent together. And her reaction was the same. Every part of her wanted to lean into his heat, to surrender and give him all her love.

Instead, she backed away.

He took the opportunity to come inside her chamber and shut the door behind him. Still, he didn't speak and he didn't come closer, just stared at her with those eyes that spoke volumes.

She steadied herself by gripping the edge of the chaise. "You—you should be heading to London. You should find your father." She paused as a terrible thought leapt to her mind. "You did get my letter, didn't you?"

He bobbed out a curt nod. "Yes." He finally took a step closer. The movement worked through her like a caress. "And it made no sense."

Her spine stiffened even as her heart softened. "It makes perfect sense. I found the proof about your father. Once that was done, there was no reason for me to stay where"—she took a deep breath and hoped he believed her lie—"to stay where I didn't want to be."

"With me." His voice was flat and his face suddenly dull and free of any emotion. She couldn't tell if he was coming to accept her refusal or somehow hurt by it.

"Yes," she whispered, longing to touch his cheek, to smooth the lines away from his eyes and mouth. To bring a rare smile to his lips with a kiss.

"Now that you've spoken the lines you wrote for yourself, why don't you tell me the real reason you left?" he asked, his voice going up a notch.

She shivered as she turned away. She feared she wouldn't be able to lie to his face anymore. Not when she was quickly losing herself in his stare. In him.

"I told you already!" This time it was her voice that elevated. "I no longer wish to be with you. When I found the evidence of your father's identity, I knew I could finally be free. I did my duty."

He caught her arm and spun her around to face him. "Tell me that while you look into my eyes, Kat," he insisted just before his lips came down to hers in a passionate, desperate kiss that devoured and claimed and softened her all at the same time.

She surrendered to it, swearing to herself it would be the last time. A niggling voice in the back of her head reminded her she'd made that vow before, but she cut it off as she wrapped her arms around her husband's neck and clung to him.

He pulled back and stepped away, leaving her empty and trembling. His jaw tightened, but not before she saw he, too, shivered with the power of the kiss.

"You can't look at me while you say those words because they're a lie. You love me."

She backed away, stumbling from his arms. He knew?

"I—" She dipped her chin. No matter how hard she tried, she couldn't deny such a direct statement. "Yes. I do love you, Dominic, but that isn't enough."

"Why?" he gasped. "It means everything."

She scoffed at that, turning from him with a shiver. Perhaps it was time to explain herself, to make him understand why she couldn't live her life loving him while only receiving desire or friendly affection in return.

Pivoting slowly, she held her shoulders back and kept from flying into his arms on sheer will alone.

"You have asked me over and over about my past. My family. I want to tell you about them now. Perhaps then you'll understand why my loving you changes nothing. Why I cannot return to Lansing Square."

Dominic shut his eyes. Katherine's admission of love rang like beautiful music in his ears, but he felt no joy. Not when she seemed so determined to remove herself from his life permanently.

"Tell me," he urged. "I want to know everything."

She sighed as she took a seat before the roaring fire. He joined her, leaning forward with his elbows on his knees and memorizing every taut, tension-filled line of her face.

"You know my mother loved my father, but he didn't return that emotion."

He nodded. It was the one glimpse she'd given of herself the night she forgave him for his lies. Or claimed to forgive him. He didn't know what the truth was anymore, except that it was buried in her stubborn heart.

"It was more than that," she continued. "He encouraged her. When he wanted something she could provide, he let her believe he cared, then crushed her when she was of no more use."

Dominic flinched. "How cruel."

"Yes." Her face softened with emotion. "He was an unkind, selfish man. But my mother was blind to his unsavory qualities. She made excuses for him, even blamed herself. I watched him hurt her, and when he left, *I* was the one to pick up the pieces. Even as a child."

Her mouth thinned. "I realized love could blind me to the truth. And I saw how easily I could be manipulated if I allowed myself to give in." Her gaze flicked to him as she clenched her fingers in her lap. "That was why I chose Colden as my husband. I didn't love him. I liked him at the time . . . before I knew the truth about his character. I felt no passion for him, so I knew I wouldn't be swept away by emotions or lose my head."

Dominic sucked in his breath. She never cared for Cole? His heart throbbed with intense pleasure and relief.

"I am sorry you endured such heartbreak," he said softly.

She shrugged. "It was a nightmare. And it only grew worse with each passing year. My father's contempt for my mother grew. He flaunted his mistresses more publicly. But her love for him remained steadfast, even as she grew more and more desperate. The night they were killed, he said incredibly unkind things to her. He vowed he wouldn't return again. In a panic, she followed him, and I her. Somehow we all ended up in his phaeton."

Her words hitched, but she fought to keep speaking. Dominic was moved by her strength and her pain, but managed to stay in his chair. Until she finished her tale, there was no use trying to console her.

"Go on," he urged softly.

"She tried to convince him to stay, even using me as an excuse. They struggled for the reins, the horses were whinnying and crying as they raced faster and faster. Then . . ."

She shuddered. "Oh God. We rounded a turn too fast. You know how rickety phaetons can be. The vehicle flipped. By some miracle, I was thrown clear, but my parents went over the side of the road in the rig."

He shut his eyes as pain laced through him. Then he shifted nearer and caught her hands. They trembled, the only indication she gave of how upsetting the memories were. He could only imagine how many times she'd relived the accident. How often it haunted her dreams.

"What happened after?" he urged with a gentle squeeze of reassurance.

Her voice shook. "I climbed down the ravine

when I could stand, but I was only thirteen. I couldn't help them. It wouldn't have made any difference. They were both dead, crushed under the rig and the injured horses."

Now her tears came freely, winding their way down her soft cheeks in silent trails of anguish.

"How long was it before help arrived?" he asked, brushing her hair back from her face. His thumb caught the warm wetness of a teardrop, and he wiped it away.

"I walked to the nearest estate a few miles away." Shaking her head, she said, "It felt like forever."

He measured his breathing as he let her story sink in. His own childhood had been filled with lies and pain, but not trauma. Not the kind of horror Katherine described in just a few short moments. No wonder she'd been afraid. No wonder she wanted to choose her mate at her own speed, not have a husband forced on her.

"Don't you see why I can't stay?" she asked, drawing her hands away from his and hardening her face.

He shook his head. "No. I understand volumes about you now, but not that."

She sighed in frustration. "You do not love me, Dominic. You told me when we met that you didn't believe in love. My God, you didn't desire this marriage, even if you grew to desire me. Even care for me in some way. But that isn't love. And I can't live like that. I won't."

Chapter 20

Dominic recoiled. Instead of the calm control that usually resided in his eyes, pain rippled across the lines of his face. Tangible. Caused by her.

"You think I would use and manipulate you the way your father did to your mother?"

She shook her head. "I know you wouldn't take things so far," she admitted. "You would never be intentionally cruel. In some ways, that would be worse. To feel your friendship and your desire, but know there was no chance for love . . . it would be too difficult. It *has* been unbearable since I allowed myself to accept I had fallen in love with you."

Dominic smiled. Warmth lit his eyes as he came out of his chair and sank to his knees before her own. He brushed a hand across her cheek and she shivered.

"Hear me, Katherine. Hear me well. I love you."

For a moment, Katherine's world lit with fireworks of pure happiness. She gasped in surprise, searching his face for a sign he was sincere.

"Please come home."

She drew back in disappointment. "Don't you see? You want me to return with you. You know what I want is your love and so you offer it. No, I can't do this, Dominic. I can't put my own child through what I endured."

The words were out of her mouth before she could call them back. She covered her trembling lips with a hand, watching through wide eyes as Dominic rocked back.

"A child?" he asked in a harsh, low tone that cut through the room to her soul.

"Dominic," she whispered.

"Is my son or daughter growing inside you right now?" he demanded. "Were you intending to keep that from me by running away?"

She tried to speak, but no words of either denial or confession would pass her lips.

"How could you?" he asked, never taking his gaze from her face, never moving so she could run from his intensity. "You read those letters. You know my father was denied access to me. You know how much he longed to see me. You don't think I would feel the same way about my child?"

She winced. Her reasoning was so selfish in the face of his accusation.

"Dominic, I experienced the worst a one-sided love can bring. I can't let my baby—"

He cut her off by grasping her shoulders. His eyes were wild and dark with emotion.

"I have never claimed to love any woman before today. I have never desired that emotion. I certainly have never made plans to use love against anyone. But I do love you. And I am *not* your father. You are *not* your mother."

She swallowed. His words sank into her soul, past the walls of resistance and fear she had erected long ago. She searched his face again. And saw . . . love. It was something she'd never seen in her father's face. It was something pure and good that she could no longer deny herself out of fear and empty memories.

"I won't let you keep my child from me." He cupped her cheek and warmth flooded her. "And I won't let you keep yourself from me, either. I *am* taking you home. If you don't believe I love you, I will prove that to you every day. I will say it until you have no choice but to surrender to the truth."

Her lip quivered as she finally allowed joy to crest over her like an ocean wave.

"Just say it once more," she whispered.

"I." He kissed her forehead. "Love." He kissed her nose. "You."

He hesitated at her lips, staring down at her.

With a cry, she wrapped her arms around his neck and surged up to meet his mouth.

"I love you," she said between kisses. "I'm sorry, so sorry."

"I know." He kissed her even deeper.

As his hot breath warmed her skin and her vision began to blur, a thought raced through her that brought her out of her haze. Placing her hands against the broad muscles of his chest, she shoved back. "Dominic, what about your father?"

He smiled. "Finding him is a resolution of my past. One I've yearned for as long as I can remember. But you . . . you are my future."

She blinked back renewed tears. "And you can still go to him now. We will find him and have all your questions answered, at last."

"We will." He nodded. "But not tonight."

Drawing her back into his arms, he kissed her. His love flowed through her, joining with her own until nothing else mattered but the moment. And the future.

Dominic pulled back the curtain on the carriage window and blood drained from his face. The Vidal town house was shrouded in black, a symbol of grief.

"Dominic," Katherine whispered as she touched his hand in comfort.

He squeezed her fingers. They had anticipated this moment might come after their investigator met them in London. With little understanding for the damage he was doing, the man informed them that Charles Vidal was very ill.

Still, knowing that fact and seeing proof of it were very different. His heart sank.

"It's too late. He's already gone."

"You don't know that, Dominic," Katherine said softly. "The house is mourning the inevitable as much as what has already come to pass. Your father may live still. You won't know for sure until we knock on the door."

He nodded at her wisdom even as his heart lurched when the footman opened the carriage door. The first step seemed so far to travel, especially after the long years of waiting. Wanting. Questions rushed through his mind, threatening to overwhelm him.

Katherine's hand on his arm brought him back to reality. A chilling reality, but reality nonetheless. "Come, we'll face this together."

He gripped her arm and walked up the steps to the door. His knock was weak and quiet, but within a few short moments, the door opened to reveal a young man. Immediately, Dominic looked to his arm for a band of black and was relieved that he wore none. Perhaps it wasn't too late, after all.

"I'm here to see Mr. Vidal," he said.

The man looked at them and for the first time Dominic noticed his eyes. Gray like his own.

"Perhaps you have not heard, sir. He is on his deathbed. He cannot receive visitors of any kind. Only family is permitted."

His voice wasn't unkind, but Dominic winced at this reminder that he was no family to this man any more than he was to his own.

He fumbled for his card. "I know it is asking very much, but I have urgent business with Mr. Vidal. Perhaps an exception could be made?"

The other man looked at the card. His eyes widened.

"You are Dominic Mallory?" he asked slowly.

Katherine stiffened at his side, gripping his arm tighter.

"Yes. And this is my wife, Katherine." He hesitated. "Are—are you Mr. Vidal's son?"

He nodded. "I'm Louis Vidal."

Dominic's breath caught. This was his younger brother.

Louis searched his face, then Katherine's. "My father once told me if you ever came to call, we were to allow you in. He never told me why. And now you are here."

Dominic stiffened at this revelation, but fought to keep his emotions at bay. Obviously, this man had never been told he had a brother. It wasn't his place to reveal a secret Vidal never told.

"If you decide to refuse me, I understand," he managed to say.

Louis cocked his head. "No. I will respect my father's wishes. Please come with me."

Dominic stared at Katherine as they followed the other man up the stairs to the family quarters. She returned his look with a kind one of her own. She understood how difficult this was and her strength helped him.

Upstairs in the hallway stood three other men. They ranged in age from their late teens to their mid-twenties. There was also a woman of about Katherine's age. All wore black and their eyes were rimmed red with sadness. His brothers and sisters.

Louis paused to whisper something to them, then opened the door to a chamber.

"Just a few moments, Mr. Mallory," he murmured.

Dominic entered the dim chamber slowly. In the moments it took his eyes to adjust to the light, he drew in several long breaths to compose himself. He needed to stay strong.

"Who's there?" came a weak, male voice from the bed.

Dominic's breath hitched as he gazed upon this man. His father. He was gaunt because of illness, with thinning hair and his pale skin. But his eyes were like Dominic's and his face held the quiet strength of a man who had seen and done much in his life.

"You do not know me, sir," he began awkwardly, finding words hard to come by and so very inadequate. "But my name is Dominic Mallory."

For a moment, only silence filled the room. Dominic stiffened. Was he going to be refused? Did his father no longer wish to see him?

Vidal's breath faltered on a cough and Dominic took an instinctive step closer.

"You came because you know." Vidal's voice was stronger through the dim room somehow. "You know the truth."

Dominic shut his eyes. How many times had he imagined this moment? So many. But in his fantasies, his father hadn't been dying. And Dominic had always envisioned an angry encounter, not this sense of peace filling him. Of forgiveness.

"Yes. I know the truth," he whispered.

There was a long silence, but then his father raised a frail hand. "Then close the door and come sit beside me, my son."

Dominic's knees nearly buckled. Son. Hands shaking, he reached back and pushed the door shut, then took the first steps toward his father.

Epilogue

Dominic stared out the window overlooking the grounds of Lansing Square. The room around him was so silent he could have heard an ant scurry across the floor. Not that Katherine would ever allow ants entry to her home.

He smiled. Come to think of it, it wasn't totally silent. No, when he stopped staring out at his estate and concentrated, he could hear other things. In the distance, there was a burst of laughter, both masculine and feminine. Then the sound of a baby's squeal.

Both brought a warm, comforting joy to his body. One that just a year and a half before, he wouldn't have believed possible.

"There you are."

He turned at the voice that interrupted his musings to watch Katherine slip into his study and tap the door shut behind her. Her ebony hair was bound up in a loose chignon, but little strands of it were determined to pull free, winding around her face. She claimed to hate it. He loved it. It brought him to mind of how she looked the first night he saw her, on the terrace in the cold.

"Yes, I'm here," he said with a smile as he opened his arms to her. Without hesitation, she slipped into his embrace and stayed there for a few long moments.

"You know, you're missing the party. Since it's in your honor, you might want to think about joining us," she teased when she finally pulled away. "Birthday Boy."

He laughed. His birthday had never been a happy time for him, but last year's had been more than he could have ever hoped for. And this year's was even better. He had a child, he had his beautiful wife. He had everything.

"And when will you give me your present?" he asked with a sinful wink that had her blushing.

"You got that lovely cigar cutter!" she protested, though he didn't miss the gleam in her eye. He cocked his head. "Oh, very well," she said with a theatrical sigh. "You know you'll have another present. Tonight. Alone. With me."

She leaned into him and kissed him, filling him

with as much desire as he felt love. He was still taken aback by how easily she could do that. Arouse and fill him with joy in such equal measures. Finally she pulled away.

"But not right now," she said, though before she turned to the door, he saw that her eyes were glazed with desire. "Because your entire family is just a few paces down the hall and they wonder where you are."

"Very well," Dominic said with a grin as he offered her his arm and let her lead him down the long hallway toward the sitting room where his guests were assembled. He took a moment to enjoy a long look at his home. Katherine had worked so hard to make Lansing Square perfect.

And it was. Despite everything, it was where he belonged. Now and forever.

"There he is!"

Dominic grinned as he entered the room and was greeted by a playful jeer from the small group of people. His family.

Julia and Adrian had made a special trip, thanks to the blessing of her doctor, who had reassured the worried couple that their miracle child would survive a brief carriage ride. His sister glowed as she rested a soft hand on the swell of her belly.

But along with the family he'd known all his life was the one he had just come to know. His brothers, Robert, Jeremy and Louis Vidal, sat scattered around the room. And his other sister, Charlotte, held his son with the care only a beloved aunt could manage.

How had he ever gotten by in life without these people? He knew the answer. He hadn't. Until he met Katherine, his life had been nothing but a meaningless blur of desire to find answers, but no joy.

His wife had changed that, and his new family had accepted him with more love than he ever could have hoped for. It had been their father's dying wish.

He brushed away the sadness that always accompanied thoughts of Vidal. Though their time together had been brief, it had been a powerful gift to him. One he cherished.

"All right, Charlotte Jean," he said with the admonishing air of an older brother. "I think you've had my son long enough. I don't want to give your maiden heart too many longings when you haven't yet set a date to marry that scoundrel of yours."

His younger sister gasped in a playful show of outrage, but held the baby out nonetheless. "The only scoundrel I know is you, Dominic," she said with a sassy wink.

He laughed and took John from her arms. Instantly, the baby giggled and did his all-new trick. Clapping wildly.

"He approves," Katherine said at his elbow, before she reached out to pinch her baby boy's cheek.

With a laugh, Dominic sat down next to one of his brothers, and enjoyed the beautiful scene of his family.

* * *

"Margeretta, will you take John upstairs please?" Katherine gently placed her baby into the nursemaid's arms. He only barely stirred, showing her a brief glimpse of the eyes that were just like his father's. She smiled.

"Of course, Mrs. Mallory."

Margeretta took the sleeping bundle and slipped from the room, leaving Katherine to go on a search for her husband. This was the second time he'd slipped away from his own party, and it worried her enormously.

When Dominic was with his brothers and sisters, she could see how happy he was, but she was also well aware of how painful his birthday was. Neither Cole, nor his mother, had made any kind of acknowledgment, continuing a coldness that had lasted since their last ugly encounter.

She slipped into the hallway. She could hear their houseguests in the same sitting room where they'd been gathered earlier, but this time they were sharing drinks before supper. Their laughter warmed her heart, for these were all the people she loved, and more importantly, who loved her husband.

Almost as much as she did.

Just as she was about to look for him on the terrace, she heard Matthews clear his throat behind her.

"Yes?" she asked with a kind smile for the butler.

He returned the expression with genuineness. "A

letter has arrived for Mr. Mallory. From Lady Larissa Mallory."

Katherine jolted in surprise but took the missive the butler held out on a small silver tray. "Thank you. I'll be sure to give it to him."

Taking a deep breath, she looked at the letter. Yes, it was Larissa's soft, flowing hand. The address looked shaky, as if her fingers trembled when she wrote her youngest son's name.

With a frown, Katherine put the note in her gown pocket and continued to search for her husband.

She wasn't surprised to find him out on the terrace behind the ballroom. The wide stone parapet offered him the best view of the estate, though in the darkness he couldn't see anything. She adjusted her thin shawl to protect her arms from the spring breeze, then slipped up beside him.

"This is the second time you've escaped me," she said lightly, watching carefully for his reaction.

"I could never wish to escape you," he said with a grin, but behind it was something heated and filled with desire. It almost melted her.

"But you're thinking about things that trouble you, and you don't want me to take on your worries," she said gently.

Briefly, he looked surprised, but then his smile grew. "Ah, you know me so well."

"I do." She sighed. "And I have something for you that may or may not improve your mood."

She held out the letter. Dominic hesitated and she knew he'd seen his mother's handwriting. Finally, he took it and broke the wax seal. The letter was short, just one page, and from Dominic's expression, she couldn't tell if he was upset by whatever Larissa had written.

"She wanted to wish me a happy birthday," he said quietly as he folded the note and put it in his jacket pocket. "And invited me to come to her town house when we return to London next month. She wants to tell me about my father."

Katherine bit her lip. "And how do you feel about that?"

Truth be told, she didn't know how she, herself, felt. Part of her was angry. It was too late to gift Dominic with knowledge now! Now when Charles Vidal was dead and Dominic had moved on with his life. But part of her knew that Dominic still longed to hear the truth from his mother's own lips. To have her take his side as she hadn't his entire life.

"I don't know," he admitted as he reached out to take her hand. "I think she must be very lonely now that Cole and Sarah have gone to the Continent. The scandal over Sarah's affair last fall put a gap between them."

Katherine nodded, thinking of the uproar Sarah's very public affair with a stable hand half her age had caused. She stifled a smile. Banishment and ruin were only part of what Cole and his wife deserved. Though she knew it was wrong to take pleasure in their pain, she couldn't help it after all they had put Dominic through.

He sighed as he looked out at the estate again. "I also know she had word of my reunion with Vidal and his ultimate death. Perhaps her irrational fears of destroying him are gone now that the truth is out."

"What do you intend to do?" she asked.

He shrugged, but as she searched his eyes, she was pleased to see the pain that once filled them when he spoke of the Mallorys was no longer present. He had put it away in the past where it belonged.

"I think I'll go to her. She is my mother. I understand how unhappy she was. And how her actions were, perhaps, meant to protect rather than hurt. I used to think she couldn't look at me because she regretted my birth . . . but now, knowing how much I look like my father did when he was younger, perhaps she only regretted losing him."

He slipped his arms around Katherine and she snuggled back against his warmth, forgetting about the past. She let out a contented sigh as she looked up at the starry night.

His voice reverberated against her earlobe. Soft, sensual. "A very long time ago, I saw you looking up at the sky like you are now. And I think I fell in love with you a little at that very moment."

She laughed as she held him tighter. "Yes. It does

seem like a very long time ago, doesn't it? Or perhaps only yesterday."

"I asked you then what you wished for and you told me nothing. That you had everything your heart desired."

Her laughter faded as she remembered her tangled emotions and the groundless fears that had haunted her all those many months before. When she thought of what she almost deprived herself of . . . what she'd nearly deprived her son of . . . it gave her a shiver.

"I didn't know what I wanted then. I was confused by false worries." She looked at him. "That night you also told me you didn't believe in wishes."

Now it was his turn to smile. "I was confused then, too."

Tears pricked her eyes as she lost herself in a wash of gray. "Then make a wish tonight, Dominic. Make a wish on the stars."

He looked up as a streak of light crossed the sky and for a long moment, she thought he *was* making a wish. But then he bent his head to press a kiss on her lips.

She leaned up into it with a sigh of surrender. When he finally parted with her, he whispered, "I spent my life wishing for the truth, but I have that now. I wished for a family, but they are all in the sitting room probably making dreadful assumptions about the fun we're having."

She smiled with a blush.

He continued, "I wished for love, but love is looking at me right now, reflected in your eyes." He reached down and brushed the back of his hand against her face. "No, Kat. I've no need for wishes. I received everything my heart desired when I married you. And I intend to spend every night for the rest of my life making *your* wishes come true."

She cupped his strong chin in her hand and leaned up until she was just a hair's breath away from his lips.

"You already do, Dominic," she murmured as she caught his mouth for a long kiss. "You already do."

Great stories, hot heroes, and a whole lot of seduction are coming this November from
Avon Romance...

This Rake of Mine by Elizabeth Boyle
An Avon Romantic Treasure

Miranda wants nothing to do with the scoundrel who caused her ruin years ago, but the students of Miss Emery's Establishment for the Education of Genteel Young Ladies, where she is a teacher, are all atwitter at the attraction that crackles between them. So the girls come up with a plan to get them together, and Miranda and Jack don't stand a chance . . .

The Boy Next Door by Meg Cabot
An Avon Contemporary Romance

Melissa Fuller is bored by her life. But then all sorts of strange things start happening when the lady next door is a victim of a suspicious robbery/attempted homicide. This young woman is determined to unmask the criminal. And most interesting of all is the man who comes to "house sit" while his aunt is in the hospital. Could she have found a boyfriend next door?

Keeping Kate by Sarah Gabriel
An Avon Romance

When Captain Alec Fraser takes custody of a beautiful lady spy, the handsome Highland officer must discover information that only she knows—and refuses to reveal. With secrets of his own to protect, Alec never expects the stunning, stubborn girl to cause him so much trouble—nor does he expect to open his closed heart ever again.

Gypsy Lover by Edith Layton
An Avon Romance

As the poor relation to a wealthy family, Meg Shaw is obliged to be a governess companion to their daughter. But when her charge runs away, she embarks on a search of her own to find the missing heiress and clear her good name. Little does she expect that her path will cross Daffyd Reynard, a wealthy and dashing gentleman with the wild spirit—and heart—of a gypsy . . .